FOUR DADDIES FOR CHRISTMAS

A MILITARY REVERSE HAREM ROMANCE

K.C. CROWNE

DESCRIPTION

**Four untamed ex-military daddies.
One very unassuming girl.
Who said Christmas miracles don't exist?**

My family's failing farm and my father's debt has me on edge.
Luckily, a chance rescue could be my ticket out.
An adorable set of twins need childcare.
And their legal guardians are four insanely HOT uncles.

THREE reasons why this can't work:
1. All four brothers are constantly working out in their mansion.
2. They're older and more experienced in **ALL** facets of life.
3. It appears I've ignited a desire in them that can't just be brushed under the rug.

And if I'm being completely honest...
I'm beyond turned on by **all** four of them.

**But the weather calls for a scary winter storm.
A storm brings that brings all sorts of trouble...
Not to mention unexpected surprises.**

CHAPTER 1

AUBREY

"**G**eorge! You get your big, fat butt down here, *now!*"
As soon as the words left my mouth, I realized how insane the situation was. It was Thanksgiving in Maryland, the sky a deep gray, the chill wind whipping snow all around me—snow that was accumulating at my feet more and more with each passing second.

Instead of being back at the farm in front of a crackling fire with a big plate of turkey and stuffing and all the fixings in front of me, I was out in the cold chasing around the unruliest llama I'd ever known in my life. And in my line of work, I'd met a lot of llamas.

"George!"

He didn't care. The big, white beast glanced in my direction from a hundred paces away for just long enough to snort, his big tongue hanging dumbly out of his mouth. If I didn't know that this particular goofy expression was his default look, I would've sworn that he was mocking me.

I broke into a run, trying to cut the distance between us a bit. As soon as he realized what I was doing, however, he broke out into a trot, heading further up Halbrook Trail, the wooded path that seemed to be his favorite place to go when he pulled one of his frequent escape acts.

"Ah, hell."

I took off my hat, shaking the snow out of the brim before starting after him. My mouth was watering as I hurried, thoughts of buttermilk biscuits topped with fresh clotted cream and homemade jam filling my mind. My best friend and roommate Aggie and I had decided to go all out this year, waking up at the crack of dawn to prepare the feast of a lifetime. We'd stocked up at the store in anticipation of the snowstorm ahead, both of us looking forward to a few days of burrowing in, eating our leftovers, and watching whatever was good on Netflix in front a roaring fire.

Sounded like heaven. That is, until I happened to look up through the window over the kitchen sink to see that George was missing.

"George!"

I was beyond frustrated. I'd been chasing the animal for a good half an hour, and my legs were starting to burn underneath me. Wanting to get to him as fast as possible, I broke out into a jog, heading up the snaking path of Halbrook Trail, the winding, snow-dusted dirt road leading me up through the hills overlooking the land I called home.

A few minutes of jogging and still no sign of the jerk. Needing a bit of a break, I reached into my pocket and took out the small thermos of cider that Aggie had sent me off with. I unscrewed the cap and sipped, the warm, tart deliciousness washing over my palate. As I enjoyed the cider, I took a moment to look out over the rolling expanse of my land.

Downing Farm, named after the man who'd started it all the way back in colonial times, was a hell of a place. Situated in the hills of the central Maryland panhandle, it was a little slice of heaven that had been in my family for generations, passed down to me when my father died last year.

It was a hell of a lot of work. Chasing down ornery llamas was the least of it all. As I stood there at the middle point of Halbrook Trail, admiring the view of the seemingly endless landscape dotted with birch, cedar, and butternut trees, with small ponds here and there looking like little teardrops, the daily grind of keeping the place up and running seemed to fall away.

I could spot the farm itself from where I stood, the two-story farmhouse situated in the center of it all, the big red barn off to the side. Truth be told, Downing Farm was more of a ranch these days, with more space dedicated to pigs and cows and, of course, llamas, than crops. But shaking off an old name like that was no small thing, so I let it slide.

Another chill wind hit me as I stared out onto the landscape, reminding me of the task at hand. I pulled my scarf tight around my neck and returned my attention to the trail, catching a quick flash of George's white-and-black-spotted fur as he peeked around the trunk of one of the many trees.

"George!" I called out as I hurried in his direction. "You get back here *now* or no more play time for you and Larry for the next... hundred years!" Larry was George's brother, and by this point I was damn sure that the two of them got a sick thrill out of egging one another on, each encouraging the other to get up to the sort of trouble that kept me up all damn night with worry.

More snow began to gather, and I broke into double-time pace as I hurried up the trail. My neck of the woods could get some serious storms, and the last thing I wanted was to freeze to death in the process of chasing down a damn llama.

"George!" I shouted up the hill. "Alright, you drive a hard bargain, but here it is—you come out now and make this easy for me, and I'll make you a little plate of Thanksgiving goodies. No telling Larry about it though, got it?"

No reply, of course. I kept on trudging, the snow deepening by the second.

Right in the middle of my trek, however, I heard something strange. At first, it sounded like the groaning of a branch about to give way under the weight of snow. A quick glance up let me see that, while the snow was gathering, we were still a ways off from that sort of thing happening.

I held my position for a moment, trying to catch another bit of the strange noise I'd heard.

Nothing. I sighed, chalking it up to one of the animals in the area. Then, right before I took a step, I heard something else. This time, there was no mistaking what it was.

The sound was the soft sobbing of a child.

A whimper drifted through the air, catching my heart and attention. The whimper was followed by sobs, then a gentle, "*oww.*"

My heart racing fast, my eyes wide, I listened carefully. More whimpering sounded from what seemed to be to my left, near the ravine along the hills of Halbrook Trail.

I cleared my throat and spoke. "Is someone there?"

The whimpering stopped, like a plug had been pulled. I listened some more, hoping to hear it again so I could pinpoint the direction.

Finally, the whimpering started again. Now there was no doubt where it was coming from. I glanced down the path one more time in the direction George had gone, as if he might've decided to have some sympathy on me and come back down. No such luck. If I headed toward the whimpering instead of George, there was a good chance that damn llama might be lost for good.

Didn't matter—if there was a kid around, I was going to find him, or her.

I started off to the left, weaving through the thick knots of trees, stepping carefully not to slip on the snow. I gripped the trunks of the birches around me, focusing on each step. Halbrook Trail was lovely, but once you were off the safety of the path, it was more than a little treacherous. Last thing I wanted was a broken ankle.

"You there, kid?" I called out as I stepped. "Hey, I know you're scared, but I'm here to help, OK? No one should be out here in the middle of a blizzard, especially on Thanksgiving."

I had no idea if I was helping or hurting. I didn't have kids of my own, and I was an only child, talking to little ones didn't exactly come naturally to me. All the same, I figured some little kid out lost in the middle of nowhere was a hell of a lot more important than any of my animals.

I broke through the trees and stepped out onto the edge of the ravine.

That's when I spotted him. The boy was laying among the rocks in the dry creek. From where I stood, about a hundred feet away from him, I could see that he was dressed in dark pants and a big puffy coat, his hair dark and matted with sweat and snow. A small smear of blood was on his forehead, giving me a start.

Finally, he opened his little mouth and called out.

"Help!"

CHAPTER 2

AUBREY

The sight of the little man in pain was heart-wrenching. I broke out into a run, hopping down into the ravine and made my way toward him, carefully moving down the stony slope.

"Hey, kid!" I called out, my voice carrying along the dip of the dry creek bed. "Stay right there, alright?"

The boy turned toward me. There was fear in his eyes, eyes that I could tell were a gorgeous hazel even from a distance. His hair was semi-long, the ends curling at his collar. Between his hair and the outfit of jeans, boots, and a tiny flannel, he looked like an adorable little rancher. His clothes were a bit dirty from his fall, but other than that, he appeared well-groomed. That meant he was almost certainly well taken care of.

Most importantly his forehead was smeared with blood. Although I'd never been all that much of a kid person, the sight of a hurt little boy activated a protective feeling in me like none other.

He didn't reply. So, I called out to him once more.

"Are you alright?" I asked, my voice projecting down the ravine. "Say something, will you?"

He didn't, and I was beginning to get the sense that he was more worried about the strange lady flying toward him than he was his injury. I closed the distance, dropping to my knees once I got to him.

"Let me get a look at that, OK?" I asked.

The kid regarded me with a wide-eyed expression, his mouth formed into a flat line. The boy was totally adorable, the kind of kid you could already tell was going to grow up into a very handsome man.

I reached for his forehead, and he responded by turning his body away from me.

Think, Aubrey. This little guy's far away from home, and now some crazy woman is looming over him trying to look at his wound.

I paused, closed my eyes and took a deep breath. After that I smiled and placed my hand on my chest.

"Hey, there. My name's Aubrey Downing. What's yours?"

He said nothing but turned back toward me.

I pointed off in the direction of Downing Farm. "You know that little place that's just over there? That's my farm, Downing Farm, just like my last name." I swept my hand toward the land around us. "This is all my property. I saw you here, and I wanted to make sure you were OK. That make sense to you?"

That got a little nod out of him.

"So, how about you start with telling me your name?"

He pursed his lips, and for a moment I was worried that he was about to clam up again.

But he didn't. Instead, he put his tiny hand on his chest, like I had, and spoke.

"Henry."

Relief washed over me; we were finally getting somewhere. A big smile took hold of me.

"Henry! That's such a cool name. Like King Henry, right?"

He nodded, still regarding me with skepticism, as if he weren't sure whether he ought to be talking to me.

"You're a stranger."

The realization of what he'd said hit me like a sack of bricks upside the head. Of course, he was going to be hesitant talking to me —I *was* a stranger. Being wary of strangers was the first thing any parent worth his or her salt taught their little one.

"I know. But you can just call me Aubrey." I grinned, maybe a little too much.

"Aubrey."

I laughed. It was so damn cute.

"There you go! Said it like a pro. Now, Henry, I've got two things I want to make sure of. First is that you're OK. Second is that we get you back to your mommy and daddy."

He shook his head. "Uncles."

"Your uncles?"

He nodded.

"Alright, I'm going to make sure you're A-OK, then get you back with your uncles. First, let's get you sitting up. Can you do that?"

"Yeah." With a bit of effort, he was able to push himself up without any help from me. It was a good sign that whatever he'd done to his head hadn't hurt him too badly.

"Awesome. Now, can I get a closer look at that?" I nodded toward his forehead.

"Um, OK."

With that, I leaned in and peeked at the injury, yanking my red-and-white bandana out of my back pocket and gently wiping away the blood.

"Look at you, not even flinching a little bit. You're a tough guy, you know that?"

My words managed to get a smile out of him. Henry sat patiently as I cleaned him up a bit. Once the blood was gone, I was able to get a good look at the wound. Relief washed over me as I realized that it was nothing more than a scuff, barely a surface injury. There was a chance he might've banged his head around a little from the fall, but so far, the evidence pointed in the direction that it was nothing more than the sort of war wound common to rambunctious kids.

"Can you stand up?" I asked.

To help guide him along, I rose to my feet and offered my hand. Once up, I took a quick look around to see that the snow was getting worse by the minute. The sky was the sort of deep gray that promised more white stuff to come.

"Uh-huh." Without taking my hand, he pushed himself to his feet. I chuckled at his insistence on doing it all alone. Once he was up, I was even more relieved to see that he was able to stand steady.

"Nice job!" I said, bending over and giving him a little pat on the shoulder. "Nothing stops Henry."

"Nope!" he affirmed with a big, toothy smile.

"Now, next step is figuring out where you need to go. This snow's getting bad, so I'm thinking we can head back to my farm and wait there with my friend Aggie. What do you think?"

"I'm hungry." He placed his hands on his tiny, round belly.

"You're hungry? OK, I think I've got something here." I reached into the little canvas pack that I always carried whenever I stepped out, unbuckled the front and stuck my hand inside, feeling around for the baggie of granola I'd put in there. Once I found it, I handed it over to Henry. "Here, this is good stuff. You like granola?"

"Does it have chocolate?" he asked, his big hazel eyes going wide at the possibility.

"Oh, you bet it does. There's white *and* dark chocolate. And my roommate makes it herself, so it's extra good."

"What's a woo-mate?" he asked.

"She's my best friend and she lives on my farm with me. She's super nice."

He opened the bag up happily, stuffed his tiny hand into it and pulled out as big a portion of granola as he could grasp. Then he shoved the food into his mouth and chomped eagerly.

"Careful now," I said. "I know you're hungry, but make sure you chew it up good before you swallow, alright?"

"OK." His eyes were on the bag as he spoke, his hand going in for another grab.

I sat there full of curiosity as he ate. Who was this kid? How did he end up on my land? And who were these uncles he was talking about? Part of me wanted to launch a barrage of questions at Henry, but I decided to let him eat in peace, as the snow fell all around us. He seemed to be in good shape and good spirits, but I knew a kid as young as he was wandering around in a blizzard-in-the-making was not a wise thing to do.

The first and most important step was to take him back to the house, get him cleaned up and his scuff disinfected and covered with a Band-Aid. Once that was done, Aggie and I could start the work of figuring out who little Henry belonged to.

Before I could give the matter too much more thought, Henry lifted the bag and stuck it out in my direction.

Kind of.

He held it out toward me, but a little off to the side. My stomach tensed at the sight. Had he banged his head to the point of being that uncoordinated? Was he seeing double? If that was the case, I'd need to get him to the nearest hospital as soon as I could.

"Henry? Thank you, but I'm over here." I placed my hands on his gently moving them in the right direction.

He quickly moved them right back. "Not for you! For him!"

"Him?"

"Yeah! Right there!"

I turned, my heart nearly jumping into my chest as I saw George standing just over my shoulder, about twenty feet back at the tree line. He had the usual dopey look on his face, his tongue hanging out of his mouth.

"There you are!" I called out, turning toward the animal. "Buddy, I swear."

I started toward him. Before I took a step, however, I thought of Henry's offer.

"That's my buddy George," I said. "He's a llama."

"A llama?"

"Yep. He's really nice, but he's a troublemaker. I came out here to bring him home. Want to help?"

"Yeah!"

"Alright. Come with me and let's give him some chow. He eats everything, so he'll go crazy over that granola. Then, once we've got him, we'll go back to my place, where we will get you cleaned up, you can meet my roommate and we'll try to find out where you belong"

"I want to see my uncles," he said, a touch of worry to his face.

"You live with your uncles?"

He nodded.

"Well, once you're cleaned up and have some real food in your belly, we can get in touch with them and get you home, OK? But it's getting super snowy out, so we shouldn't be outside."

The worry stayed on his face. "You're a stranger," he said for the second time.

"Only for now, buddy! We're neighbors! Once we get to know each other, we won't be strangers anymore, we'll be friends."

He regarded me with a bit of hesitation, then nodded. "OK."

"Perfect." I held out my hand to his, and he took it.

Together, we made our way over to George, the llama's big, black eyes still locked onto the baggie of granola.

"George! I'd like you to meet my new friend, Henry." George said nothing, of course, his eyes on the food. "Henry, this is George. Why don't you introduce yourself?"

"Hi!" Henry said. "Do you want some food?" He stuck out the bag, George doing a little excited hop in response. Henry laughed. "He does."

"Pour some of it onto your hand, like this." I took the bag from Henry and dumped a bit of granola onto my hand. That done, I lifted the food up to George. The animal wasted no time sticking his tongue out and cleaning off my palm with a single slurp.

Henry laughed again. "He's really hungry."

"He sure is. He likes to run off, but he always comes back when he remembers that I'm the one who gives him his food. Now, you try. Put a little on your hand and stick it out to him."

Henry, a huge, excited grin on his face, did just that. George lowered his head and stuck out his tongue, wrapping it around Henry's hand and licking off all the granola.

That got a huge laugh out of Henry. "It tickles!"

"I know, right?"

Henry turned to me. "Can we give him more?"

"Yep, but let's save a little for the trip back. George can get a little distracted, so we should save some food to make sure he doesn't wander off again. OK?"

"OK!" Henry looked up at me. "Can I ride him? I ride our ponies."

"You can't really ride llamas. If you try to jump on his back he'll buck you right off. But if we get going, I bet he'll let you pet him a little."

"OK!" That seemed to go over just as well with the little man.

I grabbed George's collar, leading him and Henry through the woods and back onto the trail. The snow was picking up more and more, but all I could feel was relief. Not only was Henry safe, but George was, too.

"There's my place," I said, pointing off toward the farm in the distance once we reached the hill I'd been looking out from before. "Nice, huh?"

"Yeah." He sounded a tad underwhelmed. "Our house is bigger."

I couldn't do anything but laugh at the example of kid honesty.

"Well, it's cute and cozy and it works for me." Just as I opened my mouth to say more, something clicked in my head.

Henry said he lived in a big house. He had to have wandered off from somewhere nearby. There was a large house in the area, a huge mansion about a half mile west. The place was ginormous— seated on about a thousand acres of primo land. I didn't know a darn thing about the house or who lived there, it was so far off that I'd never needed to. However, it made perfect sense to where Henry must have come from.

"Hey, Henry, do you live in that huge house over that way?" I pointed in the general direction of the place.

His eyes lit up. "Yeah! With my uncles and my sister."

More relief took hold. "Well, that's perfect." I dropped into a squat and put my hands on my knees. "How about this—I'll take you over to my place, get you cleaned up, then I'll drive you home. Sound good?"

"Yeah!"

The situation was becoming more and more manageable by the second. George's collar still in hand, I led us down the trail and back onto the main grounds of the property. The house was about twenty minutes off, and once we got going, little Henry proved himself to be quite the chatterbox. He told me about his uncles, how they worked on the ranch with all the animals, how they took care of him and his sister, Hattie.

About halfway into the walk, a gruff voice stopped me dead in my tracks.

"Hey, there. Going someplace with our boy?"

My heart skipped a beat. The voice was low and deep and impossibly masculine, with just a bit of gravel to it.

I turned slowly, confronted with the sight of two men, both tall, both insanely handsome. They were dressed in the same style as Henry, wearing rugged jeans, brown leather work boots, and flannel shirts under half zipped parkas. They both wore rancher-style hats like mine, snow collecting in the brim.

One look at them was enough to see that they were related not just to each other, but to Henry. They were both tall—one of them appeared to be just a little under six and a half feet with dark hair and hazel brown eyes, his angular face brooding and his facial hair cleanly groomed into a neat stubble. It was a bit hard to tell, but I guessed he was somewhere in his mid-forties.

The other wore his light-brown hair just long enough to hang down the sides of his face. He was clean shaven, with male-model-gorgeous features, and a cocky smile on his face as if he knew something that I didn't. I noticed that his eyes weren't hazel brown like the other man's or Henry's. They were a stunning forest green, the color of my land's grass during the brightest part of summer.

"Now," spoke the taller one. "You want to tell us what the hell you're doing with Henry?"

CHAPTER 3

MAC

S he was so damn gorgeous that I hardly even noticed the llama next to her.

That is, until the big, black and white beast let out a snort.

"Easy, George," she said, putting her hand on the back of the creature's neck and stroking him gently. "They're friends. At least, I think."

It took me a moment to collect myself. The woman standing about thirty paces from Adam and me seemed to be in her late twenties and was absolutely stunning. She was tall and slim, wearing light-wash jeans that hugged hips that were nice and round in spite of her athletic shape. She had on cowboy boots and an orange and red flannel with a shearling jean jacket, the buttons of her flannel tenting just a bit over her breasts.

The woman wasn't just beautiful, she was uniquely so. Her skin tone was olive, her hair dark and curly with faint, copper highlights that I could tell was obviously wild even under her hat. Her chocolate-colored eyes were almond-shaped, her lips full and her cheekbones sharp. Her eyebrows were arched in mild surprise, though I got a sense that they were normally that way.

"We're friends," Adam said, an easy tone to his voice. "But I gotta say, that llama looks a little on the vicious side."

The woman allowed a small smile to form on her plush lips. Adam had always been good that way, able to diffuse tension with a well-placed joke or two.

"He is," she said. "And he's especially mean to trespassers."

As if to make her point, the llama let out another snort. I couldn't help but laugh.

"Hen," I said, turning my attention to our boy. "You alright?" I looked closer, seeing a small scuff on his forehead, a tiny bit of dried blood around it.

"He's fine," the woman said. "He—"

I raised my palm. "He's more than capable of speaking for himself."

The woman narrowed her eyes. I could already tell she wasn't the type to be talked to like that. All the same, she seemed to have the good sense to understand that she was with a child that didn't belong to her.

"I'm OK!" he said. "I fell down. But Aubrey helped me."

Now I had a name.

"Is that right?" I asked. "She was nice to you?"

"Uh-huh."

"That's what I would've said," Aubrey added. "If you would've been *oh-so-kind* enough as to let me speak."

Adam raised his palms. "Easy now, all of us. This is obviously an awkward situation for all parties concerned. Listen, thanks for taking care of Henry. He's a good kid, but he's got what you might call a predilection for wandering."

"You turn your back on him for a second and he's gone," I added.

"I can see that," she replied.

"And" Adam continued, "To make things clear, that's the only reason why we're on your land. We're not the trespassing type otherwise."

She nodded. "Fine. And in the spirit of explaining ourselves, the only reason why I was taking Henry here to my place was to get him cleaned up and give him something to eat before getting in touch with you all."

I stuck my thumbs into my front pockets and shifted my weight from one foot to the other. "Fine. Now that it's all settled, we'll be taking our boy and heading home."

Her beautiful face flashed with an expression I'd seen before. It was the look people never failed to give when my brothers and I referred to Henry or Hattie as ours.

"No!" shouted Henry.

"You don't want to come?" Adam asked, surprised.

Henry stepped over to the llama. "George was lost. He has to go home."

"This woman here's George's owner," I said. "She'll see him the rest of the way."

Henry shook his head. "I want to help."

I glanced over at Adam, and it seemed as if both of us understood what was going on. Aubrey had helped Henry, and now he wanted to help her.

"Come on, now," I said. "We don't need to take up any more of her time."

He only shook his head.

"Sorry," Adam said. "Kid's stubborn as the rest of us."

"We always teach him and his sister to pay it forward—someone does something nice for you, you do the same for them in return," I said.

Aubrey pursed her lips, giving the situation some thought. "You know, if Henry here wants to help finish the job, my ranch is only another ten minutes that way. You all could come with, make sure George here gets his furry butt back where it needs to be."

"Sure," Adam acquiesced. "Sounds good to me. And we are neighbors, after all. I suppose it's as good a time as any to get to know one another."

I winced. Everyone was waiting for us back home. We didn't

have time to escort some llama to another ranch, even if that was what Henry wanted.

Aubrey smiled and nodded. "Then let's get moving. Just a short trip that-a-way." She nodded in the direction she'd been going.

"Fine," I said. "Let's move."

"Yay!" Henry shouted. "Come on, George!"

Aubrey pulled George back in the direction of the farm, Henry turning with her. I shot a hard look in Adam's direction. When he noticed, the smile faded from his face and he mouthed, "what?" I shook my head, picking up the pace of my walk in order to catch up with the trio.

My stomach grumbled. Now that we'd solved the mystery of where Henry had gotten off to and we'd confirmed he was safe and sound, my attention went back to the meal waiting for us at home. Marcus had taken the ATV to scope out the rest of the property in search of Henry, while Tyler had gone back to the house with Hattie to finish up the rest of the Thanksgiving preparations. We were all pretty handy in the kitchen, but Tyler had always had a knack for cooking.

"So," Adam said. He placed his hand on his broad chest. "My name's Adam MacDaniel. That there's my older brother Jonathan. But we just call him *Mac* for short."

"I can introduce myself," I grumbled.

"Like he said, I go by Mac."

"Short for MacDaniel, I assume?" Aubrey asked.

"Yeah. I was the first of the four of us, so I got the nickname."

"Four of you, huh?" she asked, an intrigued smile on her face. "My name's Aubrey Downing."

"So, you're the new owner of Downing Farm?" I asked. "I've been wondering just who was going to be moving into that place."

"Well, you're looking at her. Hope I am everything you boys were expecting."

My eyes flicked down to her perfect ass, the shape just visible under the hem of her coat. God, it was hard not to stare.

"Didn't have much in the way of expectations," I replied. "Though it's good to know that you're the type who'd help a child in need."

"Oh, of course. Doesn't hurt that Henry's as cute as they come."

Henry flashed a broad smile, happy as always to be the topic of conversation.

"I'm having fun," he said. "And George, too."

Adam and I shared another look, this one communicating something different. Henry was a good kid, and quite social once he warmed up to someone. That warming-up process could take some time, however, and it was unusual to see him becoming comfortable with Aubrey so quickly.

"You boys are over on the big farm?" she asked. "The huge, thousand-acre place? What do you all call that chunk of land, anyway?"

Adam laughed. "We call it 'Thousand Acres Ranch.' Our great grandpa might've been a hell of a rancher, but he wasn't the most creative when it came to naming."

Aubrey laughed too. "Hey, makes it easy to remember the name. And it's apropos."

"That it is," I agreed.

We approached her place which was a respectable-sized bit of land, I guessed around fifty acres. The main house was two stories, there was a big barn off to the side, and a good number of animal pens. The small road connected to Washburn, the main drag into the nearest town.

One of the pens had a handful of llamas within its confines.

"Interesting choice for animals," I said, stepping over to the wooden fence around the llama pen. There were five in total, including George. I placed my hands on the wood and looked at the animals. "Can't say I've seen many llamas here in Maryland."

"Hey, you might think they're a little silly, but they're worth their weight in gold. Yuppies over in DC pay a *huge* premium for real llama-wool sweaters. Plus, they love the cold—they're happy as clams outside even when it's snowing."

Adam and I shared another look, this one suggesting that maybe this whole llama thing was worth looking into. I chuckled, leaning forward on the fence and watching the animals do their thing.

"Alright, Henry," I said. "We led George back home. Let's let Aubrey here get back to her holiday."

"He's not home yet!" Henry exclaimed. "He has to go inside." He pointed to the pen.

"He can help," Aubrey said. "Don't worry, they're all gentle."

Adam glanced over at me, and I nodded.

"Sure. I suppose it's good for the kid to meet new animals when he can."

Aubrey smiled, reaching into her pack and pulling out a ring of silver keys. "See this one here, Henry? That'll open the lock. Go ahead and do that, then push open the door. Once it's open, step into the pen and call out for George. He should come to where you are."

"OK! I can do that!"

She handed over the keys and Henry took them, stepping over to the gate. The big, silver lock was just out of reach, so I stepped over and hoisted the little man up by his waist. Henry let out a laugh as he worked the key into the lock, opening it. I helped him with the latch, and once that was open, he pulled the gate.

"Ready, big guy?" I asked.

"Yep!"

I set him back down, backing up as Henry entered the llama pen. The other llamas watched skeptically, as if wanting to wait and see what was going on with this new, tiny person in their zone.

"Come on!" Henry said. "George, get your big, furry butt in here!"

"Hen!" called Adam as I let out a big belly laugh. "Is that a nice thing to say to George?"

"Aubrey said it!"

Aubrey arched her brows in surprise. "Um, well, it's true. I *did* tell him that his butt was big. And furry."

"Whatever gets the job done," I said, shaking my head in amusement.

George took a second, but after a little more calling and waving from Henry, he eventually got the hint. The animal made his way into the pen, stepping over to Henry and giving his hair a sniff. Henry laughed, petting George's chest.

"There you go, big man," I said. "Now, get on out here and finish the job."

"Say bye to George!" Aubrey called out.

Henry grinned at us before climbing the fence and waving at George.

"Bye-bye! Bye-bye!"

In response, George trotted over and began licking Henry's hand. Henry let out a big laugh, reaching over and stroking the llama's fur.

"Looks like these two don't want to part," Aubrey said as she came over to me.

"Maybe we ought to set up a sleepover?" Adam said with a grin.

"Why not?" she asked. "Your place is sure big enough for a llama to run around in." As Henry said his goodbyes to George, Aubrey turned to us, putting her hands on her hips and giving us a once-over, as if sizing us up. "Henry mentioned he lived with his uncles."

"Yes, that's right. The four of us, Henry, and his twin sister," I replied. "One big, happy family."

"Sounds like it." She nodded toward the house. "Here at the humble Downing Farm, it's just me and my friend Aggie."

"You do all the work here yourself?" I asked. "Just the two of you?"

She offered a challenging grin. "What, you don't think two women can handle it?"

"It's not that at all. I'm actually impressed, more than anything."

Henry let out a laugh, still having fun with George.

"Alright, bud!" I called out. "Time to get moving; you've been enough of a handful for Miss Aubrey here for one day."

Adam stepped over to Henry, lifting him off the fence.

"Aw!" Henry said. "I want to play with George! And his friend Larry!"

"How about this," Aubrey began. "If you want, you can come back and visit. Maybe when the weather's a little nicer. That is, if it's OK with your uncles."

Adam lifted Henry higher, putting the boy on his shoulders. Henry replied with an excited giggle.

"Don't see anything wrong with that," I said.

"OK, great. We can work out the details later. Anyway, can I send you boys off with some food? Aggie and I kind of went a little overboard and we have more than enough to spare."

"Famous last words," Adam said. "All four of us are huge eaters. Trust me—even just the two of us would be able to eat you out of house and home."

"He's right. Once we get going, we don't stop until the pantry's bare. Even Henry's been known to put it all away."

"Can we eat?" Henry asked, placing his hands on his belly as Adam held him by the ankles on his shoulders.

"Sure can," I said. With that, I pulled off my glove and stepped over to Aubrey, offering my hand. "Pleasure to meet you, Aubrey. And thanks again for handling our boy."

She smiled, taking my hand. "It was a pleasure. Come back any time."

"I'd shake," Adam said, "but, uh, I've got my hands full." Instead, he bowed a bit forward, Henry laughing.

"You boys have a good Thanksgiving, alright?" She glanced one more time at all of us before tipping her hat and turning back toward the house.

I watched her as she left, her ass swaying from side to side in a way that begged my eyes to stay locked on it.

She was going to be trouble.

CHAPTER 4

ADAM

"Something catch your eye, bro?" I asked the question with a grin, knowing the answer.

"Huh?" Mac pulled his gaze off Aubrey's backside, turning his attention back to me.

Not like I could blame the guy. Aubrey's rear was about the nicest thing I'd seen in a long, long time. Didn't matter that she had on jeans and a thick, shearling coat. One glimpse of an ass that fine was all you needed.

"Just making sure she got in alright," he said. Mac adjusted the brim of his hat and turned his attention westward. "Shall we?"

"I do believe we shall," I said, shaking my head in amusement.

"Bye, George!" Henry called out one last time, waving so hard to the llama that I had to grip his ankles extra tight.

We started off. I was giving my brother a hard time for ogling Aubrey, but truth be told, I'd been eyeing her all the same. She'd almost seemed out of place for rural Maryland.

I glanced over my shoulder, my attention going to the lights in the kitchen on the first floor of the two-story house. We were too far away for me to make out anything other than the shape of two figures moving around here and there.

"Interesting woman," Mac said, his eyes on the horizon as we made our way off the land of Downing Farm.

"Yeah, interesting." I chuckled.

"Get your mind out of the gutter," Mac said, glancing in my direction.

"What?" I asked. "I don't recall saying a single thing, big bro. Maybe *you're* the one whose mind is in the gutter."

"BS."

"What's that term called? Projection?"

"Not projection. More like predictability. I know how your mind operates."

"Yeah, especially right now because you're thinking the same thing."

Mac cleared his throat, glancing over at me once more.

"You know, it's OK to admit that a woman's attractive," I said. "I know you're Mr. Stoic, but no shame in admitting a beautiful woman is beautiful."

"What's boo-tee-ful?" Henry asked.

Mac and I shared a look that made it clear that neither of us knew quite how to answer the question.

"It's when someone or something is nice to look at," Mac said.

"Like George?" Henry spoke with excitement, as if he couldn't wait to use his new word.

"Uh, sure," Mac said. "I suppose George had a certain kind of beauty."

"Especially the way his tongue hung out of his mouth," I added. "Just breathtaking."

"Breathtaking," Henry repeated, trying yet another new word on for size.

I had to laugh at how damn cute the little man was. Even more so, it was a reminder of how brainy Henry was shaping up to be. He loved learning new words and was always asking us to read him countless books before bed.

"God, I'm hungry as hell," I said. "Thinking I might skip the turkey and go right to the pie."

"Can we?" Henry asked, eagerness in his voice.

"*I* can; *you* can't."

"Why not?"

"Because I'm a grown-up and you're not. Simple, right?"

"Aw, man!"

I chuckled. Out of the corner of my eye, I spotted Mac, silent and brooding as usual.

"What's on your mind, bro?" I asked.

"Huh?" Mac shook his head a bit, coming back into the moment.

That got a laugh out of me. "It appears that something's on your mind. I was asking what it was."

"Uncle Mac was thinking," Henry confirmed.

"That's right, Hen. I could smell the rubber burning."

"What makes you think I was thinking about something?"

"The look on your face. There's brooding and then there's *brooding.*"

"What the hell are you talking about?"

"You have a certain look when you're pissed about something and another look entirely when you're trying to puzzle something out. The one you have now is like you're trying to puzzle something out."

Mac said nothing. Instead, he shook his head and took off his hat, running a hand through his thick, dark hair.

"Maybe."

"That means yes. So, what's on your mind? Let me in so I can help."

"I can help too!" Henry called out from on top of my shoulders.

Up ahead, I could see the truck we'd taken out to do the work we'd brought Henry along for, a 2021, night-black F-350. Once we reached that, we'd have a five-minute drive back to the house. Good thing the truck was there, the snow was starting to get bad. I was ready to be inside and sitting in front of the fireplace with a big glass of whiskey and a slice of pecan pie and ice cream.

Mac chuckled, as if realizing that there was no getting out of this conversation. He was right. Once I'd opened him up a bit, I rarely let him off the hook.

"Well, I was thinking about the nannies we'd interviewed for Henry and Hattie."

"The ones we talked to last week? Why are you thinking about them?"

A few months ago, the boys and I had decided that, even with four of us, we needed a little help with the twins. Thousand Acres was, well, a thousand acres, which was a hell of a lot of work even for four men and a small crew. As much as we'd felt a bit odd outsourcing our childcare, we'd all come to the conclusion that it was the right call to make.

Not only that, but four men was a hell of a lot of testosterone for two kids to be exposed to. A little femininity around the joint could be good for them.

"No reason. Well, other than the fact that we still need to decide on one." I could sense from the look on his face that there was more to it than that.

"And?"

"And what?"

I chuckled. "Might as well save us the trouble and get right to it."

He shot me a side-eyed look, one that seemed to say that there was no sense in keeping his walls up.

"Uncle Mac hates talking," Henry said from up above.

"Now, I don't hate talking," Mac replied. "Just... don't see the use in it most of the time."

"This case is different," I said. "We're talking about the twins. They, along with the business, are the two subjects we don't keep secrets about, oh mute brother of mine."

He tapped the brim of his hat, dusting off the snow that had accumulated there.

"Yeah, you're right." He pursed his lips and cleared his throat, as if trying to figure out where to begin. "Just thinking about the women we interviewed; the ones we didn't go with."

I chuckled, thinking back on the three disastrous interviews we'd had.

"Which one were you thinking about the most?" I asked. "That hippie girl who made sure to ask within five minutes if we had a problem with her hitting her weed vape pen while on the job? Or how about the one who showed up thirty minutes late and rolled her eyes when Tyler asked what the holdup was?"

Mac chuckled, shaking his head at the absurdity of it.

"Oh, or how about my favorite—that sugary-sweet Mary Poppins-type who was all smiles during the interview and seemed perfect. Until we pull her up on the background check to find out she's a two-time convicted felon for fraud and identity theft?"

"That one was all my fault," he said. "Met her at the grocery in town and thought she was perfect."

"Not giving you s-h-i-t, brother," I replied, spelling out the word so Henry didn't pick up on it. "Just saying that this process is shaping up to be a heck of a lot harder than we'd anticipated."

"No kidding. That's why..." He trailed off, as if not sure he wanted to put out there what he had on his mind.

"Come on, now."

He sighed. "That's why I think we might want to give Aubrey a shot at it."

I couldn't do anything but regard him with total damn surprise.

"Wait, what? Aubrey? The woman we just met only minutes ago? The one who owns Downing Farm?"

"Yep."

"Aubrey's fun," Henry said. "Can she come over?"

Mac raised his brow, as if to say, "see what I mean?"

We approached the truck. I squatted down a bit, taking Henry off my shoulders and putting him on the ground. We'd parked at the border of Thousand Acres, the magnificent land stretching out into the western distance. It was nearly all white by this point, and I was eager to get out of the cold.

Mac opened one of the back doors to the four-door truck, nodding for Henry to climb into his car seat.

"I want to sit up front!" he called out. It was a discussion we'd had tons of times before. Henry was one of those kids who was convinced he was a grownup, and too old and wise to sit in a kid's seat.

"Into the seat, young man," Mac said with a gruff tone. "I won't hear another word about it."

"Aw..." Henry complied, stepping over to the truck and putting his little gloved hands onto the seat. Mac stepped over and tried to help him up. "I can do it!" he replied, a defiant tone to his voice.

Mac shrugged and chuckled, stepping back and letting Henry do his thing. It took a bit of work, but he managed to get one foot up. Mac, being as stealthy as he could, put his hand on Henry's butt and gave him a tiny push to get him the rest of the way. Once that was done, Mac strapped Henry into the seat.

A few moments later, we were seated in the truck with the heat going and I pulled my gloves off, rubbing my hands together and warming myself up. Mac was behind the wheel, and I knew better than to try and argue with my big brother about driving.

"Anyway," I said once we were on our way. "*Why* exactly, did Aubrey make you think about the nanny thing?"

"Because I think she'd be perfect for the job."

I cocked my head to the side, wanting to be sure I'd heard right.

"Are you serious? You just met this woman, and you think she's perfect for the job? The job she doesn't even know about, let alone a job that she might not even want if she did know about it? I mean, she's got a ranch to run, man."

He drummed his fingers on the steering wheel, the inside of the cab silent aside from the growl of the powerful truck engine as the truck trundled over the snow.

"Let me explain my thinking."

"That'd be a good start."

"First of all, she was great with Henry. She found him, took care of him, and was very sweet towards him."

"Can we go back and see George?" Henry asked.

"Hen, bud, we've got to get back home," I said. "We can see George another time."

"Aww..."

I turned my attention back to Mac. "Go on."

"Yeah. So, she was good to Henry, and showed a real knack for taking care of him."

"Sure. I can't argue with how good she was with the little guy. All the same, she *has* a job—she's got Downing to handle."

"Not so much in the winter," he replied. "Even with those animals, with no crops to worry about she's going to have her workload cut in half. So, I'm thinking a gig just a quick drive over where she can make a little extra dough during the off season might be right up her alley."

Mac was starting to make a little sense. All the same, I wasn't sure yet if I was on board.

"But that's all assuming she wants to do it."

"Yeah, you're right," he agreed. "She might turn us down the second we bring it up."

He shrugged. "If she does, she does. Just saying that we're looking for a nanny, and she might be exactly what we need."

I wanted to find a way to shoot him down, to tell Mac that he was being crazy. The more I thought about it, however, it started to sound like a good idea.

"Plus, I got a good sense from her."

"A good what?"

"You know... what the kids call a *vibe*."

That got a laugh out of me. I wasn't that much younger than Mac but hearing him use kid lingo like that was kind of funny.

"You mean, she passed the vibe check?"

"Huh? Sure, I guess. I'm just saying, I trust my gut when it comes to this sort of thing, and I got nothing but good feelings from her. You can't tell me you don't feel the same way."

I shifted my weight, trying to think the matter over.

"I mean, yeah. She was nice, good with Henry and seemed to be level-headed. Just saying, it's a little out of character for you to make a decision like this so quickly."

"Who said I decided? We still need to talk to the others before we present the idea to her, and even if she agrees, you bet your ass she's going to get a background check."

"Right. We still need to be on the safe side, of course. But damn, I guess I have to admit I did get a feeling from her that I haven't gotten from anyone we've considered so far."

I continued to think the matter over as we approached the huge estate of Thousand Acres. The house was a three-story, colonial-style home with a red brick front, dark blue gables, and a large balcony on each floor that reminded me of something you'd see in the deep South. Two big barns were off to each side, and there were two circles of animal pens to our left and right. The massive garage was big enough for the four trucks we owned, along with a handful of ATVs and motorcycles. Off in the distance, I watched as Marcus finished leading the horses into the barn in preparation for a snowy rest of the day.

We pulled to a stop in front of the house, a set of stone stairs leading to the huge, dark red double doors.

"Let's talk about it over dinner," Mac said. "I don't know about you, but I'm starving."

CHAPTER 5

TYLER

"**A**lright little man, what's the story?"

Henry's big eyes went wide as he clapped them onto me. I'd been ready for the crew to come home ever since Mac's text ten minutes ago and had been waiting for them sitting in the big wing-back situated in the nook of the grand staircase.

I enjoyed spending time there. Like the rest of the house, the area was dominated by rich, dark wood, the ceilings sky high and the floors covered with rugs. It wasn't quite as cozy as the study or the den or the kitchen, but few things were nicer than sitting in the chair with a good book, able to glance up at the huge, arched windows that looked out over the stretch of land in front of the house any time I wanted to.

Reading was the last subject on my mind, however. The moment Mac and Adam came into the house with Henry, the three of them dusted in new-fallen snow, all I could think about was how damn distressed I was.

"Uh oh," Adam said with a smile as he set Henry down. "You're in for it now."

I sprang out of my chair, making my way toward Henry with long strides. While I was happy as hell to see the kid, there was no way I could pretend I wasn't upset.

"Buddy!" I said, dropping to a squat and putting my hands on my knees. "What's the story? You go out with Uncle Mac and Uncle Adam and then I hear you wandered off?"

Henry's eyes got even bigger. He knew he'd done something wrong.

"Remember when you asked to go? Do you remember what Uncle Mac said?"

"Uh-huh." He nodded slowly.

"What did Uncle Mac say?"

"Um..."

"Let me jog your memory, bud," Mac's voice boomed down from his six-foot-four-inch height. "I said that you could come with me, as long as you didn't run off."

"Do you remember now?" I asked Henry.

He looked at me, then up at Adam, then Mac. The kid seemed too scared to speak.

"Mind if I talk to him alone?" I asked.

"Have at it."

"We'll check on the food. But Henry, we're going to have a little chat of our own later, you hear?"

Henry nodded. With that, Adam and Mac left, both of them giving Henry's brown hair a tussle as they did.

"Come with me, big man."

I stood and offered Henry my hand. He took it, and together we headed off to the den. The room was big and comfy and inviting as always, with two giant, overstuffed leather couches at a right angle in front of the massive fireplace, a big fire roaring behind the metal, child-safe gate. The furniture was situated on top of a big, circular Oriental rug, the walls of the room lined with bookshelves packed with colorful spines. A few paintings of the local landscape were hung here and there.

On a snowy day like today, it was the most ideal place to spend a few hours with a good book or just watching the fire, relaxing and taking a nap.

We sat down on one of the couches, the reflection of the fire casting Henry's handsome little face in a flickering orange glow.

"What happened?" I asked. "Let's start there."

He wrung his tiny hands, as if trying to figure out where to begin.

"Um, I saw a road and I went for a walk."

I knew instantly that the "road" he was referring to was Halbrook Trail, one of the landmarks that formed the border between the eastern edge of our property and Downing Farm.

"You know that Halbrook Trail isn't ours, right? We've shown you and your sister several times where our land starts and ends. But you went over there anyway."

"Yeah. I wanted to see the creek."

"And you waited until your uncles weren't looking, then ran off. Is that right?"

Wouldn't have been hard for Mac and Adam to quickly lose sight of him—there was plenty of tree cover over in that area for a kid to hide in. I could easily picture Henry ducking behind one tree or another and running in the other direction while Adam and Mac looked for him.

"That's right."

"Gotta be honest, bud. I'm not liking this story."

Henry's eyes started to shimmer with tears. I could sense he was now well aware of what he'd done wrong. While I was confident that I was doing the right thing, it still killed me all the same to see him upset. There was no denying that I had a soft spot for the kids, one that made it a touch hard at times to bring down the discipline hammer when I needed to.

"I'm sorry!" With that, the tears started flowing. Henry opened his arms and hugged me as tightly as he could, as more tears continued to fall.

It was one of the hardest parts of being a parent. Henry was ashamed of what he'd done, and understood it was wrong but all the same he needed to be punished.

"I wanted to see the trail," he said. "But then I fell!"

"I heard you met a nice lady out there. You're *very* lucky that someone was around to help you out."

"I know. She was really nice. Her name was Aubrey."

Aubrey. So that was the name of the woman who owned Downing Farm. I'd been meaning to head over there at some point to introduce myself, but it ended up being one of those tasks that I kept putting off. Her saving our boy was a hell of a way to get to know one another.

For now, I needed to figure out what to do with the little guy in front of me.

"Alright, alright," I said gently as I swept Henry's hair back away from his damp eyes. "You're in trouble, make no mistake. But for now, we need to get you washed up and ready for dinner. How about we head upstairs for a bath and a change, then we get some grub?"

The idea of punishment now far into the future, Henry's face lit up. "Can I have pie too? And ice cream?"

"Maybe. We'll see. Come on."

I hopped off the couch, taking Henry's hand and turning to lead him out of the room. Once facing the entry to the den, I realized that Henry's and my conversation had a listener. Marcus, my twin brother, stood at the entrance, leaning against the side with his arms crossed over his chest and a typical stoic expression on his three-day-old scruff covered face.

Marcus was a serious man, though not without a sardonic sense of humor that came out from time to time. Judging by the expression on his face, this didn't appear to be one of those occasions. Marcus shot Henry a hard look as he approached, one that caused the little guy to grip my hand harder.

"So much for tough love, huh?" Marcus asked. "A bath and some pie? Hardly seems the best way to hammer home that he's done something wrong." He spoke softly enough for Henry not to hear.

"Hey, he feels bad enough already."

"He should. We were all scared as hell that something had happened to him. And he's going to do it again unless he completely understands that he did something wrong."

"He gets it," I said. "We can punish later. Besides, you want me to send him to his room without Thanksgiving dinner?"

"It'd sure send the message home," Marcus muttered.

"Dude, he's five years old, not fifteen. I'll sort him out later."

Marcus snorted, clearly displeased with my call. "You're soft on the twins. Need to be a little tougher if you want them to learn."

"Thanks for the tip," I replied, a tinge of sarcasm to my voice.

Though the four of us often had different opinions on how to best raise our niece and nephew, we were united in our love for the twins, and that was far greater than any disagreements we might have when it came to the finer points of raising them.

"Come on, big man," I said. "Let's get upstairs."

Before we could take another step, however, a voice called out to us.

"Where are you going?"

An instant grin formed as I turned to see the big, smiling face of Hattie, her eager expression framed by a tussle of sandy-blonde hair. She ran over to me, letting out a squeal as she threw her arms around Henry.

"Well, hey there, little lady!" I said, bending down and joining in on the hug.

"Hey!" Henry called back, not a big fan of the hug. "Let me go!"

"Where did you go?" Hattie asked. "I was scared."

"I was in the woods."

"But it's cold out!"

I stepped back, watching the two bicker in the way only twins could. I happened to be an expert on the subject myself, having just had a small spat with my own twin. The pair loved one another like crazy, though Hattie was the one keener on showing it.

I glanced up to see Mac across the room.

"Heard you were planning on washing Henry up before dinner. Mind getting them both at the same time?"

"Sure, might as well wash the pair of them if I'm going to fill up the tub. You ready, Hat?"

"Yep!" She beamed, clearly happy to be part of the process. Hattie was the shier of the two, less rambunctious, less eager to get into trouble. When it was just family, however, she was always sunshine and smiles, blessed with the same optimism and positive attitude that her mother had had.

We headed upstairs, Hattie getting all the details of Henry's adventure out of him as we made our way to the bathroom near the kids' room. I filled the tub and got the kids out of their dirty clothes, making sure the bath was nice and bubbly before I plopped them both into the water.

I loved giving the kids their daily bath. The two of them were growing up right before my eyes, and it seemed like just yesterday that they were talking in babbles and crawling everywhere. When they were in the tub, splashing around and laughing their little heads off, they were kids through and through.

By the time we were finished with baths, the scents from the kitchen downstairs had become impossible to ignore. Marcus and I had handled most of the cooking while Henry and Mac and Adam had gone on their errand-running trip, but now that they were back, they'd taken over to put the finishing touches on the meal.

I helped the kids get dressed, Henry and Hattie putting on their best collared shirt and dress respectively while chatting eagerly about all the different dishes of food they were going to eat. The conversation focused mainly on pie and ice cream, of course, both homemade.

By the time the kids were cleaned up and dressed, I was so ready to eat that I couldn't think straight. I carried the twins down, bringing them into the kitchen where the rest of the boys were busy at work getting the meal ready to serve. The kitchen was all rustic, huge and spacious with copper pots hanging over the island, the wooden farmer's table off to the side big enough for ten.

"'Bout damn time!" Adam said.

Mac reached over and gave him a swat to the shoulder.

"Language!"

"Shi—, I mean, *shoot*," he said, screwing up his face a bit in embarrassment.

Marcus chuckled as he set plates on the table, shaking his head. We'd had the kids for almost a full year, but all the same we were still working on getting out of the habits we'd established over our years of bachelor-dom.

"I see you took the time to trim that beard of yours," Mac said to me with a small smirk.

I laughed, pretending to fluff my beard.

"You wish you could grow a beard like this, old man," I goaded.

He let out a barking laugh.

"Alright, Grizzly Adams," Adam said. "Get your butt over here and help us set the table. Faster we get that done, the faster we eat."

"Sounds da—, *darn* good to me."

We got to it, loading the table with turkey, gravy, stuffing, biscuits and all the other traditional dishes. Henry and Hattie helped, setting the silverware and napkins. By the time we were done setting up the table, I was so ready to eat that it took all the restraint I had not to grab the nearest turkey leg and bite into it like a damn caveman.

We finally sat, Mac pouring wine for us and milk for the kids. The lights of the kitchen were low, a few candles providing ambience with their flickering flames. The snow still came down outside, and the sun had dipped down enough to bring on a bit of darkness. Between the food and the company and the snowy weather, it was just about the perfect Thanksgiving.

Mac cleared his throat, signaling that he had something to say. The table silenced, all of us turning our attention to our eldest brother.

"Now, I'm not one for speeches. But I think I'd be remiss if I didn't say a few words, considering how different this Thanksgiving is compared to our last one."

A serious expression took hold of all of our faces. He didn't need to mention what he was referring to.

"It's been almost a year since we lost Kristen," he said.

He was referring to our sister, Henry and Hattie's mother. Henry was sitting next to me, and I put my hand on his tiny shoulder.

"And I don't know about you all, but not a day goes by that I don't think about her, think about how much we're all missing without her in our lives."

Mac swallowed and closed his eyes. If the way I was feeling was any indication, the mere mention of Kristen was hard for him.

"Though she's no longer with us, we've been blessed with two amazing little people. Goes without saying, but none of us imagined a year ago that we'd be raising kids together. But Henry, Hattie, I want you two to know that all of your uncles love you like crazy and having you in our lives has made us feel more complete than we ever could've imagined."

I squeezed Henry's shoulder, and he looked up at me with a smile.

"There's a lot of love in this house," Mac said. "And as we start the holidays together, I can say for certain that it's only going to grow." With that, he raised his glass of wine. "Here's to our family."

We raised our glasses, Henry and Hattie lifting their small cups of milk.

"Here, here!" I said, Adam and Marcus joining me.

"Alright!" said Mac, allowing himself a smile. "This food's not getting any hotter. Let's eat!"

With that, we dug in. After helping Henry with his plate, I went for the turkey, snagging one of the legs and drenching it with gravy. Next was mashed potatoes, along with stuffing and some green bean casserole.

We talked as we ate, going over our plans for the winter on the farm, along with what we wanted to get done for the next year. Managing Thousand Acres was no small thing, and with the success we'd had, it was looking like we'd need another couple dozen hands on the place to keep it chugging along.

"Speaking of which," Adam said with a big smile. "You want to tell the guys about your idea for the newest member of the staff?"

Mac's eyes flashed, then his expression turned hard. "You dumba —, I mean, you dummy, I'm not ready to talk about that just yet. Still thinking it over."

I was intrigued. "What? What's going on here?"

Marcus leaned in. "Whatever it is, cat's out of the bag. Might as well spill it."

Mac sighed, wiping his hands and tossing the napkin down onto the table. "Fine. Got an idea for the nanny."

"Is that right?" I asked.

"It is. The woman who runs Downing Farm."

Needless to say, I was *more* than intrigued.

CHAPTER 6

MARCUS

"What the heck?" I asked.

I was equal parts amused and surprised. Seeing Mac, the oldest of us, caught on the back foot like that was something else. The man was more stoic than I was, and I was about as stoic as they came, but there was no doubt in my mind that he was all kinds of steamed at Adam for letting that particular cat out of the bag.

"You couldn't have waited until *after* the kids were in bed to talk about this?" Mac asked, angrily slicing through his turkey.

"I liked Aubrey," Henry declared.

"Who's Aubrey?" Hattie asked.

Mac sighed. "Alright, here's the deal. If you guys want to talk about this so badly like a trio of gossiping housewives, then fine. But let's do it after dinner."

Adam leaned toward me. "Aubrey's the woman who owns Downing Farm. Evidently, Mac here thinks she'd be perfect for the nanny job."

"*Enough*," Mac stated. Tight anger was on his face, the sort of anger that always reminded me of Dad whenever he'd be on his last nerve with us when we were kids.

"Fine, fine," Adam said. "Let's talk about it in the den over whiskey once the kids are in bed."

"Sounds good," I agreed. "Because I'm all kinds of curious."

As we finished up dinner, Mac brought the conversation back to the subject of odds and ends around Thousand Acres. It was clear by the way the guys and I kept looking at one another that the subject of Mac's new nanny suggestion was the biggest thing on our minds—far more than any goings on around the place and the potential of a new mission.

We topped off the meal with sweet potato, pecan, and pumpkin pie, the six of us nearly finishing off all three. The few slices left meant there'd be a battle over them for breakfast, but that could wait.

Mac and Marcus put the kids to bed, while Adam and I got the den ready with drinks and a few new logs on the fire.

"What the hell happened out there?" I asked, pouring the two of us some bourbon. "How'd Henry get away from you?"

Adam shook his head. No doubt he was furious with himself.

"That kid loves the outdoors," he said. "So much so, in fact, that I'm quickly learning that we can't take our eyes off him for even a second while he's out there with us. All he wants to do is explore."

"Worse traits to have when you're growing up on a ranch." I stepped over to Adam, handing him the drink. We clinked glasses, then sipped.

"Yeah, especially when you spent the first year of your life in a DC apartment."

I dropped into the couch in front of the fireplace, watching the flames crackle for a bit.

"No sense in beating ourselves up over it. Henry's a kid, and a boy. Things like this are bound to happen here and there. Don't forget what we were like as kids."

"You're right about that," Adam agreed. "We got four pairs of eyes between us, though. There's really no excuse in letting him wander off like that again." Adam's expression hardened. He'd always been the happy-go-lucky type, like Hattie. Weird seeing him like that. "When I looked around and realized that he'd run off..."

He grit his teeth, his jaw working back and forth. Adam didn't finish his sentence. He didn't need to—it was obvious what was on his mind.

"Hey, I said that you didn't need to beat yourself up over it, and I meant it. Between four uncles and two kids, we're going to be making all kinds of mistakes over the years. We learn from them, and we move on."

He nodded. "Yeah. No sense dwelling on what *could've* happened."

I sat back, taking a sip of my drink. "Kristen wrote in her will that if anything happened to her, we'd be the ones to take care of the twins. She wouldn't have done that if she didn't think we were up to the task."

He smiled. "Then again, she figured it'd take all *four* of us to raise them, not just one."

I allowed myself a smile, too. "Hey, why settle for one uncle when you can have four? But she made the right call. I mean, what else was she going to do, try and get us to track down that deadbeat, piece-of-shit ex of hers?"

"Seth," he said, practically spitting out the name. "Worthless prick."

We both took sips of our booze, as if trying to wash the taste of mentioning him out of our mouths.

"Alright, boys." Mac's booming voice came from behind us. We turned to see him and Marcus coming into the room, Mac with his laptop tucked under his arm. "Had a little discussion with Markie here."

"Oh yeah?" I asked. "What's the word?"

"Figured that if we were going to bring this up," Marcus said. "We might as well just go ahead and go the whole nine."

"And what does *that* mean?" Adam asked.

Mac curled the side of his mouth as he opened his laptop on the coffee table.

"Means that before we talk about the idea of her being a potential nanny, we're going to vet her a bit."

"Now, that's thinking," Adam said. "What's the point of having all these fancy security clearances if we're not going to use them to make sure anyone who's going to be looking after our kids is on the level?"

The boys and I were all ex-military. Mac and Adam were former SEALS, Mac a commander. I was a Marine, and Tyler was a former Green Beret. While our servicemember pasts were behind us, we still kept our toes in that world. Mac, for example, owned an extraction agency called Exfil Inc. – a top-secret military contractor used by the government to extract high-value targets out of dicey areas.

We all pitched in. Truth was, that Exfil Inc. more or less ran itself at this point. We had a solid team of men, and these days the boys and I did little more than serve as middlemen between our contacts in the military and the team. We used to go out on missions, but not one of us had done that since taking in the twins.

"Anyway," Mac said, typing. "The woman's name is Aubrey Downing. Shouldn't be too hard to track her info down."

We all sat in silence as Mac did his thing, pulling up databases and searching for her. It wasn't long before a picture appeared on the screen, one from the local newspaper, the title "City Girl Makes Good."

The picture of her that accompanied the article was... something else. I nearly dropped my drink at the sight of her. The shot was of her in front of the main house of Downing Farm, a llama at her side and a big smile on her face. She was tall and slender, dressed in jeans and a T-shirt and a pair of cowboy boots. Her hair was dark and curly, her skin olive, and her body as fine as they came. Just the sight of her in the photo was enough to make my cock twitch to life.

Tyler whistled. "That her? Damn."

"Get your mind out of the gutter, bro," Adam said with a knowing smirk. "We're looking into her for professional reasons, not recreational ones."

Mac made the text bigger, giving it a quick read. "Impressive stuff. Graduated from University of Maryland with top honors, got herself a degree in accounting. Says she worked for some big tech firm up in New York City until her father died and left her the farm."

"Explains why she showed up out of nowhere," Adam said. "And why she seems a little out of her element."

"Let me look around a little more," Mac said. "Find out some info that this puff piece isn't going to have."

He clicked here and there, eventually bringing up her financial information.

"Good credit," he said. "But wait..."

"What is it?" I asked, craning my neck to get a better look at the screen.

Mac sipped his drink, shaking his head.

"Lots of debt in student loans, I mean a *lot*. Talking tens of thousands of dollars here."

"Well, that's nothing," Tyler said. "Just means that she didn't have some rich parents paying her way through college. These days, the only way an average person's getting a degree is by taking out tons of loans."

"All the same," Mac said, sitting back and taking a thoughtful sip of his drink, "I don't like it."

Adam shook his head. "Brother, if you aren't going to hire someone because of student loans then you're excluding half the pool of twenty and thirty-somethings out there. As long as she's paying it off, I don't see what the big deal is."

"I'm more interested in her criminal history," I said. "After what happened with that last woman we interviewed..."

Mac nodded in silent agreement as he leaned forward and typed. Generally obtaining criminal background info wasn't easy. For a crew like us, however, it took no effort at all.

"She's clean," he said. "Nothing other than a few parking tickets back when she was a teenager."

"That's good news," Adam said. "Anything else we can find?"

Mac put her name into another search engine, this time bringing up what looked to be a webpage for the farm. He scrolled down, and I had to admit the page was charming. There were pictures of her posing with the animals, a big smile on her face in each one.

After a bit more scrolling, however, he reached a picture that gave all of us pause—a photo of her in a bikini.

"Now *that's* the sort of background information I'm looking for," Adam said with a grin.

"Easy, horndog," I replied, reaching over and giving him a swat to the arm. "This is about finding out if she's right for the job, not ogling her like some horny teenager."

He shrugged. "Just saying what we were all thinking."

He was right. There was no way to look at the picture of her wearing barely anything at all without noticing right away how damned gorgeous she was. I was getting so turned on, in fact, that it was almost uncomfortable to be around my brothers.

"So," Mac said, closing the internet browser window and mercifully taking the sight of Aubrey in a bikini away from me. "She was great with Henry, seems on the level, and lives right nearby."

"Not to mention, she's not a convicted felon," Adam added. "Always a plus." He flashed a smile.

I rubbed my chin, thinking it over. "There's still the matter of her *wanting* the job. We don't know if she's got the time for it with running her farm and all. And if so, we'll still need to try her out with the twins. One kid is one thing, two is a whole different ball game."

"Right," Mac replied, closing the computer. "The kids come first —no matter what."

He said what we were all thinking. Strange as it seemed, however, it felt like we'd already made the decision, that Aubrey was almost fated to be a part of our lives.

Things were about to get interesting.

CHAPTER 7

AUBREY

"Y̶ou're back! *Finally!*"

Aggie Culberson, my best friend and assistant on the farm, stood up from where she was seated at the small, square kitchen table. She was dressed in light wash skinny jeans and a big, red sweater; a long braid of her sandy-brown hair draped over her shoulder.

She hurried over and gave me a quick up and down, as if to make sure that nothing was out of place.

"What the hell took you so long out there?" she asked, a tinge of worry to her voice. Between the two of us, Aggie was the more cautious one, always worried about how hard I pushed myself on a daily basis keeping the farm up and running. "Actually, never mind that right now, you look like you're freezing. Go get changed into some dry clothes, and I'll pour you some tea."

I laughed, casually slipping off my snow-dusted coat. "Thanks, Mom."

Aggie raised a thick, dark eyebrow. "Hey, you joke, but sometimes I wonder what kind of nonsense you'd get up to if I weren't here to make sure you were taking care of yourself. They'd find you frozen stiff among the llamas."

I shook my head. I was too taken with the scents of cooking food that hung heavy in the kitchen. I closed my eyes and took a big whiff.

"God, you really outdid yourself, Aggs," I said.

"I think I did a pretty good job," she replied, putting her hands on her hips and looking around at the spread on the kitchen counter. "But you're not getting one bite without cleaning up first. Change into something warmer, OK?"

I pursed my lips, eager as hell to tell her about what had happened out there. Aggie, knowing me all too well, raised a finger.

"When you're cleaned up."

"Fine, fine."

She took my coat, and I hurried out of the room, images of the men I'd just met still fresh in my mind. It seemed so surreal yet so exciting at the same time. I was already trying to figure out how I could see them again.

Mac and Adam. Their names repeated in my thoughts as I hurried up the narrow, wooden stairway to the second floor, rushing down the hallway decorated with photos of my family. Once I was in my bedroom I shut the door, a smile forming on my lips as I thought about them.

I tried to push them out of my head as best I could, slipping off my wet clothes and changing into a comfy pair of sweatpants and an oversized NYU sweatshirt. The snow was still coming down hard, making me glad I'd taken the time to put the animals in the barn.

When I was dressed, I stepped into some slippers and went back into the kitchen just in time to see Aggie pull her teal-colored Dutch oven out. The delicious scent of roast turkey blended with the smells of biscuits and stuffing and all the other dishes filled the air. I realized then that I'd been so wrapped up in the events of the early afternoon that I'd totally spaced on how hungry I was.

"Thanks for cooking," I said, my eyes locked onto the Dutch

oven. "But I'm going to have to ask you to get out of the way right now so I can dig in."

"Patience, my dear," Aggie said, lifting the Dutch oven lid and revealing the simmering food within. "We need, let's say, ten more minutes to let the meat stew in its own juices. In the meantime, we drink tea, and you tell me about what happened out there that took you so long to get back."

I grinned, sliding into one of the chairs at the kitchen table. Sure enough, a mug of hot tea appeared in front of me.

I leaned in and gave the tea a sniff, wrapping my hands around the big, ceramic mug.

"I swear, sometimes I think you and I ought to just get married. Not like I'm ever going to meet a man who knows me as well as you do."

She laughed. "Don't give up hope just yet, oh negative one. And besides, we've been over this before, you're not my type. You know I like my women a little on the shorter and thicker side."

That got a laugh out of me. I took a sip of my tea, letting the warmth run through me. Aggie prepared a mug of her own and came over to sit.

"Okay, I'm ready now. Spill."

"Alright. So, it started when I heard this weird noise off in the distance when I was chasing George up Halbrook Trail..."

I told her about Henry, how I'd found him in the ravine. After that, I gave her the full scoop about Mac and Adam.

Her eyes lit up. "You're serious? You finally met the guys from Thousand Acres?"

"Yep, turns out it's a family operation, like here."

"And? What's the story with them?"

"Well... they were hot."

She leaned in, intrigued. "Oh, really?"

"Really." I laughed. "You know, for someone who's not into guys, you sure seem interested."

Aggie shrugged. "Good looking is good looking."

"Well, they were definitely good looking, that's for sure. They were both the same kind of strong, strapping guy with broad shoulders and big hands and steely eyes and just enough stubble to be totally sexy..." I found myself trailing off, my mind totally focused on the two men. I felt a tingling down below, one that made me bite my lower lip.

"Uh, Aub?" Aggie asked, waving her hand in the air. "You OK over there?"

"Sorry, just got a little distracted."

Aggie grinned. "I can see that."

I took a moment to compose myself, a sip of the hot tea bringing me back into the here and now.

"OK, anyway..."

I finished the story, telling her about how the men and Henry came back with me to the ranch, and how they'd left with an invitation to get to know one another better.

"There's *four* of them?" Aggie asked, her eyes round as dinner plates.

"Four brothers," I said with a shrug, as if it were the most normal, commonplace thing to say. "All living together."

"That's certainly interesting. Which one of them was Henry's dad?"

"You know, I didn't ask. He called Mac and Adam 'uncle' so it wasn't either of them."

"Very interesting. Well, you definitely need to meet the other two. "

"You're right. I mean, we *are* neighbors. Makes sense that we get to know one another."

Aggie nodded, glancing off in thought.

"Oh no," I said.

"What?"

"You've got that look on your face that you always get when you have something... R-rated on your mind."

"Well, maybe I do."

"Dare I ask?"

She turned her eyes back to me, a mischievous smile on her face.

"First I was thinking about how you ought to hook up with at least one of them."

"Aggie!"

"What? I mean, why not? When's the last time you've been with a guy, anyway?"

"God, I don't even want to think about it. Not since I took over the farm."

"See? Might do you some good to knock the cobwebs out from down there."

My jaw fell open. "Please tell me you didn't just say that."

"I *did* just say that. You can't tell me I'm wrong. I mean, it's been so long for you that I bet you've forgotten what it's even like to do the deed."

"Oh, stop it. I haven't forgotten!"

"Are you sure?" she teased. "You remember what goes where?"

I threw my napkin at her. "You're terrible. But I have to admit that the thought of taking one of those cowboys for a ride does sound fabulous."

She grabbed the side of the table, leaning in with a wicked look on her face.

"Why stop at just one?"

I cocked my head to the side. There was no way I'd heard her right.

"Like what, at the same time?"

"At the same time."

I blinked hard. "How does that even work?" Something else occurred to me. "And that's totally gross! Aggie, they're brothers! I'm sure they don't want to be naked together."

She let out another laugh, as if she were totally pleased that her words were having the desired effect.

"I'm not saying they're going to do it with each other—that'd be completely messed up."

"Then what *are* you saying?"

Aggie grinned, as if she had me right where she wanted me.

"Think of it less like a five-way, and more like them all taking very, very good care of you. A pair of lips here, a nice big cock there..."

"No. Just *no*. That's way too much to even think about."

"Four big, strong guys making sure *all* of your needs are attended to, over and over."

"Alright, alright, enough of that. What about dinner?"

She threw one more smirk in my direction before glancing over her shoulder.

"I think we're probably ready to go. Let's get our feast on."

With that, Aggie and I headed over to the stove and took the lids off the food we'd prepared. After everything that had happened over the last few hours, I was starving. We loaded our plates, sat down, then went to it.

The food was amazing, delicious enough to take my mind off my handsome neighbors. Thankfully, Aggie eased off giving me the business over them, and we talked about other, farm-related matters.

A few minutes into that conversation, however, I quickly realized that the farm wasn't exactly a fun subject to discuss.

"So," Aggie said, setting down her fork and lifting her glass of red wine. "Some of the llamas are due for a shear. Thinking we can handle that in the next week, then get the wool shipped over to our distributor."

"And when are we going to get paid for that?"

"Shouldn't be more than a month."

I quickly nodded, doing the calculations in my head.

Aggie, understanding right away what I was doing, leaned over and put her hand on mine.

"We're going to make enough to cover the mortgage for next month. *And* the month after that. This llama fur is worth its weight in gold."

"The mortgage is one thing; I'm worried about the debts."

Aggie nodded sympathetically. "I know. When your dad left you this place, he left a hell of a lot of debt to go with it." She narrowed her eyes in thought, as if something had occurred to her. "You know..." Aggie shook her head. "Actually, never mind."

"What?"

She pursed her lips. "It's just... your dad left you this place when he passed, right? What if you just..."

"Nope. Not going to happen."

"You didn't even let me finish."

"Why would I? I know what you're going to say, and the answer is no."

She leaned forward. "Listen, don't get me wrong. I love the farm. It's beautiful and quaint and few things are more fun than working with my best friend and all these cute animals. *But...*"

"*But?*"

"There's still the matter of the debt. Yes, you've put that accounting degree to work and figured a way out of it—"

"Might as well use it for something if I'm going to be living the farm life."

"Absolutely. But you said yourself, it's going to take a ton of time and effort. Don't get me wrong—I'm fine with working hard. But if there's an easier solution, why not at least explore it?"

I took in a long, slow breath through my nose.

"Nope."

"Just listen! You sell the farm..."

"Nope. Not going to happen."

"You sell the farm but come up with some kind of arrangement with the new owner where you can buy the place back. Then, we both go back to New York, get jobs in our fields and work-work-work until we make the money back."

"It's not going to happen."

Aggie pursed her lips. "I get that you want to keep the place; I really do. And while I hate to play this card, I *did* invest in the farm just to keep it from going totally insolvent. You make the final decisions, but I do get some say."

She had a point. I'd had to chew through a ton of my savings just to get the farm totally out of arrears when Dad passed. And even then, I'd needed a little help unless I was going to go completely broke in the process of making the farm mine. That's where Aggie had come in.

"Anyway," she said, blowing past my objections. "We earn money in ways that we're actually good at, then buy the place back. You can't tell me this is a bad idea."

I shook my head. "There's no guarantee if we were to sell it to someone that they would make that arrangement. What would be the benefit to them to do it that way? Once you sell, it's theirs. They could agree to one thing and go right back on it the second their name's on the dotted line."

"We just have to find someone sympathetic and trustworthy to do it."

"Easier said than done." I sighed, shaking my head in frustration, more at the state of affairs than at Aggie. "Listen, I know this is a hard situation."

"I do too. Don't get me wrong. knew what I was signing up for."

"Right. And you know that I went into it with a promise to my dad that I wouldn't sell this place, not for anything. I can't risk losing it. I have to do everything I can to..."

I trailed off, not knowing what else to say. Aggie was right, the finances for Downing weren't looking good. If we were going to make this happen, we'd not only have to walk a wire across the Grand Canyon, but we'd also have to pray that no wind blew us off in the process.

"Listen," Aggie said. "When I agreed to go into this with you, I did it with the intention of seeing it through. You want to keep at it, then that's what we're going to do. And I'm going to be at your side, through thick and thin, down to the last llama."

She smiled, and I did the same.

"Thanks, Aggs."

"That's what I'm here for. Now, clean that plate! I've got some bourbon cherry pecan pie in the fridge that I've been thinking about for the last ten minutes."

She squeezed my hand, the two of us sharing a smile before returning to our meals.

It was hard to focus on the food. Between my new neighbors and the reality of my farm, I had a feeling that the way my life would look like come springtime would be totally different.

CHAPTER 8

AUBREY

"How are we feeling?"

I gave the matter some thought. Aggie and I were seated in the small, cozy den, a roaring fire in the hearth as snow came down in sheets outside. My belly was full of delicious food, a big, heavy blanket wrapped around me as I watched the flames dance. To make it even more perfect, I had another glass of wine close at hand.

Aggie was seated over in the other easy chair in front of the fire, a true crime book opened up on her lap.

"You know, pretty damn good. Thanks again for helping with the cooking."

"Hey, I did more than 'help'." She grinned. "And I'm happy to do it." Her expression turned serious, with a touch of worry. "Listen, I didn't mean to come down on you so hard at dinner. Sometimes I get a little too worked up for my own good; not all of us are as skilled at staying cool, you know."

"Don't even worry about it. One of the reasons I asked you to join me in this whole operation was because I know you've got no problem keeping it real with me. It's one of your best qualities, even when it means you're chewing me out over Thanksgiving dinner."

"Good! Because I couldn't turn it off even if I wanted to. So, as long as we're in this together, that's what you're getting."

"Wouldn't have it any other way."

She gave me a smile and an affirmative nod.

"Anyway, I have an idea."

"An idea? Oh no..."

"Trust me, this is going to be a good one. I'm thinking that since I put a little bit of a damper on our holiday, it's only fair that I try to help lighten the mood."

"What'd you have in mind?"

"Let me handle the dishes. If you ask me, this looks like the perfect weather for a hot bath and a glass of wine."

The idea was very tempting.

"You don't have to do that, Aggs."

"I know I don't have to, I'm offering, and I want to. And don't forget you're the one who braved the cold to retrieve George, the world's dumbest llama. Now, get your butt up there and have a soak. Don't forget the candles!"

I laughed, pushing myself out of my seat.

"Alright, alright. Thanks, Aggs."

She winked, giving me a finger gun before turning her attention back to her book.

I headed into the kitchen, the sink full of plates and silverware and pots and pans. After topping off my glass, I went upstairs to my bedroom's ensuite bath. The room was lovely, with a slanted ceiling and windows that looked out over the back stretch of the property, giving me a view of the blizzard in progress, and the roof of the barn already topped with white. The tub was gorgeous—a freestanding antique clawfoot. After years of living in a New York apartment with a shower that was barely big enough for me, the tub was an amenity that I made sure to take advantage of as often as possible.

I left the main lights of the bathroom off, choosing to do as Aggie suggested and light a few candles. Once those were going, hot water streaming into the tub with a little lavender bath oil, I was more than ready to get in. Once out of my clothes, I stepped into the sudsy water, letting out an *"ohh, maaaan"* as I slipped inside.

Once I'd adjusted to the heat, the water and the bath oil working their magic on my worn muscles, I took in a deep, slow breath, a big, stupid smile on my face. The window in front of the tub looked out onto the snow, and I couldn't think of any place I'd rather be during weather like this.

I took another sip of my wine, settling into a perfect buzz. Suddenly, Mac and Adam popped into my mind.

Just the thought of the two gorgeous men was enough to make my pussy tingle. I set my wine glass down, biting my lip. I thought of their steely, narrowed eyes, their sensuous mouths, their big, rough hands. The picture of them in my mind's eye was so complete and clear that I could almost feel what it'd be like to have those huge hands, calloused from hard days of work, all over my body.

As ridiculous as it had initially sounded, I couldn't stop thinking about what Aggie had said about being with all four of them at the same time. Almost out of my control, my hand began to slip under the water and between my thighs.

I moaned as my finger swirled around my sensitive clit.

I closed my eyes, picturing the brothers once more.

I focused on Mac first—the older, taller brother. I imagined his dark hair, his brooding face, his hazel-brown eyes and neatly trimmed beard over his sharp jawline. Mac's face was angular, his eyes narrow slits as if he were always gazing off into the horizon. He was so good-looking that it was almost scary—an intimidating sort of hand-someness.

Then there was Adam. While he had similar features to his brother, his green eyes and slightly softer features set him apart. He was undeniably sexy, and his overall appearance, his smile, and easy attitude gave him a warmth that was irresistible.

Both men had big, powerful bodies. I had no doubt they were shredded and built underneath their jeans and flannel.

I imagined them on either side of my bed, the brothers' eyes locked onto me as they took off their rancher's hats, tossing them to the side before undoing the buttons of their flannels, one after another.

"I hope you're not planning on stopping there," I spoke in my fantasy. "There's plenty more to take off."

The men shared a knowing look before going to work on their jeans. Their flannels gone, their big, oval belt buckles were exposed. They came off with clicks, and soon they were stepping out of heavy work boots as they pulled jeans down over their powerful, tree-trunk-like thighs. Both stood at opposite sides of the bed wearing nothing but a skintight pair of boxer briefs, Mac's stone-gray, Adam's jet black. Naturally, the men were hung, their half-stiff cocks straining against the fabric.

"Now," Mac said in his deep, booming voice. "Where to begin?"

"Why don't you both... start with your hands?"

Seemed as good a place as any.

"Gladly," Adam said.

Mac stepped over to me, putting one hand on each of my thighs and stroking my skin slowly. I shuddered with delight at his touch, the sensation of his rough skin against my legs almost too much to bear. Adam placed one hand on my belly, his palm almost as big as my entire middle. Adam's other hand went to my breast, his fingers teasing my nipples and sending out waves of delight through my body.

I glanced down, watching as the two men moved their hands over me. It was as if I were receiving the most sensual massage of my life.

Adam squeezed my breast gently, Mac's right hand moving along my inner thigh until his fingertips grazed my lips. Back in the real world, I moaned with pleasure, my fingers still doing their work. I squirmed a bit, writhing my hips underneath the water.

Back in the fantasy, Mac was touching me expertly, his fingers spreading my lips as he teased my clit with the tip of his thumb. He kept those hunter's eyes on me, his cock growing by the second. Adam's member was fully erect right next to my face.

There was simply no way I could resist seeing what was underneath the tight fabric of his underwear. I reached beneath his waistband, taking hold of his thick, warm cock. I wrapped my fingers around it tightly, Adam letting out a low, sensual groan as I took it out. Sure enough, it was long and thick, the end glistening with precum.

Adam continued to knead my breasts, Mac slipping a pair of fingers inside of me as I began to stroke Adam's cock.

I opened my mouth and took Adam's head in, wrapping my lips around him and tasting the savory saltiness of his arousal. I moved my lips forward, doing my best to take in as much of him as I could.

The pleasure stopped below, and I turned a bit to see that Mac was no longer fingering me. I didn't need to wonder what he had in mind as I watched him move onto the bed and between my legs, spreading me open as he pulled my legs up onto his round, thick shoulders. He leaned down and began licking and sucking, teasing my clit in a way that brought the orgasm I craved right to the forefront.

"You taste like heaven, gorgeous," Mac said, taking a momentary break from licking me. "I could eat you all damn night."

I moaned with delight, the vibrations traveling up and down Adam's thickness. I glanced up to watch Adam watch me, his hands still on my breasts as he gazed down at me with those gorgeous, emerald-green eyes.

Mac continued to lick my pussy, my own fingers back in the real world bringing me closer and closer to orgasm. Adam groaned, and I could sense he was about to lose control in my mouth. His sounds of pleasure only made me want to make him come that much more. I moved my mouth up and down as quickly as I could, Mac still holding me, his tongue dancing over my clit.

Finally, I couldn't take it anymore. The orgasm ripped through me, Mac not letting up for a second as I came hard. Back in my bathroom, I put my other hand over my mouth so as not to scream in a way that Aggie would hear. In the fantasy, Adam erupted in my mouth, his thickness shooting hot streams of his cum over my tongue and down my throat. I gulped it down without hesitation, glancing up to see his handsome face in a tight expression of total pleasure, his eyes winced shut.

The orgasm faded, and so did the fantasy. I was soon completely present back in my tub, slowly removing my fingers from my pussy and turning the water back on.

Adam and Mac at the same time. There wasn't a chance in hell it would ever happen, but damned if it hadn't been fun to imagine.

"I still can't believe we're doing this!" Aggie's voice carried up to me from the bottom of the ladder. "The day after Thanksgiving and you already want to put up Christmas decorations?"

I grinned, my gloved hands busy attaching the greenery to the top of the house. I pressed the red bow into place, holding it there as I gently put a nail through the middle.

"I still can't believe you think it's weird!" I called back down. "Look at this weather!"

I swept my arm toward the scene around us. The snowstorm from last night was long over, the sky a perfect blue and the white on the ground untouched. Over in the animal pens, Larry and George and the rest of the llamas watched Aggie and me silently. The other animals were in the barn, safe and warm for the day.

"This is the *perfect* day to put up Christmas stuff!"

"Or, for normal people, the perfect day to hang out inside in front of a fire and watch Netflix and pig out on leftovers."

"Don't you worry your pretty little head," I said, moving over and preparing to put up the next section of the greenery. "We're going to be doing plenty of that. I just want to get this up, and a couple strings of lights, then we can call it a day."

"Fine, fine."

The smile stayed on my face as I went back to work. The

Christmas season was my favorite by far, and I couldn't wait to sink my teeth into decorating and everything else that the holiday season would bring. In a way, it was good that Aggie was being a wet blanket, since if it were up to me, we'd be working until the entire house was covered in greenery and lights. I even had a big Santa, complete with sled and reindeer, somewhere in the basement.

"Uh, Aub?"

"Hold on!" I called out, my eyes still on the décor in front of me. "Let me just finish this and then we can take a break."

"No, it's not that."

"Huh?"

"Were you expecting company?"

"Company? What on earth are you talking about?"

I turned on the ladder, whipping around so quickly that I needed to brace myself, so I didn't take a tumble. When I was facing the other way, I saw what Aggie was talking about.

Two trucks approached the farm, and I slowly made my way down the ladder, dropping from the last few rungs onto the ground just as they came to a stop.

"What's going on?" Aggie asked, her eyes hidden behind sunglasses.

"That's a damn good question."

Aggie and I watched as the engines of the trucks turned off, one then the other. Silence filled the air.

I cleared my throat, preparing to speak once whoever it was got out of the vehicles.

Just then, the passenger-side door of the Tahoe opened, a little leg sticking out. A little boy attached to the leg came next, and when I spotted that head of sandy-brown hair I knew right away who it was.

"Henry!"

The little boy prepared to jump down, but I watched as two big hands grabbed ahold of him before he had a chance. Adam stepped out of the passenger-side door behind Henry.

"Easy, kiddo," he said, coming out and setting Henry down on the ground. "Taking a jump like that's a good way to twist your ankle."

Henry locked eyes on me, a big smile spreading across his face that I couldn't help but match with one of my own.

"Miss Aubrey!" he ran over to me, all kinds of excited.

It was a bit surreal, and I didn't have time to react before he closed the distance and threw his arms around my leg. Aggie raised her eyebrows and chuckled.

"Hey, kiddo!" Strange as it felt, I was happy to see Henry. I dropped down to give him a little hug back. I watched as men piled out of the trucks, four in total. And they weren't alone. A little girl about Henry's age was seated on the shoulders of Mac.

I suddenly remembered Mac and Adam mentioning yesterday that Henry had a twin. There she sat, her sandy-brown hair pulled into a thick braid and dark eyes darting about, checking out the scene before her. While Henry was all kinds of energetic and rambunctious, however, the girl seemed more reserved, as if she were taking it all in and making mental notes.

"Hen!" called out Adam. "Go ahead and ease up on poor Aubrey before you squish her legs, y'hear?"

"OK!" Henry let go of my legs.

"You want to introduce me to your sister?" I asked.

"Oh, sure! Hattie!" As his cute kid voice carried across the way, Hattie's eyes lit up with recognition. "Come over here!"

"Sounds like you're being summoned, little lady." Despite Mac being a few dozen feet from me, his booming voice carried over clear as a bell. He squatted down and took who I now knew as Hattie off his shoulders and set her down.

She and Henry were dressed in puffy coats and little snow pants and boots and hats, looking so cute that I wanted to scream.

Hattie looked at me with the same big hazel eyes as her brother. While Henry showed no fear in running over to me and throwing his arms around my legs, however, his sister was far more reluctant.

"I don't wanna," she said. Her voice was so small and quiet that there was no way I'd have been able to hear it if it weren't still and silent out.

She grabbed onto Mac, holding him tightly. "That's ok kiddo. You don't have to if you're not ready."

I nodded. "That's right."

I took note of the other two men that had come with Mac and Adam and realized with a jolt that they were identical twins. The only way to tell them apart was the length of their beards. One was cropped close to his face, while the other wore his a little longer.

"Sorry to just roll up on you all without notice," Mac said. "But since we're here, want to meet the rest of the gang?"

CHAPTER 9

TYLER

To say that I was awestruck would've been the understatement of the century.

She was damn gorgeous, the prettiest thing I'd seen in my life. Even in her bundled-up winter gear it was obvious that she was something special. Her skin was a stunning olive, her eyes dark and her beautiful face framed by the dark curls that dangled down from her knit cap.

I couldn't stop staring.

"Yo, Ty! You alright?"

"Huh?"

A response came, but instead of words it was a sharp blast of pain to my arm. I snapped back into reality, flicking my eyes in the direction of where it came from. Marcus was next to me, an expression of confusion and annoyance on his face.

"What?"

"Get your head out of your ass, we're meeting the neighbors."

I felt like a damn idiot. It wasn't like me to get so distracted by a woman. I shook my head quickly and got back in the game. Marcus and I stepped over to the two women. As we approached, I noticed something interesting in the way the other one looked at us—nothing more than pure skepticism.

Aubrey stepped over, pulling off her glove and offering her hand.

"My name's Aubrey," she said. "Really nice to finally meet you guys."

I took off my own glove, reaching over and taking her hand. Her skin was warm and soft, enough to distract me once again.

"Pleasure," I said. "I'm Tyler, this is Marcus."

"Now, I can introduce my damn self," Marcus said, his voice gruff. "Marcus MacDaniel. Great to finally meet you both."

When the shake was over, I didn't want to let go of her hand. There was something about her touch, her glance, that was completely irresistible. It sure as hell didn't help matters that I'd seen a picture of her in a bikini and knew just what she looked like under that heavy winter coat.

"Agnes Culbertson," spoke her friend. "But everyone calls me Aggie. I'm part-owner of Downing."

She shook my hand, and the way she grasped my palm was sharp and a bit aggressive, though not in a hostile way.

"George is so funny!" Henry's voice carried over to us, interrupting our introductions. We all turned in the direction of Henry, he and Hattie standing with their hands on the wooden fence of the llama corral.

"He's cute!" Hattie added. A big smile was all over her precious face, which was good to see; normally, the girl was so shy that it took her hours to warm up in front of strangers.

"Excuse me," Aubrey said with a grin. "Let me make sure that the kids and the llamas get properly introduced." If she was upset that the kids were messing with the llamas, she sure as hell didn't show it. Aubrey headed over to the twins while we watched.

"You guys like tea?" Aggie asked.

"Wouldn't say no to something warm," Marcus replied.

"Yeah, tea sounds great."

Aggie smiled. "Good, I'll put on some hot water."

With that, Aggie headed inside. Marcus and I made our way over to the twins and Aubrey, watching the trio interact with the llamas. A pair of them came over, one white and black, the other a peach-color. The rest of the pack was off on the other side of the pen, watching the show with careful eyes.

"Now," Aubrey said. "George is nice, but he's kind of a knucklehead. If you're not careful, he might try to eat your hand."

"He will?" Henry asked. "Cool!"

Sure enough, right as Henry reached for the black and white llama, the animal opened his mouth and wrapped his lips around Henry's tiny hand. Now, I was no llama expert, but I knew enough to understand they weren't carnivores. So, I wasn't too worried about what I was seeing. Hell, it was pretty damn cute, really.

"That's damned adorable," I said. "We've got mostly pigs and cows over at Thousand Acres, nothing big and fuzzy like him."

"Maybe I ought to let you all borrow him for a while," Aubrey said with a smile as she stepped over to the fence next to the twins.

I said nothing, and neither did any of my brothers as we watched her with Hattie and Henry.

"Quick," she said to Hattie as the llama continued to lick Henry's hand, "get in some pets while he's distracted."

"OK!"

"Here, let me help."

Aubrey scooped the little girl off the ground and onto her shoulders, leaning forward a bit so Hattie could reach George. Hattie laughed as she pet the llama, the smile on her face the biggest I'd seen in a long time.

"He's so soft!" she said, scratching the top of his head.

Aubrey kept at it with the twins, one of the other llamas coming over to join the fun. And as Aubrey turned her ranch into an impromptu petting zoo, the guys and I shared a look—one that made it clear that we all could see how good our neighbor was with Henry and Hattie.

"Tea's on!" Aggie stuck her head out through the open front door of the house.

"Let's go inside and get warm, OK?" Aubrey said to the twins. "Then we can hang out with the llamas a little more. That is, if it's OK with your uncles."

"Getting warm sounds awful nice," Mac said easily.

"Then come on in," Aubrey said with a smile, waving for all of us to follow her as she started toward the house, the twins close behind.

"You sure?" I asked. "I know this was all a little unplanned. Don't want to put you out."

"Not at all," she said, opening the front door for us. "We're neighbors, this has been a long time coming."

Her friendliness was like a cool breeze on a warm day, her smile as inviting as they came. Our group made our way into the house, Aubrey taking our coats and gloves and hanging them up. The scent of brewing tea was in the air, and as I pulled off my gloves and slipped out of my coat, I glanced around the place.

The house was nice, cozy, even. The floors were solid oak, rugs here and there along the length of the entry hall, the stairs to the right. The furniture was antique, nothing Ikea in the place. Framed photos hung from the pale-yellow walls, some of them pictures of Aubrey at various points in her life, posing with friends and family.

The house wasn't the only sight that caught my attention. Aubrey slipped out of her coat, the flannel she had on fitted to her slender but curvy body, her breasts big enough to strain the buttons over her chest. Her jeans were tight, making it nearly impossible to take my eyes off her perfect, round ass. My cock moved down below, and all I could think about was her in that bikini, or in nothing at all.

"Come into the kitchen!" Aggie called out. "Got some tea and leftovers!"

Together, we stepped into the kitchen, the room sunny and bright from the big windows that looked out over the property.

"Can we play with George and Larry some more?" Henry asked, his eyes wide as he tugged on my pant leg.

"Maybe in a bit," I said. "And that all depends on what Aggie and Aubrey have to say."

"Fine with me," Aggie said as she passed out mugs, the group taking seats around the big farmer's table in the center of the room. "But I need some food in me first before I think about anything else."

Aubrey and Aggie let us go wild on their leftovers, the six of us putting together some big, hearty sandwiches.

Over the course of our meal, we got to know Aggie and Aubrey a bit. We learned a little more about Downing, how it'd been in Aubrey's family for centuries. As Aubrey spoke, giving us a brief history of the farm, I found it impossible not to notice just how beautiful she was.

"Dad died less than a year ago, so Downing's my job now."

"How long have you had the place for?" Mac asked. "And my condolences about your father."

"Thank you. And... let's see... by the time the legal stuff was all said and done, it was..."

"February twenty-fourth," Aggie said with a grin. "Sorry, scheduling's kind of my forte."

"There you have it," Aubrey nodded. "But we didn't jump into running the place right away. We had to buy the llamas and do some repairs before the day-to-day stuff could begin."

Marcus leaned back, crossing his arms over his chest. "So, this is the first real winter you're going to deal with?"

A touch of worry formed on Aubrey's face. "Yep. Most of the money here's wrapped up in livestock, so it's just a matter of keeping them warm for the winter. But come spring thaw, we're going to have to hire a mess of staff if we want to get the crops up and running."

"That reminds me," Aggie said with a grin. "You boys got anything going on this spring? We're going to need quite a few hands, and it looks like you've got more than enough between the four of you."

"I have hands!" Henry stuck his palms up as he spoke, as if to illustrate his point.

"*Grown-up* hands," Hattie said, shaking her head.

That got a laugh out of everyone. As we chuckled, however, I noticed a tinge of worry flash on Aubrey's face again. Something about the subject of hiring hands for the spring season made her tense.

"We'd love to help," Mac said. "But we're booked up solid for the spring. And our winter's looking packed, too."

Adam cocked his head to the side. "Huh? What do you mean?"

Mac formed his mouth into a flat line. I got the impression he'd said something that he hadn't meant to.

"We'll talk about it in a little bit. In the meantime, there was something else we wanted to discuss with you, Aubrey."

"Yeah? What's that?"

Aggie raised her eyebrows. "Is this something private? I can leave."

Aubrey raised her hand. "Nope, not at all. If it's about me and the farm, then Aggie's going to be here for it."

"It's nothing dire," I said. "Just a proposal."

Before we had a chance to continue the conversation, Hattie pushed her plate away and sat up.

"Can we play with the llamas again?"

"Yeah!" Henry called out. The boy took after us, which meant that his plate was already clean.

"In a bit," Marcus said.

Aggie got up. "How about this—I can take the twins and let them hang out with their new best friends while you guys discuss business. We'll be just out back, so you guys can keep an eye on the kids through the window If you want."

Aubrey opened her mouth to speak, likely to tell Aggie that she could stay.

"I got it!" Aggie said with a smile. "Come on, dudes, you want to see the llamas?"

The twins, their minds one-track as always, jumped up from their seats and let out happy cries as they headed out with Aggie.

"Give me a shout if you need anything!"

With that, they were gone. My brothers and I were alone with Aubrey, a strange sort of tension falling over the group.

"Alright," Aubrey said, leaning forward. "What's up?"

"Simple," I said. "We've got a job for you—if you're interested."

CHAPTER 10

MAC

There was no doubt in my mind that she found all of us attractive, she didn't hide it in the slightest. Her eyes jumped from me to my brothers, her gaze occasionally dipping down to our chests or arms. There was also no doubt we all felt the same way about her.

We had business to discuss, however. That didn't leave any sort of time for flirting or bullshit.

"I want to know why our winter's looking packed, Mac," Adam stated. "There something you're not telling us?"

I shifted in my seat, crossed my arms, and tucked my hands underneath my biceps. I'd misspoken, shared information that I hadn't been ready to let out.

"It's a mission," I said. "One that we're all going to need to be on."

Adam's eyes flashed, Marcus and Tyler sitting up in their seats.

"A mission?" Adam asked. "You mean, like a real-deal mission? The kind we haven't done since we got the twins?"

I sighed, shaking my head. "Didn't mean to mention it now."

Marcus narrowed his eyes. "And you've been keeping this to yourself? I thought we were a team?"

"Hold on, I didn't agree to anything yet. And the reason I didn't mention it is because I'm still waiting on the details. It accidentally sort of slipped out now."

"Boys, boys," Aubrey said. "If you're going to fight, there's plenty of space in the backyard."

She smiled as she spoke, but her words reminded all of us that we were there to talk to her about *her* job, not ours.

"Fine," Marcus said. "We'll table the conversation about the mission, for now."

"Deal," I replied.

Aubrey took a sip of her tea, leaning back in her seat with her hands wrapped around the big mug. There was something about her —maybe it was the way she was totally at ease with all of us, four men who weren't the easiest in the world to get along with—that was irresistible.

"I have to admit, I'm curious about this mission. I was raised on this land, and I've never heard anything ranch-related referred to as a mission. So, what exactly is it that you all do?"

"We run a party clown operation," Adam said with a smirk on his face. "You know, dress up, entertain the kids. We call the gigs missions because it sounds cooler."

Aubrey laughed, nearly spitting out her tea. "You almost had me there for a second."

"You'll have to excuse my jackass brother," Marcus said. "He's got a sixth sense for when it's the exact wrong time to make a joke."

"We're military," Tyler said. "Well, *were*. All of us have been in the service at one point or another."

"So what does that mean? You're farmers who moonlight in mercenary work?"

I leaned forward. "Not quite. We run a side operation called Exfil Inc."

"Exfil?" she asked.

"It's short for 'exfiltrate'," Tyler explained.

"Basically, it means getting people the hell out of places," Adam added.

"Oh, like rescue operations?"

"More or less," I said. "Not just military, but civilians that find themselves in jams and need to be extracted as smoothly as possible."

"We're damn good at it, too," Tyler said. "But we haven't gone on operations ourselves in years. Most of the work is done through contractors that we hire."

"This client wants Exfil," I said, "wants *us,* not some newbies three years out of their tours. But that's really all I know so far, aside from the fact they're offering the payday of a lifetime." I turned my attention back to Aubrey. "That's where you come in."

"Uh, what, am I supposed to be the bait or something?"

Laughs sounded in the distance, catching all of our attention. We turned, spotting Aggie with the twins. Both kids stood on the lower rung of the wooden fence of the llama pen, nearly half the herd of llamas over in their direction. The twins were having the time of their lives, reaching out and petting as many of them as they could. Aggie was near, watching attentively.

"How much you want to sell those for?" Adam asked with a smile that made it clear he was only joking around. "Looks like our kids have made a dozen or so new friends."

Aubrey laughed. "Not a chance. Those fuzzy goofballs are the most profitable part of this farm so far. Anyway, the job."

I decided to get right into it. "Simply put, we need a nanny."

Aubrey cocked her head to the side. "A what? A nanny? Like a Mary Poppins kind of thing?"

"You know, we almost had a Mary Poppins type for the job," Tyler said. "Ended up being a convicted felon."

Aubrey blinked hard, as if she wanted to make sure she'd heard me right.

"Seriously though, you want me to be a *nanny*? Why me? I mean, I don't have any experience taking care of any living thing that doesn't get around on four legs."

"They're twins," Adam said. "There's four legs between them."

Aubrey chuckled and shook her head. "But for real, why do you want me for the job? What makes you think I'm qualified?"

"Because we're looking for someone who's good with the kids," Marcus said. "And so far, you're the best we've found."

"I wasn't *that* great with them. I mean, I just did what anyone would've done with a lost little boy."

"It was more than that," I said. "You gained his trust, knew just what to do to make him feel better when he was scared."

She smiled. "Didn't seem scared to me. That's a brave guy you've got there."

"He's also reckless," Marcus said. "Takes after Tyler; always getting into trouble."

Tyler shrugged, not bothering to argue the point.

Aubrey pursed her lips, glancing aside in a way that made it obvious she had something on her mind.

"OK, I know it's none of my business. But if I'm going to think about doing this, and make no mistake, I'm only *thinking* right now, I want to know what the situation is over at Thousand Oaks."

"Makes perfect sense," Adam said. "Not every day you meet twins with four uncles and no parents."

Aubrey nodded, as if Adam had said in plain language the question she'd had on her mind since meeting us.

I drummed my fingers on the table for a moment, gathering the nerve to speak about a subject that was hard to bring up.

I took a deep breath and began.

"There used to be five of us."

"Five brothers?" she asked, the softness of her voice suggesting she had a sense of the subject to come.

"Four brothers," Marcus said, his voice gruffer than usual. "And one sister."

Tyler nodded. "Kristen, our baby sister. We lost her about a year ago."

"Car accident," Marcus added. "Some piece of shit drunk driver slammed into her, barreled through a red light." There was tightly controlled rage in his voice—the mere mention of the driver who took our kid sister away was more than enough to get him, or any of us, good and pissed off.

Aubrey's face turned serious and sympathetic. "Oh my God. I'm so sorry. I don't even know what to say to a tragedy like that."

"Thanks," I replied. "And might as well answer the question you've no doubt got in your mind."

She nodded. "The father."

"He's a loser, through and through," Tyler said through gritted teeth. Out of the corner of my eye, I could see that his right hand was clenched into a tight fist, as if he wanted to deliver a hard punch right to Seth's face. "Barely there when he and my sister were together. More interested in drinking and stepping out on her."

"Thankfully, Kristen had the good sense to divorce him when she realized he had no interest in being a father. She'd been on her own since six months after their birth."

"God, what a prick," Aubrey said. "And what happened when he found out about your sister?"

"Guy didn't even bother flying in from LA to come to her funeral. Guess he figured that if he were to come in and face us, face his kids, he'd understand that it was his turn to step up, to be a man and a father."

"The dickhead sent us a card," Marcus said. "A *fucking card*." After he dropped the f-bomb, he closed his eyes and composed himself. We were all hard men, but we knew better than to swear like that in front of company. "Sorry."

I picked up where he left off. "Sent us a card that said, 'his current situation didn't leave room for the kids.' Left it to us to tell the twins that their dad wasn't coming back."

"Sounds like a real charmer," Aubrey said sarcastically, adding an eyeroll. "Now those poor kids don't have any parents, really."

"That's how we looked at it," Tyler said with an affirmative nod.

"Lost their mom *and* their dad, just in different ways. One's gone for good, the other one might as well be."

"You hear from him at all over the last year or so?" she asked.

"Not a word," I said, rage building in me more and more the longer we talked about the asshole. "Far as we know, he's still in LA, still living the loser barfly life."

Aubrey shook her head, her expression darkening. I could tell that she was moved by the story, that she cared enough to be bothered. It was a good sign—it meant she had a healthy sense of empathy.

"Well, the less said about him, the better," Aubrey said. "I'm sure you guys don't want to waste any more breath on a piece of shit like that. Excuse the language."

We all chuckled. While we did our best to hold our tongues when it came to talking foul, there was something about a woman who didn't mind swearing now and then that was hard to resist.

"So," she went on. "Tell me more about this job you're offering me."

"Well, like we said it's a nanny gig. You'd be looking after the twins for the upcoming winter. You'd be responsible for them while we're on our mission, and during the day while we're in town."

She shook her head, running her hand through her hair. "I can't believe I'm even considering doing this. I don't have a damn bit of experience as a nanny, and besides that, I'm not all that experienced with kids in general."

"But you've got a knack," Adam said. "I saw you with Henry, and we all saw how you handled things just now when we showed up unexpectedly. You're a natural."

She pursed her lips. "Listen, I hate to jump to this, but... the pay. Don't get me wrong, the kids seem great, and I'm sure it'd be a pleasure to look after them. But I'm so damn busy around this place that it's hard to justify taking time away for another gig without knowing the compensation."

I reached into my back pocket, pulling out a small notebook and pen.

"Not to mention that I'm still doing freelance accounting work when I can," she said.

I chuckled. "Trust me, we can offer more than any freelance gig. I jotted down a number, showing it to the guys. We'd discussed the subject of compensation before, but I wanted to make sure they were all still on the same page. The boys nodded all around, and I folded the piece of paper and handed it over.

Aubrey, a touch of hesitation on her face, reached forward and took it, sitting back as she unfolded the paper and read the amount.

Her eyes widened and her brows arched.

"Uh... are you guys serious?" she asked. "This is the amount you're offering?"

"Not enough?" I asked.

"No, not that at all. It's... it's more than generous. Just seems like, um, a lot for someone who's not a professional nanny."

"We're willing to pay whatever it takes for the right person," Marcus said. "And right now, we're all in agreement that you seem to be her."

I nodded. "Right. And, naturally, we'd cover any expenses that you incur during the job."

"Plus," Adam said, "If all goes well, we'd be happy to include a bonus at the end."

Aubrey let out a long puff of air, setting the piece of paper on the table and sitting back. I could sense she was trying to process everything. Once the shock of the news settled, however, a different look came over her face, one more thoughtful, as if she were working out all of the logistics there on the spot.

We collectively held our breath, trying to silently will her into saying yes.

CHAPTER 11

AUBREY

I was still trying to process not only the job offer but the compensation offer as well.

Damned if it wasn't hard to focus on the subject at hand with four gorgeous as hell brothers sitting across from me.

"She looks like she needs some more time to think about it," Marcus said. It seemed he rarely spoke, and when he did, it was in a low, gruff voice. He was so different from Tyler, who exuded warmth and eagerness. Nevertheless, they were both sexy in their own ways.

"No, that's not necessarily true."

Part of me wanted to jump up and down and accept it right then and there. The amount they were offering me was insane, far more than I would've guessed and more than enough to keep my head above water during the winter. Between that and what I'd make from the llama wool over the next few months, I'd have enough cash to hire hands come spring, which meant that I'd have the chance to get the ranch up and running in order to start making a profit.

It almost seemed too good to be true. I'd make a ton of money, and all I had to do was hang out with two adorable kids. Sure, it'd be plenty of responsibility, but I felt up to the task.

"Then you want to do it?" asked Adam, his eyebrows arched.

I pursed my lips. "Let me ask you this—how am I supposed to take care of the animals on the farm if I'm going to be performing nanny duties? Aggie's a hard worker, but she's still only one person."

"When do you take care of the animals?" Tyler asked. "Probably in the morning?"

"Yeah, usually. I wake up bright and early and feed them, make sure they're not sick or anything like that. Aggie does it in the afternoon, then I check on them once more at night. There aren't many others besides the llamas, but it's still a lot to do."

"Believe me, we know," Mac said. "We've got our share of animals over at Thousand Acres, but we do have a few hands on staff to help us."

"Then you get it. Doesn't leave much room for nannying."

"What if we bring them here?" Adam asked. "You wake up and tend to the animals, and we drop the kids off after. Then you bring them home in the evening, or we pick them up. It's only a ten-minute drive door to door, not a long commute by any means."

"Right," Mac said. "Bring them over around, say, six, feed 'em, bathe 'em, get them ready for bed, then you're done."

It would be a lot of work, for sure. All the same, with the amount of money they were offering me, it seemed like a steal.

"That's definitely doable. As long as we're all willing to work with one another's schedules if anything comes up."

"Of course," Mac said. "As long as you're able to be consistent and reliable, we can make modifications to the schedule now and then."

"How long do you normally spend on your freelance work?" Marcus asked in his gruff way.

"God, too much time. I get to it when I can, either in the mornings or after all of the work is done. Sometimes I stay up pretty late."

"Maybe I'm biased," Adam said, a slight twinkle in his eye. "But this arrangement is starting to look better and better. You'll be able to work a normal set of hours and get some beauty sleep come nighttime instead of squinting at your MacBook Air at midnight moving around numbers in Excel."

"Hey," I said, raising a finger and smirking. "You're totally wrong... I use a ThinkPad."

Adam laughed, shaking his head.

"Got another question," Mac said. "How would you feel about the twins staying here every now and then? Like, spending the night. I haven't taken the tour of this place, but it looks like you've got more than enough space."

"That sounds like a question that you'd ask someone who accepted the job," I said. "Keep in mind that I'm still thinking about it."

He smiled. I hadn't noticed it before but seeing the light smile Mac wore in that moment made me realize how rarely he shared such an expression. The smile was warm, and just a little cocky.

"I know you're still thinking about it," he said. "But I've got a darn good feeling on which side you're going to come down."

"Someone's a little confident. Some might say *cocky*."

"Just got a feeling in my gut. And I always trust my gut."

"You'd be perfect for the job," Adam said. "Henry loves you, and Hattie already seemed on the verge of warming up to you. Trust me, even getting her to the verge is a process that takes weeks. You did more in ten minutes than what most people have been able to do in hours. You've got the touch."

I sighed, shaking my head.

"You alright over there?" Tyler asked. "We can give you some time to think about it."

"No, it's not that. I don't know; I can't believe I'm right on the precipice of agreeing to do this."

"Then that begs the question," Mac said. "What can we do to, well, push you right over the edge of that there precipice?"

I grinned, leaning in and placing my hands on the edge of the table.

"Two words. Signing bonus."

Mac grinned, sticking out his big, rough hand, a hand that I wanted right between my thighs.

"Deal."

CHAPTER 12

MARCUS

One week later...
"Man, you look like shit, bro. I mean, even more than usual."

I grumbled as I ran my hand through my hair. Didn't matter that I'd spent as long as I had in the service, where getting up at the ass crack of dawn was part and parcel of the whole thing. No, a nice morning for me was waking up at around eight, easing into things with a strong coffee and a good breakfast before work.

Tyler grinned at me from across the kitchen, looking bright-eyed and bushy tailed as he always did in the morning.

"Keep it to yourself, man."

He laughed, shaking his head as he poured a little bit of fresh cream from one of our cows into his coffee. Tyler raised the bottle of ivory-white cream, waggling it a bit side to side in an enticing way.

"Gimme that," I said.

He tossed the bottle over and I caught it, taking the lid off my thermos and pouring some of the cream into my coffee, the color lightening instantly.

"You're grouchier than normal. What's the story?"

I sipped my coffee, my eyes on the kitchen window over the table. I could tell by the gray sky above that we were in for a chilly day. Not to mention that the forecast had said to expect a bit of snow that morning.

"Didn't get much sleep," I said. "Too busy getting ready for the mission."

Tyler nodded, his expression one of understanding.

"Two days," he said after taking a sip. "Two days and we're off on the biggest mission we've been on in years."

"That's right." Mac's booming voice filled the kitchen as he entered, his expression one of total seriousness. "And you all better be planning on spending the day getting prepared."

Tyler laughed, giving a faux serious salute. "You got it, Commander Big Bro."

Mac shook his head as he strode over to the coffee maker, grabbing his favorite SEALS mug and pouring himself a good measure.

"Any news on the specifics?" I asked. I raised the bottle of cream, but Mac only shook his head.

Tyler raised his hand, silently offering to catch. I tossed the bottle, a surge of pain running through me as I threw. I rolled my shoulder a few times to work out the kinks an old bullet wound had left behind.

"You about ready to take the twins over?" Mac asked, leaning against the counter behind him. "Adam's getting them ready upstairs. Should be just another couple of minutes."

"Always ready for that. Hell, seeing Aubrey is one of the few good things about getting up this damn early." My eyes went wide as I realized what I'd said. "Shit, that was damn near unprofessional of me. Just kind of slipped out."

The boys didn't react in any strange way, however. The fact that we were all into Aubrey like crazy was about the worst-kept secret the household ever had.

"Don't worry about it," Mac said. "You're not saying anything that we haven't all been thinking for the last week."

Tyler let out a snort of a laugh, shaking his head. "You guys think that she suspects anything?"

Mac allowed himself a small smile. "What, that all four of us are sweet on her? She's a smart woman. I'm sure she has to have some idea."

"I'm sure she does," Adam chuckled. "You know what I think's going on? Bet you anything that she knows and that she's just sort of pretending it's not the case. I mean, how the hell would you even begin to deal with the fact that your four bosses are all eye-screwing you whenever they come over."

"Speak for yourself," I said. "I'm good about keeping my interests hidden."

Adam laughed again. "I bet you think you are. Brother, I was there with you the day before yesterday when we both went to pick the twins up. Good thing I was driving. If you had been the driver, I was damn sure you would've driven the Tahoe right into that damn llama pen with the way you were ogling her."

"Now, that's not true."

"Can we go to Miss Aubrey's now?" Henry's tiny voice carried through the kitchen. We all turned to see the twins at the entrance, Tyler with them. The look on his face suggested that he knew that he'd walked right into the middle of a conversation that the kids most definitely shouldn't have heard.

"I want to ride Larry today!" Hattie called out.

"You can't!" Henry replied. "Larry's too big."

The kids looked cute as hell bundled up in their winter gear, their little faces underneath their big, flapped hats. Relief washed over me as I remembered that the twins were so young that they had no conception of such a thing as two adults being attracted to one another. Or, in this case, four of them.

"But I'm big, too!" Hattie retorted, scrunching up her little face in protest. "I can do it."

"No, you can't!"

The two went back and forth as I found the lid for my thermos.

"Alright, kids," I said, taking the lid down from the cupboard and placing it on the container of coffee. "You can debate about who's big enough to ride the llama on the way over."

I slipped my phone out of my pocket, typing up a quick message to Aubrey letting her know that I was about to head out. It was only ten minutes to get over there, and she knew what time to expect us, but I liked to let her know all the same. She responded with a thumbs up moments after I sent the text.

"Let's go, buckaroos," I said as I approached the kids, putting a hand on each of their shoulders and leading them out into the entry hall.

Snow was coming down in soft flurries by the time we stepped outside. The Thanksgiving snow had finally finished melting just a day or so ago, and this upcoming storm was looking to be even more substantial.

The kids and I piled into the Tahoe, the engine rumbling to life as I pressed the ignition.

"Can we listen to AC/DC?" Henry asked.

"No!" Hattie shook her head. "Frozen!"

I chuckled as I opened Spotify on my phone, scrolling to AC/DC.

"We listen to what Henry likes on the way there, then what you want when I pick you guys up, alright?"

"How come?" Hattie asked. "I hate stupid AC/DC."

"It's an important lesson that everyone has to learn as they get older, Hats – the idea of compromise."

I put the Tahoe into gear and pulled out of the parking spot. "Back in Black" started blasting—Henry's favorite song. He sang along, but because he didn't precisely know the words, the lyrics were mostly gibberish. It was cute as hell all the same. Hattie endured the ride, her face in a little pout and her arms crossed over her chest.

The kids got all kinds of excited when they spotted Aubrey, who looked to be in the process of feeding the llamas. She turned toward us as we approached, waving a gloved hand as I parked the Tahoe.

"Miss Aubrey!" both of the kids shouted at the same time as I killed the engine, and they piled out of the car. Aubrey opened her arms and gave them both a big hug. It'd only been a week since we'd started this whole nanny thing, but the kids were already crazy about her.

Couldn't blame them one bit. Aubrey was a gem—a wonderful woman who went out of her way to open her heart to Henry and Hattie. Didn't hurt matters that she was about the best-looking woman I'd ever seen in my life.

"There's my terrible twosome!" she said as she hugged the kids hard, giving each of them a quick kiss on the forehead. "You guys ready for some fun today?"

I stepped out of the car, taking in the sight of her. Aubrey was dressed in a skintight pair of light denim jeans, the bottoms tucked into her cowboy boots. Up top she had on a cream-colored Native American style pullover, with a design that looked like deer. She wore a rancher's hat, her curly hair pulled into a thick ponytail draped over her shoulder.

She flashed me that gorgeous smile as I approached.

"Hey, you two. Why don't you head to the barn and grab a few handfuls from the big bale of grass in there? I think Larry's looking a little hungry. Oh, and please pick up the bucket of chicken feed that's in there. You can't miss it; it's big and red."

The kids wasted no time running off to the barn, laughing with excitement all the while.

"You know, it's like pulling teeth to get those two to help out over at Thousand Acres," I said as I approached. "But for some reason over here they're jumping all over one another to help out."

"You've just gotta make it fun. At their age, chores don't really register. If they think it's a game, they want to play."

We stepped over to the fence of the llama pen, leaning against the wood perimeter. I watched the snow as it fell on the pack of llamas, the big, fuzzy beasts not seeming to care in the slightest about how cold it was.

"Truth be told, we weren't sure how to get them started with taking care of the animals."

"Really?" The morning sun played on her features in a way that made her face somehow even more striking. It damn near hurt to look at her.

"Yep. Their mother was as allergic as they come. She couldn't be near any kind of fur or dander or anything without breaking out in hives. We learned pretty quickly that the twins didn't have the same allergies—got 'em tested and all that. But all the same, we were a little hesitant about it. When we saw how they were with your llamas, we all seemed to realize that we'd been keeping them a bit too sheltered when it came to the livestock."

"Well, happy to facilitate. They're naturals, by the way."

The kids emerged from the barn, each with a red pail in their hands, one filled with grass, the other with chicken feed.

"Perfect!" Aubrey shouted at the twins as they approached. "I swear, you two are shaping up to be better and better little farmers with each passing day."

Henry and Hattie shared the same beaming look that made it clear they were more than happy to receive such a compliment.

Aubrey put her hands on her hips. "OK, first, let's start by finishing feeding the llamas. After that, we can move on to the birds. Once we're done with that, Aggie's got some treats inside for you to snack on while we work on our reading. And if we get all of our work done by the afternoon, we can pick out a movie to watch when the snow hits. How does that sound?"

"Yay!" they both shouted, Henry picking up the bucket of llama feed and using a handful of it to get the animals' attention.

I watched them for a time, the twins laughing their little heads off as the llamas slowly came over and began eating out of their gloved hands.

"They're great," Aubrey said, her eyes on them. "You're lucky to have them. And they're lucky to have you."

The way I felt watching the twins, knowing that they were

being well taken care of by a woman who cared about them... it brought up... *feelings* in me. I didn't like dealing with that kind of shit.

"Yeah," I grumbled. "Thanks for taking care of them. Adam will be around at the usual time to pick them up."

I didn't wait for her to respond before turning away, giving a quick wave over my shoulder as I strode back toward the Tahoe.

"See ya..." Aubrey's words and tone made it obvious that she was a touch confused by my abrupt departure.

I couldn't afford to worry about that. I climbed into the truck and started the engine. I watched as Aubrey went over to the kids and put her hands on their shoulders, the twins smiling up at her before turning their attention back to the animals.

She was a natural. At first, Aubrey had justifiably been hesitant about the idea of nannying for the kids. If she still felt that way, however, she did a damn good job hiding it. I watched her for a moment, unable to take my eyes away.

Only a text shaking my phone in my pocket brought me back into the moment. It was from Mac.

Come on back ASAP. Got some news you're going to want to hear.

The house was only minutes away, so I didn't bother responding. Instead, I put my phone into the cupholder and pulled the car around, driving as quickly as I could back home.

The entry hall was packed full of bags and suitcases when I stepped through the front door. We were all military men, which meant that we didn't wait to get ready when a mission was on the horizon. Tyler was there heaving a big bag onto a pile of others as I arrived.

"All good?" he asked, flicking his eyes up at me for just long enough to speak.

"Fine." The word came out in a terse tone.

Tyler paused, flashing me a smile that made it clear he knew what was up.

"Uh-oh, someone's all hot and bothered."

That's one of the problems with having a twin; there's no bull-shitting them one bit.

"Stuff it," I said. "What's this news I needed to hear?"

The grin stayed on his face. "Mac said he's not sharing the info until you got back. In the meantime, I'm curious what went down over on Downing Farm. You guys get nice and close? Starting to look pretty cold out there, good chance to warm one another up..."

"Fuck off," I snapped. "And don't give me that bullshit like you're not just as into her."

He let out a loud laugh.

I shook my head. "Mac?" I called out. "Where are you?"

"Study!" the voice came from upstairs.

"Get your ass in gear, bro," I said. "More important things to worry about."

He chuckled, shaking his head in amusement. Tyler didn't say another word on the subject. Even a goof-off like him knew that the mission was more important.

Tyler and I headed up the stairs to the third floor. The door to the study was open and we went inside. The study was a huge space, as big as the den, a massive round window in the back over the desk letting in tons of light and giving us a good view of the incoming snow. Towering bookshelves were on both sides of the room, a fire going in the hearth. Off to the side was a meeting area with couches and chairs, a big table in the middle covered with maps and printed-off documents.

Mac was seated at the huge, oak desk, his eyes flicking back and forth between his computer and the papers in front of him.

Adam showed up right behind us.

"Alright," Mac said, sitting back and folding his hands on his belly. "Let's get into it."

"You mind if we sit in the actual meeting area? Always feels like I'm back in middle school in trouble with the principal when we do the desk thing."

Mac shook his head, heaving out of the seat and grabbing some papers before heading over to the meeting area. I said nothing, eager to find out what Mac had learned about the mission.

When we were seated, Mac sighed, sitting back and glancing in my direction.

"What is it?" I asked. "You going to make us wait all day?"

Mac nodded. "Nope, going to tell you what I learned right now. Just found out who the bad guy is on this mission. It's Balaban."

CHAPTER 13

ADAM

To tell the truth, I'd actually been a little excited about the mission. We'd spent so much time at the ranch over the last year or so that I was beginning to get a little stir-crazy. There was nothing quite like hopping on a plane to the other side of the world, to jump head-first into danger with my brothers.

That sentiment went away as soon as Mac mentioned the name Balaban.

The instant the name came out of his mouth I was back in Bosnia three years ago, bullets whizzing around my head as me and the guys struggled to take cover and exchange fire. The mission was supposed to be simple—a quick evac of the remaining staff at the German consulate. The intelligence had told us that Balaban, some local warlord, was still a day off.

The intelligence had been wrong. We hadn't been in the consulate for more than an hour before Balaban hit us hard. What was supposed to be a simple hand-holding operation had turned into a nightmare, dozens and dozens of mercs coming at us from all sides while we screamed into our radios for the helicopter evac.

We'd been heavily armed, however, our one saving grace. Marcus had been manning a hastily-setup machine gun nest on the top floor, peppering Balaban's men with M60 fire in a desperate effort to buy time.

That is, until he'd been shot.

I'd come into the office room that Marcus had been using just in time to see him take the bullet, his face wincing in a tight expression of pain as he fell backward, his hand clamped onto his shoulder.

I'd run over to him, my blood running cold at the thought of my brother dying right in front of me.

"It went clean through. Get on that thing!" he pointed with his free hand to the machine gun, relief taking hold of me as I went to work with the powerful gun.

The moment I had my eyes on the iron sights, I saw him. Standing at the blown-open perimeter of the consulate, men swarming onto the property all around him, was a man that I instantly knew was Balaban. He was tall, easily six and a half feet, with broad shoulders and a bald head, his face craggy and scarred, his thin mouth formed into a smirk that suggested everything was going according to his plan. He wore the greens and browns of DPM forest camo, splatters of blood here and there that suggested he'd killed more than a few people up close and personal to get to the consulate.

In his hands was a rifle, one that I had no doubt was the weapon that had shot my brother.

I'd let out a yell, opening fire with the M60 and hoping to end the fight right then and there by taking out the leader. Balaban stepped back behind the stone wall, the bullets missing him as the rest of his men rushed the property.

"We have to get out of here," I said. "Now."

Marcus nodded, groaning as he rose to his feet. I pulled the M60 out of its nest, checking the belt feed as Marcus withdrew his 1911 sidearm. Together, we hurried out of the room, the sounds of Balaban's men carrying up from the first floor.

"We're leaving, now!" Mac's booming voice came down from above.

"Can you make it?" I asked, worried eyes on Marcus. His shoulder was soaked with blood, and while I knew a clean through-and-through wound to that area was pretty manageable as far as gunshots went, it was still a concern at the moment.

I reached my arm to support him. Marcus quickly swatted it away.

"I'm not dead yet," he growled.

"I'll lay down some covering fire," I said, propping up the M60 on the railing looking down the stairwell. "You get upstairs and get ready to move out."

He shook his head. "Not leaving you alone. Not a fucking chance."

"Bro, you're shot through the shoulder, and you've got a pistol against an army. Get up there and help those people evac."

He opened his mouth, as if wanting to protest.

"Don't stay down here for long," he said. With that, he shot me a hard look that I knew was the closest Marcus came to concern.

He hurried up the stairs and I wasted no time turning the M60 on the mercs coming up. I let out a war cry as I opened up with machine gun fire, the men taking immediate cover down below. I fired in bursts, keeping the mercs pinned down, hoping to buy time for the rest of the team. When the belt was spent, the gun clicking dry, I heaved the weapon over my shoulder and rushed up the stairs as quickly as I could.

"We're up on the top floor!" Tyler called down. "Hurry!"

I rushed up the stairs, spotting the rest of the group right away. To my relief, Mac, Marcus and Tyler were all there, along with the half-dozen members of the staff who we'd been charged with evacuating.

My relief turned to horror, however, when I saw that one of the staff members was slumped against the wall, his eyes closed, and his white shirt stained with blood.

"Is he..."

Mac nodded. "Got him a few minutes ago in the same burst that hit Marcus."

Balaban had claimed a staff victim after all.

Before we'd had any time to process what was going on, Marcus got the call from the evac chopper. We gathered what gear we could, Tyler escorting the staff up to the rooftop. Moments later, we were on the helicopter and taking off, rising higher and higher as we watched the consulate swarm with mercs. The last image in my mind of the mission was of Balaban, standing on the roof with his hands on his hips, that same smile on his face as if to suggest that he knew this wasn't over, that he'd see us again in time.

If that had indeed been the case, it was looking like he was getting his wish.

Back in the present moment, I watched out of the corner of my eye as Marcus rubbed his wound, as if the mere mention of the man that had given it to him was enough to make it hurt again.

"Fine," he growled. "If it's Balaban, then it's Balaban. Maybe I'll get a chance to even the score for the man he killed... not to mention what he did to me."

"What's the mission, Mac?" Tyler asked.

Mac nodded, eager to get on with it.

"Mission's in Croatia, down the very tip of the coast a hundred kilometers near the town of Gruda. Got some more intel on Balaban. Turns out he's the son of a general killed during the Balkan conflicts of the 90s. Got aims to cause as much trouble as he can with the legitimate government in hopes to even the score for what he believes they did to his father."

"So, he's basically a bad penny they can't get rid of," I said.

Another nod from Mac. "More or less. He and his small army of a few hundred men raid villages for supplies, disappearing into Bosnia whenever the heat gets on them. That changed, however, when he decided to take over a compound near the southeastern border, make it a little base of operations for whatever other trouble he might want to cause in the region."

"A compound?" Tyler asked. "Just some random compound in the middle of nowhere?"

"Not random," Mac said. "It was an old military base that dates all the way back to World War II, actually. But it hadn't been used in a military capacity for over two decades. Since then, it's been used as a base of operations for the Catholic Church – a missionary operation."

"Shit," I said, sitting back, the issue dawning on me. "And let me guess—Balaban isn't too keen on sharing."

"Yep," Mac replied. "There were around fifty missionaries in total. Most were out in the field when Balaban moved in and were easily able to get clear. Four in the compound, however, remained to make sure some of the sick and injured they'd been caring for were able to be evacuated. They were, but the missionaries weren't. So, our operation is to evac the three remaining missionaries."

Tyler cocked his head to the side in confusion. "Wait, you just said *four* missionaries."

Mac's expression turned grim. Didn't take a genius to put it all together.

"The mission's moved up to two days from now. And the reason for that is Balaban decided to execute one of the missionaries to make a point. He's demanding that the Croatian military essentially cede the lower arm of the country to him, believe it or not."

"What, he wants to make his own little country?" I asked. "Is he insane?"

"Insane, delusional, what's the damn difference?" Adam asked. "Either way, he's a dangerous madman and needs to be taken out."

"That's what the Croatian military has in mind," Mac said. "And that's where we come in. We're being paid *big* to move in and evac the three remaining missionaries. Once that's done, we give the all clear to the military to wipe the place off the map with long-range artillery. They're done playing around with Balaban. They're ending this once and for all."

"Good call on their part," Marcus said, his voice tight with anger. "The fewer pricks like him in the world, the better. Hell, give me the chance and I'll take him out myself."

"Hopefully, it won't come to that," Mac said. "We want this mission to go nice and smooth. The Croatian military is coordinating with us, planning on running some distraction ops in the region. With any luck, the compound will be nearly empty, and we can simply sweep in and rescue the missionaries without firing a single shot."

"Just saying," Marcus added. "If a shot *does* need to be fired, I want to be the one to do it."

"What about the B team?" Tyler asked, referring to the usual group of mercs to whom we typically contracted out our missions.

"The Croatians wanted *us* for this operation, not anyone else. Between our reputation and our experience with Balaban, I guess they figured we were the best bet for the job." Mac ran his hand through his hair. "Who's getting the twins tonight?"

I nodded. "I'm on duty to go pick them up."

"Alright. We've got tons of intel to go over, not to mention planning our actual assault on the place. Let's spend today getting that sorted out, then finish packing our gear tomorrow."

The rest of us made noises of approval. With that, we went to work. The hours flew by as we planned, drawing up how we were going to get in and make the extraction with minimal fuss. We were all roughneck men, not one of us afraid to get our hands dirty, whether on the ranch or in the field. Still, one of the first things you learned when running ops was how quickly they could go sideways. The infil and exfil mission was planned to the letter, and if all went according to plan, we'd be in and out with the missionaries without having to fire a single shot.

An alarm from my phone chirped.

"That's the call," I said, reaching for the phone and turning the alarm off. "Time to get the wee ones."

I stood and stretched, realizing that I'd been sitting for hours. I made a mental note to get in a workout before the day was over; nothing made sleeping harder than sitting on your ass, I'd learned.

Right as I prepared to get moving, a text arrived from Aubrey.

Hey! Snow's starting to come down hard, so I figured I'd bring the kids over. That work?

Sounds good to me.

I tucked my phone into my pocket, looking over at the guys.

"She's bringing the kids back now."

The boys regarded one another with long looks.

Mac reached forward, closing the laptop in front of him. He sighed when it was shut, looking around at all of us.

"Boys... we need to talk."

"About what?" Marcus asked, his voice gruff.

"You know about what," Tyler shot back. "We've all been ogling Aubrey for the last week."

Marcus shrugged. "So what if we have been? Not a crime to look."

"That's just it," Mac said. "We've all been doing *more* than looking, we've been thinking."

Marcus formed his mouth into a flat line.

"Even so," I said. "What can we do about it? Hot girl is hot, end of story, right?" As soon as I said the words, I realized how hollow they were. Aubrey was more than just some hot girl.

Mac shook his head. "We're about to go on the mission of a lifetime. And that means we can't afford to have *anything* taking our minds off the goal. If the four of us ship out all thinking about Aubrey..."

"It'll be a distraction," Tyler said.

"Then what the hell are we going to do about it?" Marcus asked. "What *can* we do?"

"We talk about it," Mac said. "When she comes over, we sit her down and put it all out in the open."

Marcus snorted. "You're serious? We have a little powwow over tea about how much we all want to screw her? What possible good could that do?"

I put my hand onto the back of my chair and thought it over.

"It's not a bad idea. I mean, not like anything has to happen.

Right now, there's confusion and mystery about it. If we were to sit down and talk it over, get it out there, we might dispel that, you know? Nothing kills mystery faster than dragging it out into the cold light of day." I glanced over at the round window, snow coming down hard. "Or into the gray light of this shitty afternoon."

Tyler leaned forward. "Guys, what if she says she feels the same way?"

"Huh?" Marcus asked. "What do you mean?"

"I mean what I just said. What if we sit her down and tell her about the way we've all been feeling toward her and she's just... cool with it, you know?"

None of the other guys said anything. What was there to even say to something like that?

"No way," I said. "No way would a woman be cool with four guys."

"Why not?" Tyler said with a shrug, sitting back and draping his arm over the couch.

"Too damn weird." Marcus shook his head. "That's what she'd think. Managing four different guys."

I chuckled. "And how the hell would sex even work? I mean, think about it."

Tyler laughed. "It's not impossible. More than one guy can please a woman at the same time, and if things get too crowded, any of the other dudes can back off for a while."

"I can't believe we're even talking about this," Marcus said. "I give it nearly one-hundred-percent odds that she runs screaming in the opposite direction when we bring this up. Might as well start looking for another nanny now."

Mac had a strange smile on his face as the three of us went back and forth.

"Alright, big bro," I said. "What's on your mind?"

"Oh, nothing. Just something I noticed."

"And what's that?" Tyler asked.

"That with all the talk about this, not one of us dismissed the idea outright."

The rest of us shared a look, no one saying a word. We knew he was right. Silence fell over us, no sound in the room but the crackling of the fire in the hearth.

"Well?" I asked. "Might as well come out and ask it... does anyone here have a problem with the idea of all of us being with her?"

I waited for any of the guys to say something. Surely, Marcus at least would have an issue.

Not one of them said a damn word.

"I kind of like it," Tyler said. "We're all into her, and if she feels the same way... what's the problem?"

"Mac?" I asked.

"Mom and Dad always told us sharing was caring."

My eyes flicked over to Marcus.

He only shrugged. "Seems cool. Aubrey's a babe, why should she only have to stick to one of us?"

"And you, Adam?" Marcus asked. "What're your thoughts?"

I laughed, unable to believe what was on my mind.

"It's definitely unorthodox," I said. "But the more I think about it... I'm into it. We've always done everything together, ever since we were kids. Why stop now?"

The conversation didn't get a chance to continue. My phone buzzed once more.

I'm here.

CHAPTER 14

AUBREY

"**E**asy, dudes!"

The kids didn't waste any time kicking off their boots and shucking off their jackets, hats and gloves.

"You guys know that you need to put those where they belong, right?"

They both looked at me, my tone serious enough for them to understand that I wasn't messing around.

"OK..." Henry turned slowly, bending over and picking up his winter gear.

"Fine..." Hattie did the same, gathering her things and going over with Henry to hang them all up.

"Good job, kids," Adam said. I looked up to see that he was on the stairs, a glass of whiskey in his hand. He stood against the railing in his effortlessly sexy way, a smirk on his face and one boot crossed over the other. "Next step is getting ready for your bath."

The kids moaned, Adam raising a finger and his eyebrows.

"Do we have to?" Henry asked.

"You bet your little butts you do. Now, get on up there and wait for me, OK? I've got something to talk about with Miss Aubrey."

"Is she going to give us baths?" Hattie asked.

"Sure. Let us have a grown-up conversation first, alright?"

That got the kids in gear. They hurried up the stairs and down the hall, the little pitter-patter of feet sounding as they rushed to the bathroom.

Adam trotted down the stairs. Before too long he was close enough that I could smell the whiskey on his breath, an impossibly sexy scent.

"The rest of the guys are planning the mission," he said. "They've got it just about under control, so I figured I'd come down and give you a hand with the bath."

"Thanks. I mean, I can handle it on my own for sure."

He raised his palm, shaking his head. "I insist. It's crummy out and you've probably had a long day."

My instinct was to object. "Sure. Let's do it."

He swept his hand toward the stairs. "After you." We headed up, and I found myself lost in his looks and his smile and the smell of his whiskey. "How's Aggie?"

"Good. I was kind of glad to get out of the house, actually."

"Problem over in paradise?"

"Nah, she's got this girl coming over tonight. Don't want to cramp her style, you know?"

"Totally understandable." We reached the top of the stairs and he paused. I could tell that there was something on his mind, something that he wasn't sure how to say. "Speaking of cramping one's style... you mind sticking around when we're done with the bath?"

"Sticking around? What's up?"

That strange look stayed on his face. The guys were decisive without fail, so it was extra strange to see one of them look so hesitant and unsure of himself.

"The four of us have something we want to talk to you about."

"Is it bad?" I asked.

He shook his head. "Not bad. Just... something that needs to be discussed."

Was I getting fired? As we made our way to the bathroom, I struggled to come up with an explanation for why all of the guys would want to have a sit-down with me like that. Being paranoid didn't come naturally to me, but everything about the way Adam was speaking and acting put me ill at ease.

Those feelings went away the second I stepped over the threshold of the bathroom. The twins were in the middle of the big, spacious room, already in the process of stripping off their clothes.

"Alright, dudes," Adam said, stepping over to the tub. "We ready to get clean?"

They let out their cries of excitement in response as they got out of the rest of their clothes.

Adam turned on the faucet, getting the water nice and warm as I poured some bubble bath gel into it. I laughed as the kids clambered over the rim of the tub, wasting no time splashing in the water.

"So!" Adam said, sticking his hands under the water and getting them wet. "How was the day over with Miss Aubrey?"

"Amazing!" Hattie said. "Extra amazing!"

"That's her new favorite word," I said, sitting down next to Adam beside the tub and rolling up my sleeves. "Everything's amazing."

"Worse things for everything to be," he said. "Tell me all about it, little lady."

Hattie and Henry went into it, recounting the events of the day. Adam took Hattie, getting her soaped up and clean, while I did the same to Henry. As we did our work, I couldn't help but notice how damn *cute* Adam was with the kids. He splashed with them in the tub, listening attentively as they told their stories.

All of the men were as tough as they came, steely-eyed military guys down to the last. When it came to their kids, however, none of them were scared to show their soft sides. It was impossible to ignore how much love was in this house, how crazy all the guys were for their twins.

"I'll get them ready for bed," he said, the two of us standing over the twins as we dried them off after the bath. "Why don't you go downstairs and get comfortable? Help yourself to whatever you want to drink, alright?"

I wanted more than anything to ask him what was going on, why he was being so weird. I kept it to myself, however, figuring my questions would be answered soon enough.

"Uncle Adam?" Hattie asked as she wrapped the towel around her. "Can you braid my hair?"

Adam chuckled. "Sure, sweet pea. But first thing's first, if you want me to braid you, you're going to need to get that hair good and dry. You know how we do it, right?"

"Right!" Hattie wasted no time snatching another towel from the rack.

"We put it on our head, and we go woosh-woosh-woosh!" as he made the noise, Adam moved his hands vigorously over his head. "You too, Hen – woosh-woosh-woosh!"

I handed Henry a towel and he did the same thing, the two of them standing in front of Adam as they all said "woosh-woosh-woosh" together, mussing and drying their hair. It was so damn adorable I couldn't stop smiling.

"Very good!" Adam said as he stood up, the kids' hair wild and messy. "Now we tidy ourselves up before bed." He reached over to the bathroom counter and picked up a plastic, black comb and a brush, handing the comb to Henry and the brush to Hattie. "Get neatened up, alright? Then we'll get into our jams, and I'll braid you, Hats."

The kids went to work, stepping up on their little stools in front of the mirror. Henry combed his hair carefully, making a neat part, while Hattie brushed slowly and made her hair nice and straight.

"Here's the thing," Adam said, stepping over to me and speaking quietly as the kids finished their hair. "I *just* learned how to do a French braid off YouTube... I'm hardly an expert."

I grinned, knowing what he was asking. "Want me to supervise?"

"If you wouldn't mind."

"Don't mind at all. And I'll get Henry ready for bed while you do it."

"Perfect."

When the kids were done in the bathroom, we headed down the hall and into their big bedroom. The space was so adorable—Henry's side done up with cowboy décor, Hattie's with an under-the-sea sort of vibe.

Henry turned to me with a smile on his face. "Can you help me put my jams on?"

"Sure can, kiddo." I stepped over to the dresser, opening it and letting Henry pick out what he wanted to wear for the night. As he did, Adam sat down with Hattie and moved himself into position to do her hair.

"Alright," he said. "You ready?"

"Ready!"

Henry was good about dressing himself for bed, so I barely had to do anything other than put away his wet towel. As I did, I watched as Adam braided Hattie's hair, his big hands moving slowly and carefully as he worked, an expression of total concentration on his face. Hattie held her favorite stuffed animal, a big blue dolphin, as he braided. It was so damn precious.

I sat on Henry's bed with him and read through *Little Blue Truck*, the story Henry picked out for the night.

"And... done!" When Adam finished, he pulled his hands away. "What do we think?"

I looked over Hattie, nodding my approval. The braid wasn't perfect, but it was pretty damn good.

"Not bad at all," I said. "But I think the client has the final say."

Adam laughed, reaching over to the dresser and picking up a small hand mirror and giving it to Hattie. She regarded her reflection, turning her head from side to side to see the braid.

"It's so pretty," she said. "Thank you, Uncle Adam!" With that, she tossed the mirror aside and threw her arms around Adam. "I love you."

"And I love you too, Hats." He glanced over at me. "I'm just going to read these two another story before they hit the hay. Thanks for sticking around. There's wine down in the kitchen if you want a glass."

"Sounds perfect."

I rose to leave, Henry wanting a hug, which I happily gave, before scrambling over to where Hattie was nestled in at Adam's side for story time. I glanced at them over my shoulder, my heart practically hurting at how cute the little scene was.

As I made my way out of the bedroom and down the stairs, I considered what good caretakers they all were, each in their own ways. Hattie and Henry might've lost their mother, which no one could truly replace, but they'd gained the love of four wonderful uncles.

Four wonderful uncles who wanted to talk with me about... something. Tension tightened my belly as I entered the kitchen. Off in the distance I could hear them speaking to one another in the den, their low voices reverberating through the house. What they were saying, exactly, I couldn't tell.

I spotted a bottle of opened red wine on the counter. Normally, I wasn't a coping sort of drinker. The prospect of the conversation to come, however, made me reach for it. I poured a healthy glass and took a sip. Through the big windows in the kitchen, I could see the snow coming down hard enough that I started to wonder if it might not be a good idea to try to make the drive home. Not to mention that I didn't really feel like walking in on a make out session in the living room.

"Looking bad out there." Mac's booming voice snapped me out of my trance. I turned to see him enter the kitchen.

"No kidding. And my car's no good in the snow."

"I've seen it, that little Subaru. You need something a little more substantial if you're going to live this kind of life." He stepped next to me. The moment he was close, the tension that I'd felt whenever not just Mac, but any of the guys, were near came rushing back. My pussy clenched, my heart racing.

Maybe it wasn't the worst idea in the world if they wanted to fire me. While it'd hurt like hell, how else was I supposed to deal with the way the brothers made me feel on a daily basis? All the same, knowing I wouldn't see them, or the kids again made me almost sick to my stomach.

Mac leaned onto the counter, the two of us watching the snow for a time. He turned to me, his impossibly handsome face only inches from mine.

"We, uh, we're ready in the other room. Feel free to bring your wine."

The tension between us was thick as molasses. All I could think about was him leaning forward and kissing me hard, the softness of his lips blending with the roughness of his stubble against my face. It was just like that morning with Marcus, the tension between us thick in the air before he'd gruffly broke it and stormed off.

"Yeah. Sure."

He closed his eyes and pulled away, as if it had taken major restraint not to kiss me the way we both clearly wanted. Mac opened his mouth to say something. Whatever it was, however, he didn't let it out. Instead, he closed his lips and left without another word.

Once more, I was alone. The conversation we'd just had was a perfect little summation of my relationship, such that it was, with all of the guys; warm and friendly and easy but dripping with sexual tension that made it nearly impossible to even speak.

Maybe this was what the conversation was about? Fear and excitement boiled up in me in equal measures—excitement at seeing the guys all at once, fear that it might be for the last time.

Wine in hand, I entered the den. The four of them were there, glasses of whiskey for each, a warm fire crackling in the hearth. The two big, arched windows on both sides of the fireplace allowed for a view of the swirling snow in the darkness. The guys had been chatting with one another when I'd entered, the small smiles on their faces letting me know that it likely hadn't been about anything serious.

When I entered, however, the smiles faded. Their eyes turned to me, not one of them saying a word. Despite the fear, I felt myself grow wet and tight down below, my body yearning for the men. It worried me. After all, how the hell was I supposed to have a normal conversation if all I could think about was them taking turns with me?

Mac sat up a bit out of his chair, the rest of the guys doing the same.

I couldn't help but chuckle. "All of you are so polite, real gentlemen."

"Believe me," Adam said. "If our ma was here and saw us not getting up when a lady entered the room, she'd pull one of those logs right out of the fire and smack us each upside the head with it."

I realized I didn't know all that much about their parents, a conversation for another time. I was hoping to get the chance.

"Please," Mac said, gesturing toward the sofa across from the fireplace. "Have a seat."

I did as he asked, sliding onto the extremely comfortable couch and settling in. Between that, the wine, the fire, and the snow, I had all the makings of a perfect little winter evening in front of me. The company didn't hurt, either.

Of course, there was still the minor detail of the very real chance I was about to get fired.

"Thanks for staying a little longer, Aubrey," Mac said. "Means a lot that you took the time to chat with us."

Adam craned his neck, glancing out of the window. "Though, unless you've got snowshoes it doesn't look like you're going anywhere."

I sipped my wine, nervous energy building by the second.

I couldn't take it anymore. I had to ask.

"Alright," I said, setting down my glass on the coffee table. "If there's something you guys want to tell me about my job performance, let's hear it right now. I can handle rejection; I can handle getting fired. But if there's one thing I'm *not* good at, it's anticipation."

The words tumbled out of my mouth.

The guys regarded one another with the same quizzical expression, as if they weren't sure they'd heard me right.

Adam was the one to break the silence. "You think that we brought you here to *fire* you? As in, tell you that you're not going to be working for us any longer?"

Tyler chuckled. "If we did that, our next move would be to hire some bodyguards to protect us from the twins. I swear, they'd take us down in flurries of tiny fists if we fired you."

I was confused. "So, this *isn't* about firing me? But is it about my performance?"

"No," Marcus said, his tone gruff as ever. "Not that."

"Then... what is it? Sorry to press, but this all seems a little out of the ordinary, you know?"

The men looked at each other again. I could sense that, whatever it was, they weren't sure where to start.

Mac, taking a deep breath, began. "You've been a real pleasure to have around, and the kids are already crazy about you."

"All the same," Adam said. "There's a damn good chance that what we want to talk to you about is something that very well could have you reconsidering whether or not you want to keep working here."

The more they spoke, the more confused I became.

Mac formed his mouth into a flat line, as if realizing that they were all speaking very cryptically.

"Aubrey, I'll get right to it. The four of us... we have feelings for you."

My blood began to run faster.

"And what sort of feelings are we talking about?"

Tyler grinned. "We're all into you. As in, each one of us thinks you're hot as hell." He looked away for a second, as if he wished he'd said it more eloquently. "Well, it's more than just us thinking you're hot. We all like you, feel a connection."

"And we think you feel the same way," Marcus said.

"Not to put you on the spot," Adam quickly added.

"Well, I *do* kind of feel like I'm on the spot," I admitted.

"You want to do this one-on-one?" Adam asked, leaning forward with an expression of concern in his eyes. "Or two-on-one? It wasn't our intention to overwhelm you or anything. Just figured it was easier to get it out in the open together like this." Adam was being kind and accommodating as always, and it went a hell of a long way toward making me feel better about what was shaping up to be a very strange situation.

"No, it's fine. I think. But you're right – it's better to talk about it all together." I closed my eyes and raised my palm. "But let me get this straight. All four of you wanted to talk to me because, well, all four of you have a thing for me? Do I have this right?"

"You've got it right," Mac said. "We all find you extremely intriguing."

"More than that," Tyler went on. "You're wonderful. You're funny and smart and beautiful and amazing with the kids... you're one of a kind. A guy would have to be out of his mind to not notice how incredible of a woman you are."

I shifted in my seat, not sure how to handle the barrage of kind words coming my way.

Marcus folded his hands over his chest. "There's a reason we wanted to tell you this tonight. We're going on our mission the day after tomorrow, and we didn't want to be distracted."

"Distracted? Because of me?"

Adam nodded. "Yep. How the hell are we supposed to focus on taking out the bad guys if we're all thinking about the gorgeous woman back at the house, wondering how she feels about us?"

"How she feels about... *us?*" I asked.

The reality of the situation, along with its strangeness, began to dawn on me.

It wasn't simply one of them that was into me but *all four of them*.

My gaze jumped across the room, going from one pair of eyes to the next. I couldn't believe what I was hearing, what this conversation was truly about.

"How we *all* feel about you," Mac said, as if sensing my difficulty grasping what was happening. "That's what this is about. We're... well, we're all four of us crazy about you."

I opened my mouth then quickly closed it, not even remotely sure of what to say. I stared intently at the glass of wine in front of me, shooting my hand out and grabbing it, bringing it to my lips and taking a long sip.

"You'll, uh, have to excuse me," I said. "I'm not exactly used to the idea of four men, four brothers at that, sharing something like this with me."

Warm smiles formed on all of their faces, even the normally stoic and taciturn Marcus and Mac. It was surreal, but the calm and cool attitude with which the guys handled it went a long way toward making me feel better.

"I get that," Mac said. "Hell, we *all* get it. It was strange for us too, the first time it happened."

"The *first* time this happened? You're kidding me, you guys have been through this before with another woman?"

"Yes. And it was the last thing we'd expected to happen."

"About two years ago," Mac started after taking a sip of his whiskey, "we'd needed a few extra hands on the farm for the first big harvest. We put up an ad in town, and before we knew it, we had a dozen workers ready to pitch in. We've got the guest house, so most of them stayed here on Thousand Acres for the season. One of them was a woman named Tiffany."

I felt the air change at the mere mention of the name. The men regarded one another, each of them giving off the impression that this woman, whoever she might've been, was a subject that rarely, if ever, extended beyond them.

"Tiffany," I said, trying the name on for size. "Who was she?"

"Long story short," Adam said, "she was a woman that couldn't decide between the four of us, so she decided to have all of us."

I blinked hard, trying to wrap my head around the idea. "She had you... *all*? Sorry to pry, but you're going to have to fill me in on the logistics here."

Marcus took a sip of his whiskey before he began to explain. "One after the other. That's how she got us. Mac first, then me, then Adam, then Tyler."

"Saving the best for last, naturally," Tyler said with a smile.

"Wait, so she hopped from one bed to the next?" I asked. It was so bizarre, almost too much to process.

"Pretty much," Adam replied. "But she didn't do it in a predatory sort of way. She liked all of us equally, so things just sort of happened in the way that they did."

I thought about my experiences with the men over the last week, how I'd nearly come close to kissing all of them more than once. I didn't know this Tiffany woman, but I sure as hell could empathize with her.

"What happened?" I asked, hooked into the story.

"We'd all been suspecting that something was going on," Mac said. "Hard to keep a situation like that hidden for long. We chatted and..."

"None of us really cared," Adam chimed in. "We still liked her, that didn't change. Fists didn't start flying—there wasn't any jealousy; not even a little."

"Then what?" I asked, intrigued.

"Poor Tiffany must've been going insane," Tyler said. "Keeping something like that a secret. Anyway, she brought us all in for a meeting, figuring it would be easier to tell all of us at the same time."

"Like this," I said with a smile.

"Except in reverse," Marcus said, matching my smile with one of his own.

"She broke it to us," Adam said. "Must've been thinking we'd beat each other up, then boot her ass out of Thousand Acres. But that's not what happened. We just... didn't care. We liked her, she liked us... what's wrong with a little sharing between brothers?"

"Tiffany was stunned, naturally," Tyler went on. "But once she got over the initial shock, once she realized that we weren't upset, the conversation took on a different tone. We started talking about where to go from there."

"And what did you decide?" the words shot out of my mouth. Maybe I sounded overeager, but who could blame me? I was desperate to know what happened with Tiffany.

Mac spoke. "We decided to just keep the good thing going. Only now, we didn't have to pretend about it. We were open with one another. It was a bit odd at first, but you'd be surprised how quickly one gets used to an arrangement like that."

Tyler went on. "Started out that she'd pick which of us she wanted to spend the night with. In time, however, we started sharing."

"Sharing?" By this point, I was leaning forward in my seat, almost at the edge.

"She'd pick one of us," Mac began to explain. "Or two. Then two became three... three became four. It was a little hard at first."

"I'll bet," I said, unable to resist the low-hanging innuendo.

The guys laughed. "Took the words out of my mouth," Tyler said. "But it's not that complicated. The four of us, we'd take our time with her, listen to what she wanted, then give it to her. It was nice. No rush, just the four of us making sure she was pleasured in every which way she wanted."

I was already wet, but hearing the guys talk about all four of them with her at once was enough to make me feel like I needed to change my panties. My breath was slow and shallow, my heart beating fast. I wasn't sure how much more of this I could handle before demanding it for myself.

"And when we weren't in the bedroom with her," Mac said, "we were taking care of her in our own ways around the house. She still worked, of course. But once we'd had our conversation with her about where we stood, she ended up taking one of the guest bedrooms, or choosing one of our beds to stay in."

I didn't know what to say. Silence was in the air, and I felt the urge to fill it with something.

"What happened to her? I mean, after she was done working the season?"

Mac picked up the thread of conversation once more.

"One morning we all got up, ready to start the day. We were used to not knowing which bed she'd spent the night in, so we all assumed that she was in one of the other brother's rooms. When we settled in for breakfast, we all realized she was gone."

"Left a note," Marcus added. "It said that while she'd loved the time she'd spent with us, she knew she needed to move on."

Tyler smiled. "Guess she figured she didn't have it in her to break up with four men all at once."

I laughed lightly.

The story over, however, it began to dawn on me just what they were asking, why they were telling me all of this.

"You... want this with me, right?" I asked, my heart beating somehow even faster. "Is that what this is all leading up to?"

The men shared another look before turning their attention back to me.

"Sure is," Mac said.

CHAPTER 15

AUBREY

With that, we'd gotten right to the heart of the matter. Too bad I didn't have any idea what to say.

The fire crackled. I took one more sip of my wine, blinking hard as if I were in the middle of some insane dream and all I needed to do was wake up.

"Well?" Tyler asked. "What do you think?"

"Give her a second, dumbass," Marcus shot out, narrowing his eyes. "We just brought up a *huge* thing. She needs to process it."

He was damn right about that. I shifted in my seat, draining the last bit of wine. It was hitting the spot, making me feel just a bit more mellow.

"You don't have to answer now," Mac said, with his calm attitude. "We can pick this up another time. Or, we could never mention it again, if that's what you want."

"No." The word shot right out of my mouth. "I don't want to not mention it again. It's nothing I've ever considered before but I have to say that I'm intrigued."

"We're going to be gone for a bit on this mission," Adam said. "You could take that time to think about it, let it marinate."

That idea didn't sit well with me either.

"No, I don't want that. I... I like all of you guys, each and every last one of you. Whatever's going on between us, I don't want to wait for you four to come back to find out for certain."

"We don't have to wait," Mac said. "We can explore this right here and now."

I glanced over at my empty glass of wine. Part of me wanted more just to deal with the strangeness of the situation. The greater part, however, understood that I needed to keep a clear head about it all.

"Where would we start?" I asked, tingling spreading outward from between my thighs. "I mean, if we were to hypothetically, um, explore."

The guys shared another look.

"First thing's first," Adam said. "We go somewhere a little more private."

"You down?" Marcus asked.

There it was. After all of the talking, it came to that one, simple question. With a yes or a no, I knew that I would be changing my life forever, that nothing would be the same after this moment.

"Yes."

The guys smiled. Stoic and strong as they were, I could sense that they had a hard time holding back their excitement.

"Top floor," Mac said. "There's a guest bedroom with more than enough space."

"Lead the way," I replied.

The men quickly polished off their whiskey, getting up when they were done. The anticipation was so intense, I could hardly stand up, barely think. Mac, seeming to sense this, placed his hand on the small of my back, keeping me steady as we left the room.

Together, we made our way upstairs. I found myself growing more and more nervous and excited with each step. The men formed up around me, their musky scents swirling in the air and composing a manly bouquet that was most intoxicating.

By the time we reached the third floor I was lightheaded, so eager to see what the men had in store that I could barely think straight.

"Right here." Mac swept his big hand toward a door on the far end of the third-floor hallway.

We approached, Adam opening the door. On the other side was a room that was both big and spacious yet cozy. The hardwood floor was covered with a big Oriental rug, a large four-post bed up against the wall. The big window at the far end of the room afforded a sweeping view of the property. The snow was coming down hard, but I could still see the majesty of Thousand Acres through the window.

The room had a big fireplace, just like the den. Mac wasted no time stepping over and igniting the gas, the fire big enough to fill the room with flickering orange light. Adam shut the door behind us.

"First things first," Tyler said. "We know this is something new for you. That means if you ever don't feel comfortable, just say so."

Adam nodded. "Right. We're only going to have fun if you are too. You're in control here."

Their words went a long way toward making me feel more at ease.

"Where do we start?" I asked.

Marcus curled his lip. "Wherever you'd like to start, gorgeous."

His compliment sent a thrill up my spine. All the same, the idea of four impossibly handsome men in front of me, all waiting on my wishes, was more than enough to make me feel just a touch overwhelmed.

"Why don't we start with clothes?" Mac asked. "Good a place as any."

I nodded, happy that he'd said something.

I took a deep breath, placing my hands on the buttons of my shirt, opening one after another. The men had their eyes on me, each watching eagerly, as if every little bit of my skin being uncovered was a new delight.

The guys pulled their shirts off, each exposing his sculpted, powerful body. All of them had stunning physiques—each muscular body a unique collection of tattoos and scars. I noticed Marcus had a strange, circular scar on his shoulder that looked to me like a bullet wound.

I tossed my shirt off to the side, the boys doing the same.

One by one, the men unbuttoned their jeans and pulled them down. Each wore a different color pair of skin tight boxer briefs, the fabric pulled taut over powerful thighs. I wanted to pinch myself; the sight before me of four stunning brothers stripping out of their clothes, all of them ready to pleasure *me*, was almost too much to wrap my head around.

The guys kicked off their pants and boots and socks, stepping forward and regarding me with painfully lustfull stares. Four sets of eyes were on me, and below the waistlines I saw that each brother was hard, their cocks straining the fronts of their boxer briefs.

"Alright, gorgeous," Mac said. "You're next."

I glanced down at my body, moving my hands nervously toward my belt.

"Let me help."

I turned my attention forward to see Adam coming toward me. Once he was near, he smoothly moved behind me, wrapping his big, muscular arms around me. I felt better the instant he had me in his embrace, his body warm and solid.

"Sorry," I said. "This is all a little new to me."

He placed his hands on my belly, his palms rough in just the right way.

"Don't apologize for anything." His breath was warm against my neck. "We're a little more experienced than you when it comes to this sort of thing." He kissed me softly on the neck as he moved his hands down toward my pants. "Let us take the reins here, alright?"

I wanted to respond, but the sensation of Adam's hands, the musky scent of his body, the feeling of his breath against the curve of my neck, not to mention the hardness of his cock against my back, was a sensual overload.

"O... OK." It was all I could manage to get out.

I leaned my head back against him, taking in slow breaths as he opened the button of my jeans. Once that was done, he pulled the zipper and took my pants down. I helped the rest of the way, kicking them off when they'd reached the floor.

"There you go," Tyler said. "We're naked; you're naked." I didn't have my eyes open, but I could easily imagine the grin on his face. The thought of him grinning in that way he always did helped even more to put me at ease.

Once my pants were off, Adam moved his hand slowly over my bare thighs, making his way between my legs. I shivered in the best possible way at his touch, my nervousness melting away by the moment.

"Now, let me tell you how this works," he said. "We're here to make you feel good."

"Four men, one goal," Marcus said.

Adam grazed his fingers over the front of my panties, pressing in just the right spot to send a surge of pleasure running through me. I moaned, my knees going weak at his touch. His hand went to my hip, holding me in place and making sure I didn't drop right down to the floor.

"You know what I'm thinking?" Adam asked.

"What's that?" I replied.

"I kinda want to make you come right here and now." After he spoke, he moved his hands between my thighs and pressed up against my pussy, the sensation forcing an "Oh, God" out of my mouth. It was so intense that I don't know how I managed the words.

I gathered my thoughts, his hand now moving back and forth over my lips.

"That feels so good," I groaned.

"That's the whole point, honey," Adam replied.

He rubbed me a bit more, my knees going weak once again. I moaned, pressing the side of my face against his solid, rock-hard chest, the dusting of hair on his pecs tickling in just the right way. After a bit more teasing, Adam brought his hand up, along my back, stopping at the clasp of my bra. With a quick, effortless motion, he undid the clasp, then slid the straps down my arms.

I was nearly totally exposed in front of the men. Even though my eyes were closed, I could feel the heat of their stares. To my surprise, I loved it. The strangeness of being with four men at once was fading with each second, replaced by the heady knowledge that each one of them desired me, wanted me like mad.

Adam slipped his fingers underneath the waistband of my panties, moving over the small patch of hair above my pussy. I squirmed against him, wanting more by the second. By the time his finger moved between my soaking wet lips, I was ready to scream.

He touched me expertly, teasing my clit, making slow circles around it. His other hand stayed on my breast, my nipple going hard against his touch. There was no doubt in my mind that I was in the hands of a seasoned lover, someone who knew exactly what it took to make a girl feel good.

Adam kissed along the slope of my shoulder, his fingers moving down until he was right at my opening. I pressed my ass against him, moving until I was grinding against his stiff cock.

"I want this," I moaned. "I want it so damn bad." I had a hard time believing what kind of words were coming out of my mouth. There was something about these guys that made me put away my inhibitions in a way I never had before.

"I know you do," he said. "But you're going to come for me before you get it."

He went right back to touching me, slipping a finger into my pussy. I moaned as he penetrated me, my mouth forming a perfect "O" of pleasure. My walls gripped his finger, beckoning him deeper inside. As good as his finger felt, the sensation of him in me only made me want more.

Adam moved his finger in and out, his thumb still working my clit. I moaned and sighed, each second of his touch bringing me closer and closer to the orgasm I craved. My knees shook, my breath grew shallower. Opening my eyes and seeing each of the men watching me on the verge of climax only heightened it all.

"Now," he said. "Come for me."

That was all I took. The orgasm broke, hot pleasure exploding through my body. I arched my back, Adam's hand moving to my belly and holding me in place. Between his touch, and the way his body felt against mine, I was helpless before the pleasure.

Adam knew just how to guide me through it. He touched me as I came, his lips moving along my shoulder and neck. When it faded, I turned my head and opened my eyes, greeted with the sight of his impossibly handsome face.

I couldn't resist kissing him. Judging by the intensity with which he kissed me back, Adam felt the same way. His taste filled my mouth along with his tongue, and once more the world around us faded away.

As we kissed, I reached down and grabbed hold of his cock, stroking its length through his underwear.

"Let me return the favor," I said, my voice low and sensual.

To my surprise, he shook his head.

"As enticing as it sounds, I've hogged you enough. There are three other guys here, remember?"

I smiled, having almost forgotten about them. I glanced over my shoulder to see them approaching, a smile spreading across my face as I prepared for the fun to come.

After kissing Adam one more time, I turned my attention to the others.

"Come here, beautiful," Tyler growled.

His body was lean and muscular, with thick shoulders that made it clear his physique wasn't just for show.

I stepped forward and placed my hands on his chest, sighing at how solid and sculpted it was.

I stepped onto my tiptoes and kissed him, Tyler's mouth opening and his tongue finding mine. He tasted just as good as his brother; Tyler's flavor differed just enough to be interesting. After a long, lingering kiss, I backed up, flashing him a smile as I lowered myself down onto my knees. I kissed him here and there on the way down, teasing him a bit.

When I was at waist level, his stiff cock right in front of me, I was so excited that I could hardly think straight. I leaned forward, kissing the sculpted notches of his Adonis belt, hooking my fingers under the waistband of his boxer briefs and pulling them down. His cock, thick and long and stiff, sprang out to greet me.

I glanced up at him one more time, flashing him a devilish smile as I wrapped my fingers around his length. Tyler gazed down at me, the look in his eyes making it clear he was very happy with what he was seeing. I stroked him slowly, a groan reverberating throughout his body. I leaned forward and placed my lips on his head, kissing his tip once before moving my tongue all the way down to his base, licking and sucking his balls before going back up.

Once I was at the top again, I opened my mouth and took him in, sealing my lips around his thickness. I closed my eyes, savoring the sensation of his warm hardness in my mouth before pushing my lips down, taking as many inches of him as I could.

"Just like that," he said, running his fingers through my hair. "That feels so damn good." His words of encouragement put a smile on my face, or at least, they would've if I could smile with my mouth full.

One hand stayed on my leg, the other working Tyler's length. It didn't take long before I tasted the salty tang of his precum, the flavor making me want nothing more than for him to explode down my throat. At the same time, I didn't want to make him finish too quickly.

I took my mouth off his cock, looking at the other guys.

"Can we try something?" I asked.

"Sure can," Mac said. "What do you have in mind?"

I gestured for Marcus to come closer. He stepped forward, and once he did, I reached into his underwear and pulled out his cock. It was long and thick, something I imagined the brothers all had in common, and I began stroking. Marcus closed his eyes and growled, my touch seeming to have the effect I wanted. Once I got into the rhythm of stroking Marcus, I returned my attention to Tyler. I leaned forward and took him into my mouth once more, moving my lips up and down.

It wasn't long before I had it down. The feeling of pleasing two men at once was... thrilling.

I wanted more.

I brought Tyler close to the edge, taking my mouth off him when I could sense he was about to come.

"Don't tell me you're leaving me hanging like that," he said with a grin as I took my hand from Marcus's cock and rose.

"Just for a second."

"Anything you want to share with the class?" Adam asked.

The men stood around me, my pussy aching at the sight of them. Tyler and Marcus were nude, the twins so delicious looking that I almost felt dizzy at the sight of them. There were two other men, however, each of them needing their own attention. Not to mention that I needed one of them inside me, and soon.

"Come here, big brother," I said, stepping toward Mac and placing my hands on his solid chest.

"What've you got in mind, lovely lady?" he asked with a grin as I gently pushed him back toward the bed.

"I'll show you."

With one more push, I guided him onto his back on the bed and slid off my panties. Once he was in position, I reached forward and grabbed the waistband of his underwear, pulling them down and exposing one more gorgeous cock. Mac was just a bit thicker than the others and my mouth watered at the thought of having him inside me.

I climbed onto the bed and straddled him, positioning myself over his cock. Sensing what was coming, he placed his hands on the softness of my hips and held me in place.

"Forgot to ask, beautiful," he said. "You want us to get some protection?"

"We get regular checkups," Adam said. "If you're worried about that sort of thing."

Their words put me even more at ease. "I'm on my own kind of protection."

The matter settled, I began lowering myself onto Mac, his head grazing my wet lips and opening around him. I closed my eyes, ready to feel his thickness inside of me. His thick cock slid in slowly, my walls stretching around him.

"Oh... oh my *God*." It was all I could think to say. Mac filled me with all of his length, pushing all the way in. When he was fully buried, I leaned forward and put my hands on his shoulders.

"How's that feel?" he asked, brushing my curls out of my face with a sweep of his hand.

"So damn good."

A smile on my face, I turned to the other brothers and nodded for them to join us around the bed. They did just that as I brought my eyes back to the stunning man underneath me, the man who was at that moment inside of me.

I raised my hips and brought them down, my pussy so slick and wet that Mac glided inside of me like nothing at all. Mac growled with pleasure as his eyes took in every inch of me, his hands sliding up my thighs and coming to a rest on my breasts.

"Tyler," I said. "Come here. I want to taste you again."

"Don't need to ask me twice."

Tyler crawled onto the bed, the space more than big enough for the three of us. Once he was there, I took him into my mouth and began sucking, my lips and tongue moving over him, tasting him, savoring him.

I bucked hard on Mac, and it wasn't long before he began thrusting from below, his cock shoving up into me driven by his powerful muscles. I moaned, pulling off of Tyler's cock.

"Come for me," I said. "Both of you."

That was more than enough for Tyler. As soon as I sealed my lips around him once more, he grunted hard, his cock pulsing in my mouth as he unloaded. His cum shot down my throat in spurts, hot and thick and salty. I savored every drop, bringing it down in a hard swallow. Underneath me, Mac came to the line and crossed over it, his cock throbbing as he pumped deep within my pussy.

When Tyler was done, I took him from my mouth, smiling up at him as I licked his cock one last time, then my lips.

"That was something else," he said. A pleased smile on his face, he swept his hand over my cheek before stepping back and taking a seat near the fire.

Mac slid out of me, his cum tickling as it dribbled down my leg. He reached around and gave my ass a final squeeze before rolling off the bed.

"Stay right there," Adam said. "I've got you just how I want you."

"Is that right?" I asked over my shoulder.

Adam nodded, coming to the end of the bed and putting his hands on my hips, bending me over. My ass sticking out toward him, he slid into me slowly.

"Oh... oh, *wow*." I savored the sensation for a long moment, opening my eyes long enough to gesture for Marcus to come onto the bed.

He did, his thick manhood sticking up and into the air. I lowered my mouth down onto him, looking up with blissed-out eyes as I wrapped my lips around him, sucking him hard. Marcus was long, maybe the longest of the four, and his cock was flawless. I bobbed my head up and down his prick, using my tongue and lips in ways I never had before.

It wasn't long before an orgasm arrived, moving through my body like a hot wave of pure delight. I closed my eyes, moaning hard on Marcus's cock as I came, my mind focusing on the way Adam's cock felt inside me.

"I need more," I said over my shoulder. "Please."

I placed my lips back on Marcus's cock just in time for him to come, his cock shooting hot warmth into my mouth. I drank it just as eagerly as I had his brother, savoring it all. Behind me, Adam grunted hard as he had his orgasm, his cock throbbing as he tightened his body, his cum spraying deeply.

It was all enough for one last orgasm to rock my body. I held Marcus's cock in my hand as I moaned and screamed, Adam's thickness inside of me carrying my pleasure over the edge.

When I was done, all I could do was take one deep breath after another, trying to wrap my head around what had just happened.

I rolled over, Adam's seed dripping out of me, Marcus's still fresh on my tongue.

"That was *incredible*."

CHAPTER 16

TYLER

The four of us said nothing for a time. What even needed to be spoken after something like that? Adam had thrown on a robe, running down into the den to freshen up our drinks. Once he'd returned, we'd gathered in front of the fire, all of us watching the flames dance as we sipped our wine or whiskey.

I was on Aubrey's right, tracing a figure-eight over her perfect, flat belly. Her curly hair was draped over her slender shoulders, her breasts coated with a lovely sheen from the sweat she'd worked up. She hadn't said a word since we'd all finished our fun, and I couldn't help but fear that she'd regretted it.

Finally, she spoke.

"Wow." The word tumbled out of her mouth. "I mean... *wow.* Seriously, did that really just happen?"

The boys and I, all of us still naked, looked at each other with the same amused expression. We chuckled, taking sips of our drinks.

"It sure did, gorgeous," Mac said. "Now, here's the million-dollar question—how do you feel about it?"

She pursed her lips and looked away, as if she wanted to give the matter some serious thought. When she was ready, Aubrey glanced back at us and nodded.

"I feel good. I mean, *really* good. I think I might want to explore this further."

"Sounds good to me," I replied, and my brothers all agreed.

She held up a finger and Mac narrowed his eyes. "I feel a 'but' coming on."

Aubrey nodded.

"Seriously, if we're going to do this, I want to have rules. Or, to know the rules, at least."

"Fire away," Adam said. "What's on your mind?"

She looked at all four of us. "As much fun as this was having you all together, what's the rule on sex? Do we all need to be together for it? I mean, I don't want you guys getting jealous if one or two or three of you are left out."

I put my hand on her gorgeous, silky thigh. "You don't need to worry about anything like that. We don't get jealous. We can all be together, or separate, or in any other way you want us."

She nodded slowly, processing it. "So, any combination is fine – one-on-one, two-on-one, all the rest."

"As long as you're down, we're down," Adam said. "We've got our responsibilities with the twins and the farm, and our business, but other than that, you say when, we'll be there."

She grinned. I got the sense she was liking this more and more with each word out of our mouths.

The grin faded, however, a wince replacing it.

"What's wrong?" I asked.

"Nothing. It's stupid."

"If it's stupid," I said with a smirk, "then I definitely want to hear it."

She pursed her lips, as if not sure whether or not to reveal what she had on her mind. With a sigh, she began.

"It's Aggie. She's a total gossip. If there's something going on with me and you guys, she's going to want to know about it. Like, she'll sense it."

"You're worried about her telling people?" Mac asked.

"Not that. She can keep a secret, it's just that she's going to sense something is up the second she sees me. I need to know whether or not I can tell her something's going on between all of us."

We all shared a look that said none of us cared if she told her.

"Go right ahead," Adam said. "Might want to have her keep it to herself and not blab it to the whole town though. People tend to be judgmental about things they don't understand, you know?"

Adam's words made us share another look, this one more serious. We knew what he was referring to.

"You don't need to worry about anything like that. She's nosy when it comes to me, but she's good at discretion."

"Good," Mac said. "Anything else on your mind?"

She shook her head slowly. "I think the next step is to process all of this. I've... kinda got a ton to think over."

"Naturally," Adam said. "Take all the time you need."

Silence fell over us, and I turned my head to the nearest window. The snow was still coming down hard, with no signs of letting up.

"Slight change of subject," I said. "But I don't think you should be driving anywhere in this weather. Not even back to your place, even though it's close."

She nodded. "Oh, I know. Aggie already texted me and told me to stay over, that she'd take care of the animals in the morning."

Mac threw back the rest of his whiskey, putting his hands on the ground and pushing himself up.

"Then let's get you settled in one of the guest rooms. I'd put you up in here, but, uh, you probably don't want to sleep in those sheets."

"Or maybe I do," she said with a wink. "They smell like you guys now, after all."

My cock shifted a bit at her words, not to mention the sultry expression on her face as she said them.

"As much as I appreciate the sentiment, there will be no sleeping in the wet spot in this house," Mac replied. He stepped over to the nearby closet, fishing out some spare clothes. "Come on with me, Aubrey, I'll get you settled in."

Aubrey stretched out her willowy, slender arms, taking in a big yawn as she did. "Yeah, kinda thinking some rest is in order after all of that." Mac handed her one of our old Navy sweatshirts and a pair of sleeping pants. I said nothing, taking in the sight of her slipping them on over her impossibly sexy body. Her shapely legs extended down below the bottom of the sweatshirt, and I couldn't take my eyes off of them.

Aubrey grinned as she stepped into the sleeping pants, her glances jumping from one of us to the other.

"You guys never seen a girl put on clothes before?"

The boys and I chuckled at being spotted so easily.

"Not a woman who looks like you," I said.

"Alright, alright." Mac put on some sleeping clothes of his own. "Calm yourselves down before I bring in some buckets of cold water." He nodded to Aubrey, and she flashed us all one last smile before leaving with Mac.

"Good night, boys," she said with a wink. The look on her face, and her lingering gaze, let us know without a doubt that we were going to be on her mind that night as she drifted off to sleep.

Once she was gone, the door to the bedroom shut, the guys and I settled into silence as we watched the fire and sipped our drinks.

I'd never been one for silence, however.

"Holy hell," I said, shaking my head in disbelief. "She just might be the one."

Marcus shot me a hard look. "You serious? I mean, you're really saying something like that after our first time together with her?" He stood up, making his way over to his underwear, snatching them up and putting them on. "You're getting a little ahead of yourself, brother."

"What?" I did the same, my underwear within arm's reach from where I sat. "Are you two really telling me you don't feel something a little more intense than just a physical connection?"

Adam said nothing, his eyes on the fire. I knew my brothers well enough to be able to tell when they were in the middle of deep thought.

"He's right," Adam finally said. "Marcus, I get that you're not comfortable with this kind of stuff, but—"

"What the hell is that supposed to mean?" he snapped, stepping over and swiping his glass of whiskey from the side table where he'd put it.

"You know damn well what that means," Adam said. "You don't like feelings – especially ones that bring you closer to other people."

Marcus scoffed, shaking his head as he dropped into one of the chairs in front of the fire.

"You don't know what the hell you're talking about." He followed this up with a long draw of whiskey, but no other words, meaning that he understood that Adam had a point but didn't want to admit it.

"Yeah," I said with a smirk. "We all feel it; the faster we can accept it as a fact and go from there, the better."

"She's something special, alright," Adam said. "I'm glad we discussed this before we left on the mission but all the same, we're going to have to table the matter of Aubrey until we get back, make sure we handle the task at hand, first. Still, it's hard not to get excited about this."

Marcus shook his head. "Are you guys really being this naïve? Do you need me to remind you of what happened with the last woman we tried this with?"

The mood in the room cooled, neither Adam nor I said a word.

He was right. We'd mentioned Tiffany to Aubrey. What we hadn't done, however, was tell her *why* that whole situation had gone south and why it had ended.

"This is just how it was with Tiffany," Marcus went on. "All of us were stupid and giddy about how perfectly everything was working out, how we couldn't believe our luck at this amazing, beautiful woman going for the insane idea of being with all of us at the same time. You two might be looking back at all that with rose-colored glasses, but I'm sure as hell not."

Adam and I shared a look.

Images from those few days came back into my mind as clear as a movie. I remembered us all going into town, hitting one of the local bars as a group. We drank, joked, flirted. A group like ours, four brothers and one woman, attracted all the attention that one might guess.

I remembered that feeling in the air, that tenseness that arrived as the bar patrons slowly put it together that we weren't just a group of folks out on the town – we were something more. People stared; people talked. By the time we paid our tab and headed out for the night, we'd unknowingly set the stage for the gossip that would bring everything down.

We'd known something was wrong two days later, after Tiffany had gone into town to pick up our weekly grocery haul. She'd left with a smile on her face, eager to get back and spend the evening with all of us. When she'd returned, however, her expression was dark.

Something had happened.

It'd taken some time to coax it out of her, but we'd eventually gotten to the bottom of it. People had been talking at the store, whispering to one another as she passed. At first, she'd tried to ignore it. So what if people talked? By the time she'd reached the register and the girl running it refused to take care of her, telling her that she didn't even want to look at someone who participated in something so "unnatural," Tiffany had enough.

We'd tried to calm her, to tell her that it didn't matter, that the townspeople would get used to it. At first, it seemed like we'd gotten through to her. She'd gone to her room to be alone that night, sure, but I'd felt confident that we'd calmed her nerves.

Maybe we had. Over the next few days, however, she reached her breaking point. It all came to a head during the farmer's market that weekend. We'd been there with her and had a chance to see first-hand what she'd been dealing with. The five of us couldn't take a step without someone pointing or glaring or whispering. Halfway through the outing, Tiffany broke into tears and ran back to the car.

We tried again that night to put her at ease. However, there was no doubt in my mind that each of us knew that it was over, that she'd hit her limit. The next morning, she was gone, leaving nothing but a note that said while we'd be in her heart forever, she was done.

That was the last we'd seen of Tiffany. While we'd only known Aubrey for a short time, the idea of her leaving like that, of never seeing her again, was enough to make my heart hurt like mad.

"She'd never do that," I said. "She'd be able to handle the talk, the whispering."

Marcus shrugged, seeming unconvinced. "Maybe. Maybe she'd find it funny, like we did. Good chance that she won't, though. Good chance that she'd leave, just like Tiffany did."

I opened my mouth to speak, but nothing came out. As I watched the flames dance, I knew for damn certain that there was something special about Aubrey, something different.

What I didn't know, however, was if this *something* would be enough to keep her at our sides when the heat came on. And it *would* come on.

CHAPTER 17

MAC

"How are you feeling?" Although I'd never been one to pry, I couldn't help but ask the question as I made my way down the hall with Aubrey.

"Good." She said the word with confidence. "Very good. How could I not after experiencing what I just did with you guys?" She smiled at me as we walked.

"You sure?"

She laughed. "What, you don't think I understand my own feelings?"

"No, not that," I said quickly. "Not that at all. Just... want to make sure that you know there's an open dialogue about these things. All of our doors are wide open if you want to talk."

"I appreciate it. I'm happy with it, Mac. And I'm even happier that you guys are going out of your way to make sure I'm feeling good about what we did. Still, all I can do is be honest with you about how I'm feeling now, then process the rest later."

"Honesty. That's what this is about. Anything that comes up, let us know."

We reached the door at the far end of the hallway, stopping and turning to one another.

"I will. Right now, I need some rest."

I allowed myself a smile, pleased at her directness.

"You should be all set in here," I said, opening the door and revealing a small, but cozy room with a double bed, dresser, and connected bathroom. "I'll have your clothes washed and ready for you in the morning, breakfast ready for you, too."

"Thanks, Mac, for everything."

I shook my head. "No, thank you."

The way she looked in that moment, her slender body covered in baggy clothes, her curls still mussed from our fun, the snow-dappled moonlight casting her face in silver light... there was no way I could resist kissing her.

So, I did. I leaned in and placed my lips on hers. Part of me expected her to push me away and tell me again that she needed rest, time to process things. She didn't. Instead, she stood up on her tiptoes and kissed me right back. My mouth opened and so did hers, and for a few, fleeting moments, her delicious taste washed over me.

My cock stiffened, and I knew I was ready for more. My resistance waned more and more as the kiss went on.

It wasn't a good idea. Using all the will I had, I placed my hands on the softness of her hips and gently pushed her away.

"Got some things I want to do to you," I said. "But they might interfere with your processing, and your rest."

She smiled that gorgeous smile and looked away for a moment.

We kissed one more time.

"Good night, Aubrey. Sleep well."

"You too."

With that, we parted. I shut the door behind her, fatigue washing over me as soon as I was alone. And as I made my way back to my room, I allowed myself about the biggest smile I'd worn in God-only-knew how long.

~

"Got a surprise for you two!" I said, heading into the twins' room as I roused them for the morning.

"I'm tired." Henry spoke the words as he rubbed his eyes.

"A surprise?" Hattie was a little more eager, she loved unexpected stuff.

"Yup." I scooped Henry out of bed, bringing the big guy over to the dresser and pulling out some clothes. "First of all, check this out." I pulled open the nearby curtains, revealing a gorgeous sweep of pure, white snow. The clouds had cleared, the sky a perfect blue above the endless expanse of white.

"Wow!" Henry's fatigue was gone the second he laid eyes on the snow. "Can we play in it?"

"You're going to have to ask our special breakfast guest. So, the faster you two get ready, the faster you can do that."

Henry got his butt into gear at my words. The kids were all kinds of excited, eagerly chatting with one another about who could be waiting for them downstairs.

"Aubrey!" The twins said her name at the same time as we entered the kitchen, rushing over to throw their arms around her.

"Morning, dudes!" she said, getting up and squatting down to meet their hug with one of her own.

The rest of the guys were already in the kitchen, Tyler and Marcus putting the finishing touches on a big breakfast of sausage, eggs, fresh squeezed orange juice and pancakes. I'd never been a big breakfast guy, but the sight of the spread made me damn hungry all the same. On top of that, I was plenty glad to be spending the day ahead indoors packing instead of out in the snow.

"Miss Aubrey," Henry said, getting really serious. "It snowed last night." He pointed to the nearest window, as if she hadn't noticed.

"I can see that. It's why I'm here, in fact."

"Really?" Hattie climbed up onto Aubrey's lap as she asked the question.

"Really. It got super icky out when I dropped you guys off yesterday. So, your uncles were nice enough to let me stay here for the night in one of the spare bedrooms."

"You had a sleepover?" Henry asked. "Aww..."

"Wasn't a sleepover for kids," Marcus said. "You guys were already asleep, too."

"Can we play out in the snow?" Henry asked. "Right now?"

"Well, right now we're going to eat. Then, sure, I think after that we can do some outside stuff. But remember that your uncles are going to be packing all day, so we're going to need to stay out of their way."

The twins' faces fell at the reminder that my brothers and I were about to go away for a little while. My heart hurt at the sight of it. After all, this was the longest that all of us had been away from the twins since we'd brought them into our lives.

"Do you have to go?" Hattie asked, her eyes moving to each of us in turn.

I stepped over to her, scooping her up from Aubrey's lap. "We do, Hats. But don't worry, you and Aubrey are going to have so much fun together, alright? And we'll make sure to call you both as often as we can on FaceTime." I wished like hell that I could say we'd be talking to them every day. We'd be on a mission, however, which meant that would've been a promise I couldn't keep.

Hattie said nothing, throwing her arms around me and squeezing me tightly. I patted her on the back, planting a kiss on her forehead.

"So," Aubrey said, "since I'm going to be spending some time over here for a lengthy bit, I was thinking it'd be a good idea for me to pack some stuff from my place. But with the snow..."

"No problem at all," Adam assured. "We've got a plow we can mount on the truck. It's the next best thing short of driving a tank."

"I can handle that," I said. "I'll get the plow mounted and drive you over."

"Maybe we can do lunch at my place?" Aubrey asked. "And you

two can take your nap in the guest room I've got ready for you. What do you think?"

The kids let out happy noises at the idea. I couldn't help but smile knowing the twins were in more than good hands. All the same, I didn't even want to think about the time ahead being apart from them.

"You guys ready to eat?" Marcus asked, bringing over a big plate loaded high with pancakes, a pitcher of syrup in the other hand.

"Ready since I opened my eyes this morning," Adam said as he slid into one of the open chairs.

The gang piled around the table and wasted no time digging in. Breakfast was damn near sublime. All the dairy was from our cows on the farm, the meat and all the rest from ranches around the area. I started with pancakes, slathering them with butter and syrup and digging in.

"You know what's *really* good?" Aubrey asked, the kids on both sides of her.

"What?" Henry replied.

"Watch." Aubrey picked up one of her sausage links, waggling her eyebrows as she dipped it into the pool of syrup on her plate. Once that was done, she popped the end into her mouth and took a big bite.

"Gross!" Henry said, shaking his head. "Syrup is for pancakes!"

"It's sweet and savory," Aubrey said. "Try it!"

"What's savory?" Hattie asked.

"Mmm, it's like the opposite of ice cream; salty and rich, like chicken noodle soup."

"Hmm." Hattie made an interested noise as she picked up one of her own sausages and tapped the end into her syrup. Next, she brought it to her mouth and took a big bite. Her big, hazel brown eyes lit up right away as she chewed. "So good!"

Henry, still a bit suspicious, reached over and did the same with one of his sausage links. He dunked the end in his syrup and brought it to his mouth. Just like his sister, his eyes lit up.

"Wow!" he shoved the rest of the link down so quickly that I had to say something.

"Easy, kid," I said. "Don't forget to breathe."

"Can we have sausage on our ice cream tonight?" Hattie asked.

That got a laugh out of us all.

"Let's not go crazy, Hats," Adam said. "There *are* limits to the sweet-salty combo."

"Bacon on ice cream," Tyler said, thoughtfully running his hand through his beard. "Now *that's* got potential. Maybe a little syrup, a splash of bourbon..." he took out his phone and began typing away, no doubt adding the idea to one of his notes.

"Speaking of dinner," Adam said. "Aubrey, we were thinking that, since you're going to be here in the morning anyway to see us off, you ought to spend the night here again tonight. And we can do a big family dinner this evening."

Her eyes lit up. "Seriously? I don't want to overstay my welcome."

"Have dinner here!" Henry said. "*Please!*"

"*Please-oh-please-oh-please,*" Hattie added.

I laughed. "You're not overstaying your welcome as far as we're concerned. And you can see what the twins think of the idea."

She smiled. "OK, that does sound nice. But I do need to meet with Aggie and make sure she's on the same page as far as farm duties are concerned. She's got most of it covered for while you guys are gone and I'm going to be with the kids, but I don't want to spring more on her than necessary."

"Understood," I said.

With that, we finished our meal and cleaned up. I threw on a coat and went into the garage after breakfast, spending the next hour or so getting the plow hitched onto the front of the F-350. Once that was done, I took a little time to shovel the walkways around the house. Aubrey spent the time with the twins, the guys getting our gear in order for our flight the next day.

As I worked, I couldn't help but think about how, as strange as it might've been, I already *missed* Aubrey. I'd known being away from the twins would be hard, but Aubrey was another matter altogether. The connection we'd made last night had been intense; intense enough for feelings to sneak up on me.

I put it all out of my head as best I could. We had the mission of a lifetime in front of us, and none of us could afford to have matters of the heart taking up too much mental space if we wanted to come home in one piece.

When I got back to the house at noon, Aubrey and the twins were in the den, a fire crackling in the hearth as she read them a story. I leaned in the door frame, watching as their little eyelids grew heavy as she spoke.

"Looks like it's time for a nap," I said when Aubrey closed the book.

"I think you're right," she said. "But... I still need to get over to Downing."

"No problem at all. Won't be the first time I've toted around a couple of sleepy kids. You get Hats; I'll get Hen."

Together, we scooped the kids off the couch, carrying them into the entry room. Henry rested his head on my shoulder as I carried him, and I could sense that he was right on the verge of falling asleep.

"Let's get them in their coats and boots," I said, speaking in a low whisper. "Truck's ready to go, got the car seats strapped in."

She gave me a thumbs up, the two of us going to work getting the twins prepared for the cold and snow. Hattie and Henry were in a sleepy stupor, barely able to stay awake. Once they were ready, we carried them outside, the sky still bright and clear. The truck was right out front, and each of us strapped in a twin before climbing into the front seats.

The drive didn't take too long, the truck plow pushing effortlessly through the foot or two of snow. I followed the main road, clearing a path for when she needed to come back to the house while we were gone.

During the drive, I couldn't help but stare at her out of the corner of my eye. She was so damn beautiful, effortlessly gorgeous. Her curls were stuffed under a blue knit cap, the cold of the day making her olive skin glow. She was like something out of a damn dream.

We pulled in front of her place, unbuckling the kids and heading inside. I couldn't help but notice how much I loved her house. It wasn't as big as Thousand Acres, but it was homey and cozy. I was glad as hell that the kids would be spending so much time at a home like this over the next couple of weeks.

Aubrey silently led the way to the guest bedroom on the second floor. We'd had a couple of twin beds ordered for her, and they were set up and ready for the kids. The rest of the room was perfect, stocked with clothes and everything else the kids would need.

We took the twins out of their winter gear and tucked them in. They'd been so sleepy on the drive over that it took no time for them to zonk completely out. We watched them for a time from the front of the room, making sure that they were out before shutting the door and entering the hall.

"Aggie's not going to be here for a little bit," she said. "Had some errands in town."

"OK, then. If you want, I can leave you here with the kids and pick you all up later."

She nodded. "We *could* do that."

I was confused. Her tone suggested that she had other plans in mind.

"Got a better idea?"

She flicked her eyes up at me, chewing gently on her lower lip.

"Remember what you guys said last night? About the rules?"

My cock shifted down below. I had a good idea where this was going. Without even thinking, I stepped forward, closing the distance between us.

"Which rule did you happen to have in mind?"

She grinned. "The rule about one-on-one. I mean, it was really nice having you all at the same time. But right now, I've got something more personal on my mind."

I put my hands on her hips, feeling the softness of her curves through her jeans.

"I think I know just what you mean, gorgeous."

"Then why not show me?"

No more words were necessary. I leaned in, and placed my lips on hers, that same magical electricity that I felt when we'd kissed last night returning with a vengeance.

I pressed her body against mine, letting her feel my erection. She moaned as my cock pressed against her, Aubrey's lips grazing against mine.

"Come on," I said. "I need you in the bedroom and underneath me right now."

"Sounds perfect."

I scooped her off the ground, carrying her down the hall and into the master bedroom. Once there, we shut the door and pounced on one another, kissing hard and stripping out of our clothes until she was in nothing except her bra and panties, and I was only in my boxer briefs.

I kissed her mouth, moving down as I opened the clasp of her bra, her breasts tumbling out just in time for me to wrap my lips around her nipples, one then the other, sucking and licking as she sighed, her hands running through my hair. She had about the most perfect pair of tits I'd ever seen in my life, round and perky, her nipples a gorgeous light brown.

I rose and reached around her, putting my hands on her ass.

"You know, I haven't been able to stop thinking about those skills of yours I saw last night."

She smirked. "Yeah? What skills did you have in mind?"

"The ones you have with that sexy mouth of yours."

She stood up on her tiptoes to plant a quick kiss on my lips before dropping down to her knees, making a slow, lazy trail with her tongue as she made her way down to my waistline.

Once there, she slipped her fingertips beneath my waistband, pulling my boxer briefs down in a quick yank, my fully hard cock springing out. She let out a groan of happy surprise, taking hold of my length and stroking me slowly, that smile still on her face.

She placed her lips on my head, kissing me softly starting there, then moving down my length. I brushed her curls out of the way, wanting a clear view of her work. She kissed and licked me, traveling all the way down to my balls and sucking on them for a bit before repeating the process in reverse.

"I could watch this all day," I said, brushing her cheek with the back of my hand.

"Too bad you wouldn't be able to *last* all day with me doing this," she said with a smile.

I laughed. "Is that a challenge?"

"I don't know, let's see."

She opened her mouth and took my head into it once more, sealing her lips hard and lashing me with quick strokes from her tongue. I groaned, the pleasure immediate and intense. The sight of her mouth full of me was something else, about as perfect an image as I could hope for.

Aubrey went down, cupping my balls in her hand as she took as many of my inches as she could. Once she'd hit her limit, she came back up, then back down. Soft, wet noises filled the air as she sucked me, my muscles twitching from the pleasure. It didn't take long at all before I felt an orgasm rising in the base of my cock.

I closed my eyes, focusing on holding back. Seeming to sense this, Aubrey took her mouth away and stood.

"See? You were right on the verge of letting go."

"You think so?"

"I could tell. You should've done it; I'd love to taste you."

"I bet you would. But as nice as that sounds, I've got better ideas."

"Oh yeah?"

"Yeah."

I picked her up, and carried her over to the bed, setting her down on the edge. Once she was there, I positioned myself between her legs and spread them apart, peeling down her panties and tossing them aside.

Her pussy was beautiful, glistening and inviting. I leaned in, kissing her thighs and spreading her legs until I was right on her lips. She sighed as I opened them, her pussy pink and perfect. I set my eyes on her clit, covering it in licks and presses with my tongue, moans pouring out of her.

"Yeah, just like that... please."

I loved the way she talked during sex, this perfect blend of pleading and commanding.

The delicious tang of her pussy flowed into my mouth; her juices as sweet as they came. When I slipped a finger into her, Aubrey fell back onto the bed. I watched her as I pleasured her, her breasts rising up and down, her hand pressing on her belly.

"Don't-stop-don't-stop-don't—"

Her chant changed as she came, turning into a high-pitched squeal that left no doubts whether or not she was in the throes of an orgasm. It rose and fell, her juices flowing as I carried her through the pleasure.

"Come here," she said, once the orgasm faded. "I need more."

CHAPTER 18

AUBREY

I couldn't believe how hard he'd made me come, and how effortlessly.

One orgasm wouldn't be enough, however. Lucky for me, the hungry glint in Mac's eye as he climbed up over top of me made it quite clear that he wasn't even close to being done.

Right when he was above me, his heavy, thick cock tantalizingly close to my pussy, he grabbed my hips. Before I could realize what was happening, he flipped me over, slipping his arm underneath my belly and pulling me up, my ass sticking into the air.

It was all so quick, so rough, that I couldn't help but love it. I felt the stone-solid head of his cock drag over my lips. The sensation was so intense that all I could do was close my eyes and moan.

"You want this?" he asked, positioning his cock at my entrance and holding it there, spreading my lips just enough to make me crazy.

"I want it. I want all of it."

"Then ask for it. Ask nicely."

It was a fun game, I had to admit. I played along, glancing over my shoulder and gazing back at him with a hungry expression. It wasn't a lie; I was aching for him to be inside of me.

"Can you *please* give it to me?" I asked, a bit of a teasing tone to my words. To make my point, I lifted my ass just enough to bring an inch or so of his length inside of me. The sensation of his thickness stretching me out was more than I could bear, and the smirk vanished from my face.

Finally, he gave me what I craved. Mac thrust his hips forward, his cock plunging inside and splitting me in two in the best way imaginable. I moaned, grinding my ass against him, begging with my body for all of him.

Soon, he was buried to the hilt. I glanced over my shoulder again, taking in the sight of his powerful body over top of me, his muscles shredded, his shoulders broad, his chest powerful and thick.

Mac pulled back, driving hard into me, the sensation of his thickness pushing deep enough to make my eyes go wide. It was intense, almost too much to bear. The feeling only increased when he reached forward, and placed his hands on mine, holding me in place, making me his, claiming me.

His pace quickened, his thrusts fast and deep, the pace more than enough to put me in a trance-like state. I moaned and sighed, another orgasm creeping up on me and flowing through my body, making me feel like I was about to melt.

I came, gripping the blanket as his hands stayed on mine, his grunts filling the air and blending with my moans. He pounded me through the orgasm, knowing just when to keep going and just when to stop. When I was done, he slipped his cock out of me, placing his hands on my hips and turning me onto my back.

He moved his eyes slowly up and down my body, making sure that not a single square inch of me was ignored.

"God, you're about the sexiest damn thing I've ever seen in my life."

"Right back at you, handsome."

I reached up, placing my hands on his chest, feeling the soft bristle of his chest hair, tracing the outline of one of his scars. His body was beautiful and rugged at the same time, a body that I had no doubt he could count on when he was in danger.

In that moment, however, it was a body that was making a certain woman very, very happy.

I watched as he took hold of his cock, bringing it between my legs and easing it inside. I gasped once more, writhing underneath him as his thickness stretched me out. Once he was fully seated, I opened my eyes just enough to see him over me, a strange expression in his eyes, one that I could barely make out, one that resembled *tenderness*.

Without thinking, I placed my hand on his cheek, his stubble coarse against my soft skin. He pulled back and pushed into me once again, his entire body flexing and tensing as he released. I wrapped my legs around his hips, bringing him as close to me as he could possibly get.

Mac returned the favor, slipping one of his huge arms under my back and lifting me up against him, my breasts going flat against his solid chest.

He moved in and out of me, the pleasure building and building, soft moans flowing from my mouth.

"You gonna come for me again?" he asked, his voice gruff, heavy with pleasure.

"Yes. Yes, I am." I was so gripped by the delight that the words were nearly impossible to get out.

"Do it." His voice was firm and commanding. "Come for me now."

The words were enough to allow my release, an "ah-ah-ah" shooting from my mouth as I let go, giving myself over to Mac and coming for a third time. The orgasm was the most intense of the three, powerful enough to make the world blur around me, nothing existing but the pleasure and the man on top of me, the man who was giving it to me.

Mac's thrusts picked up in pace, his breathing letting me know that he was right on the verge. Finally, with one final hard thrust he let out a groan, his body stiffening. His cock throbbed and pulsed inside of me, and even in the throes of pleasure I was able to focus on it, to savor the sensation of his warmth erupting into me.

We came together, and we descended together. When it was all over, he gazed down at me with warmth in his eyes, saying nothing, only coming in close for one final lingering kiss before rolling off and to my side.

He wasted no time scooping me into his arms, bringing me flush against his powerful body. We said nothing for a time, simply holding one another and staring into each other's eyes. He was so damn handsome that it was almost hard to look at him.

"Hell of a lunch break," he said.

I chuckled. "More than one way to satisfy an appetite."

"You're telling me."

He came in for a kiss. Before we touched lips, however, a chime sounded from a phone somewhere in the room.

"Shit. That's me." He rolled over and put his feet on the ground.

"Can't wait?"

"I wish. We're doing some important packing and planning today. The boys and I need to be instantly available if one of us needs something."

As much as I wanted his body against mine once more, I understood. Not to mention the little fact that I was able to get a very nice look at his ass as he made his way over to his pants on the other side of the room to retrieve his phone.

He picked it up and read a text on the screen. "Gotta go into town." Mac then cocked his head to the side, as if something had occurred to him. "Speaking of lunch, I'm damn hungry. You feel like some pizza?"

I grinned, pleased as hell to spend some more time with him.

"Always down for a slice."

∼

Westbrook, a town of about 30,000, and the closest urban area to Downing and Thousand Acres, bustled with a surprising amount of activity for a Friday afternoon. The holiday season vibes were well underway, and excitement filled the air. Tinsel and greenery were everywhere, lights and holly hung from the streetlamps, and a towering tree loomed large in the small, square park in front of City Hall, a classic Greek-revival building.

The main drag of town was as cute as they came, the road packed with businesses and townhomes. Just being there was enough to make memories of my childhood come flooding back.

"Busy," Mac said as he glanced over his shoulder at the scene while helping Hattie out of the truck.

Henry in my arms, I stepped over to a nearby telephone pole and read a flyer attached to it.

"Oh, wow. I totally spaced on what was going on down here."

"Winter farmer's market," Mac nodded, seemingly remembering at the same time as me. "Last chance of the year to offload your goods before the market shuts down for the winter."

"Aggie's down here running our booth. Lots of llama wool, if you're interested." I followed my words up with a smile.

Mac chuckled. "Think we're good on that."

I loved his laugh. Mac was rough and gruff as they came, making it even more noteworthy when he cracked a smile or allowed himself a little laugh. I savored it whenever it happened.

"Alright," I said. "Sam's Pizza is just down the block. You guys ready?"

"Yeah!" They said in unison.

"What do you guys want to get?"

"Cheese!" Hattie exclaimed.

"Pepperoni!" Henry added. "And green peppers!"

I cocked my head to the side. "Peppers, huh?"

He grinned. "They're crunchy."

"Kid's got unusual taste," Mac said with a shrug. "Don't know where he gets it from."

"You know what *I* like?" I asked, deciding to have some fun with the kids.

"What?" Hattie asked.

"Mushrooms. Lots and lots and *lots* of mushrooms. So many mushrooms that the pizza is just one *big* mushroom!"

"Eww!" they said in unison.

I gave both of their arms a gentle squeeze before standing up. Mac stood there, a strangely warm expression on his face.

"Thanks," he said, leaning in. "Don't think I say this often enough, but you're so damn great with them. Appreciate it like hell."

His words warmed my heart. It took all the restraint I had to hold back the big grin that he'd just inspired.

"Hard not to have fun with great kids like these."

As I spoke, Mac reached back and pulled his thick wallet of worn leather out of his back pocket.

"Here. For the pizza."

"You're not coming with?"

"I'll join you in a few. Adam hired a crew to work the market and I want to check in on them while we're here. I'll meet the three of you there in a little bit." He opened his wallet to reveal an inch-deep stack of hundreds, taking one out and handing it to me.

"You don't need to do that. You guys give me enough to treat the kids; I can handle the occasional slice of pizza."

"Answer's no," he said firmly. "We handle all of this. You're the one helping us out, remember?"

Before I had a chance to retort, he put the hundred back in his wallet, taking out a pair of twenties instead.

"Alright, you two – you're buying lunch. You think you both can handle that?"

"Of course!" Hattie said, taking the money.

"Be careful with that, money is big kid stuff. I'm testing you two here."

I loved how he spoke to the twins, stern and loving all at the same time. He may not have planned to be the kids' guardian, but he was a damn natural at the job as far as I was concerned.

"Alright, I'm going to head over," he said. "Don't eat all the pizza before I get there, alright?"

The kids grinned. "OK!" Henry agreed.

Mac gave me one last look, a glance of muted warmth, before turning and heading in the opposite direction. The man was so big that I was able to see the top of his head as he melted into the crowd.

"Hey, dudes!" I said, turning my attention to the kids. "You want to go visit Miss Aggie? I bet she wants some pizza too!"

The kids let out happy noises of agreement. They were both crazy about Aggie.

Together, we set off. The farmer's market was packed and lively, everyone dressed in their winter gear with thick coats and caps and gloves. The dozens and dozens of booths sold goods of all kinds—from food to crops to handmade crafts. And no matter where you went, the Christmas tree in the town center rose high above it all.

"Aubrey?" Hattie asked. A twin was on each side of me, each holding one of my hands.

"What's up, Hats?"

"Can we get a tree?"

"I'm sure your uncles will get you one." After I said the words, however, I realized that we were a week into December and the guys still hadn't put up so much as a bough of holly. That was no good at all – especially with kids. I was certain it was because they'd been so busy with the farm and planning for the mission, it must have just slipped their minds. All the same, Christmas decorations were a must when kids were around.

"In fact," I said. "I think I've got an idea…"

A smile formed as I hatched a scheme. The timing was perfect – at that moment we were walking by Merry Way, the town's holiday décor shop. I set the idea aside for the time being, spotting Aggie at our booth.

"There she is!" I said, pointing to Aggie up ahead. "Let's go!"

We hurried through the crowd, making our way to Aggie's booth. She was there with a pair of workers from town she'd hired to help, a small line of customers looking over the booth's wares. Her eyes lit up as she saw us coming.

"Hey!" she shouted. "What're you three doing here?"

Aggie placed her hand on her assistant's shoulder, saying something into her ear. The assistant smiled and nodded, taking over the line as Aggie came over to greet us.

"What's up, party animals?" she asked, squatting down to give the kids hugs.

"We're getting pizza!" Henry said.

"Yeah! Come with us!" Hattie added.

"Gosh, some pizza really does sound good... and I *did* skip lunch." She rose and called over her shoulder to her assistant. "Yo, Jenn! Mind holding down the fort for thirty minutes while I take lunch? There are a couple slices of extra cheese from Sam's in it if you can!"

Her assistant gave her a thumbs-up. With that, we were off.

"How's business?" I asked, the four of us making our way through the crowd over to the sidewalks on the far side of the street.

"Not bad at all. I just about off-loaded the rest of the wool. Between that and what you're making at Thousand Acres, things are looking pretty good for the winter. Oh! And Jenn hooked me up with this crew from Vermont that's going to be in the area in a few months, and they sound *perfect* for the staff we'll need come planting season. With the money we're making, we should be able to afford them."

"And if we can afford staff, that means we stand a chance of making a profit this upcoming year."

Aggie smiled and nodded. "Yep. Still a lot of work ahead of us, but we've got a fighting chance now."

Relief washed over me. I'd spent so much time worrying about the farm tanking before I'd even gotten settled. Hearing that things were turning around, the year ahead looking somewhat bright, made the day even better.

Aggie opened the door for all of us, the sights and smells of fresh pizza right from the oven instantly greeting us. The shop was done up with tons of Christmas décor, Frank Sinatra serenading us with carols from the speakers. The kids wasted no time rushing up to the counter, all the delicious-looking pizza behind a glass partition.

"So," Aggie started as we approached the counter. "How're things at the Stud Ranch?" she followed this up with a wicked smile.

"The what?" My eyes went wide, and right then and there I knew that I'd already blown whatever secrecy that I'd hoped to have on the subject of the guys.

Sure enough, Aggie narrowed her eyes and cocked her head to the side.

"Wait a minute, what's going on here, Aub?"

Shit. "Uh, pizza's really looking good today, huh?" I asked, going for the lamest attempt at deflection I'd ever tried in my life. "The veggie slice is really calling out to me. How about you?"

Aggie kept her eyes narrowed, the smile on her face making it clear she'd realized something was up.

"Aubrey! Aubrey Downing!"

A voice called out to me from within the crowd of people in the shop. I turned and was greeted with a face that seemed strangely familiar. It was a woman, around my age, with wide, eager eyes and a face framed by bright red, frizzy hair. She was slender, her body almost nothing wrapped up in her winter gear.

"Hey?" I said, the word coming out like a question. The twins, who'd already ordered their pizza, turned and regarded the woman with no small amount of suspicion.

The woman pursed her lips, making a facial expression that suggested she realized that she was maybe coming on too strong.

"It's me, Janet Lovell!"

It took me a second, but the name soon clicked in my memory.

"Oh, Janet! Hey!"

I turned to Aggie, who had her own look, one that seemed to say that she was wondering if she needed to jump in and tell a potentially crazy woman to back off.

"Aggie, this is Janet Lovell. She and I went to high school together over in Sienna."

"Nice to meet you," Janet said, her slightly manic energy still there, though kept slightly in check.

"Aggie Culbertson," she said, hesitantly offering her hand in return for a shake.

"I know this is kind of weird," Janet said. "Aubrey and I didn't exactly run in the same circles. You were more track and field; I was the nerd on the yearbook committee."

"Something like that," I replied.

"This is so crazy seeing you," Janet said.

"Not really, it's a small town, right?"

"Very true. But the reason I say that is because I was actually planning on getting in touch with you."

"Really? Why?"

"I'm doing a piece on some of the local farms that've come into the hands of the children of the farms' owners. Most kids don't wait a second before selling old property, but a few actually moved back home, left their old lives behind and kept the farm in the family – like you." She nodded over her shoulder toward one of the nearby tables. "I was actually just speaking to someone connected to Thousand Acres."

I glanced in the direction she'd indicated. Seated at a nearby table was a tall, skinny man with shaggy blonde hair and a gaunt face with big circles under his eyes. Everything about him screamed tired, except for the oddly active light in his eyes. He said nothing, instead staring at something near me.

I realized right away that he was staring at the kids.

"It's just a little puff piece, nothing too crazy. You think you'd be down to talk sometime next week?" Before I had a chance to respond, Janet turned her attention to the kids. Neither of them said a word, both watching the man with wide, worried eyes.

Everything about the encounter, even just a minute into it, seemed *off*. I wanted to be done with it right away.

"Who's he?" I asked.

"An associate of Thousand Acres Ranch," she said. "Just someone I'm getting a pull quote from. No one you'd be meeting. Anyway, what do you think?"

"Maybe. Depends on how busy the next week is."

"Totally understandable." She reached into her purse and pulled out a business card, handing it over. "Give me a shout if you have some time. Might be good for the farm, you know? Get the word out that business is up and running? Think about it, OK?" she waved to the kids. "Hey, cuties!" With a little scrunch of her nose, she was off.

The man kept staring. Then, suddenly, he rose out of his seat and strode out of the place. Janet's eyes flashed, and she waved at us one more time before hurrying after the man.

It was all so strange, and as we tried to go back to our business, I couldn't shake the taste the encounter had left in my mouth.

CHAPTER 19

ADAM

I was pissed; so goddamn mad that I couldn't think straight.

"Seth," I growled, practically spitting the name.

"Lotta nerve that prick has showing his face around here," Mac added.

"You get an address for him?" Tyler asked. "Might want to pay him a visit before we leave. You know, just to talk."

Marcus said nothing, the working of his jaw making it obvious how he'd felt about the matter.

It was evening, after dinner, the kids in bed and the five of us in the den with our whiskies, a glass of wine for Aubrey. She'd just filled us in on what had happened in town earlier that day.

"I knew something was off. Janet told me he was with your farm, but I've never seen him around. It just didn't feel right to me," Aubrey said."

"I'm glad you picked up on it and told us," Tyler said. "But we now know that he's lurking around, and that's what is most concerning."

"I don't understand," Aubrey said. "Why is he nosing around?"

Mac shifted in his seat, just the mention of Seth getting him good and pissed off.

"He scampered off with his tail between his legs. But this isn't the first time he's come back. Not sure why he comes back around every so often. Maybe he gets a whiff of conscience about abandoning his kids, being so much of a screw-up that their own mother didn't trust him to watch out for them."

"You ask me," Marcus said, "he's more interested in the damn ranch. Bet he's wondering if he can get money from us somehow."

Mac nodded slowly, giving the possibility some credence. "Either way, he's not coming anywhere near Thousand Acres and definitely nowhere near the kids. I'll break his goddamn neck before that happens." He clenched his fist as he spoke, as if part of him wished that Seth was there at that moment so he could take care of the problem once and for all.

"The kids didn't seem to be aware of what was going on," Aubrey said. "Seth was staring at them, but they were more weirded out than anything."

"They don't know who he is," I stated. "Seth was in their lives for maybe two months total. For all they know, he's a stranger."

"Kids have a way of sensing things," Tyler said. "In this case, they didn't know who Seth was, but they knew he was no one good."

We all nodded in agreement.

Mac ran his hand through his hair before regarding his whiskey. I could sense he wanted to drink a hell of a lot more of it but knew it wasn't a good idea with the mission ahead of us.

Aubrey set down her wine. "The important thing is to figure out what to do from here, right?"

"Right," Marcus agreed.

"What's the security situation like on your farm, Aubrey?" Mac asked.

"Security?" Her eyes flashed with panic. "You don't think he'd..."

"We don't know," I said. "So far, Seth hasn't been anything more than just a pain in our asses. But if he decides to take things to another level, we want to be ready. Especially if he gets wind that we're out of town."

Aubrey's beautiful features took on a worried expression before she nodded. "There's not much of anything at Downing. Doors have locks, but that's it."

"How would you feel about staying here most of the time?" Tyler asked. "There's plenty of space, and the security system here is top-notch. A few button presses and the place locks up like a bank vault."

"Probably makes the most sense," she said. "Kids are more comfortable here, anyway. But I can't leave Aggie totally on her own – I'll need to drop by the farm to do a little work, at least."

"Understandable," I said. "But if you could do it during the day, that'd be perfect."

"And Aggie's more than welcome to come over," Mac said. "You all can stay here the entire time, if that's what you want."

"I'll talk to her about it." Aubrey sighed, shaking her head. "Sorry, just processing all of this."

"You're doing fine," I said. "A lot to think about. Taking care of twins is one thing, and this is a whole other matter on top of it."

"I'll manage," she said. "In the meantime, you guys have your trip to finish packing for. Leaving bright and early, right?"

"Five A.M. sharp," Marcus replied. "Speaking of which, we should get back to it. Longer I sit here, the more I want to drink." He threw back the rest of his whiskey and got up, the rest of the guys joining him.

"You OK?" I asked Aubrey.

She offered a weak smile in response. "I guess as good as I can be knowing that I might have a psycho former brother-in-law to worry about."

I opened my mouth to speak but then, an idea occurred to me.

"Want to get some fresh air? The back patio's heated. A little outdoors always clears my head."

She smiled. "That sounds nice."

We stood, grabbing our drinks and heading out of the room. The rest of the guys were busy on the top floor, the bottom floor quiet. Moments later, we stepped out onto the back patio, and I flicked on the heat. The view was gorgeous—the snow still fresh and untouched, the sky glittering with stars cast over the faded band of the Milky Way.

"I never get tired of this," she said as we sat down, waving her hand toward the sky. "After a few years in New York, you forget what the stars look like."

"That bad, huh?"

"That bad. I swear, there's so much light pollution that you see maybe five on a given night."

"Couldn't do the city," I said. "Too damn much going on."

She laughed.

"Now, what's funny about that?" I asked.

"Nothing. I mean, just funny how guys like you who go on secret missions for a living think that New York has too much going on."

"Hey, there's a difference between an overseas special op and a bustling metropolis."

She grinned. "Listen to that disdain in your voice. You practically spit the words out."

"Not shy about what I don't like."

"Have you ever been to New York?" she asked. "It's not so bad."

"Been through it and seen enough to know how dirty and hectic it is." I nodded toward the snowscape before us. "No, this is more my speed. A big house, family, peace and quiet – that's the life."

"Peace and quiet, except for when you're on *special ops*. Any chance you guys are going to tell me about this mission of yours?"

I sipped my whiskey, giving the matter a moment of thought.

"It's in Europe. That's all you need to know."

She laughed. "That narrows it down."

"Southeastern Europe – how about that?"

"Slightly better. I mean, don't get me wrong; I'm not trying to be nosy here or anything."

I grinned. "Could've fooled me."

She laughed, putting her hand on my arm and giving me a shove.

"Seriously! I'm going to miss you guys, you know? And knowing that you're off on some mission where I have no idea how to get ahold of you... it makes me worried. I can't help it, sorry."

"You don't need to be sorry. Feels good to know that there's someone back home thinking about us, taking care of the kids." I glanced down, the next words out of my mouth a little hard to say. "We're all glad you're here, Aubrey. Not just us, but the kids, too. You've brought something into this house that we hadn't realized we needed."

"A woman's touch?" she asked with a smile.

"That's one way to put it."

"How about you show me how much you'll miss me?" The playful smile that formed on her lips after she spoke left no doubt about what she had on her mind.

I'd been thinking the same damn thing.

"I'd love to. How about you get that sexy ass of yours over here? I'll do all the showing you can handle."

With that, I wrapped my arm around her, bringing Aubrey close and planting the kiss on her lips that I'd been fantasizing about all damn day.

CHAPTER 20

AUBREY

I melted into the kiss instantly. Adam's lips met mine, and all I could do was surrender to his touch, his smell, his everything.

I opened my mouth, wanting to feel every bit of his. He responded without words, kissing me more aggressively, wrapping his arm around my waist and bringing me closer. With each second the kiss passed, my pussy grew wetter. The need I felt for him was indescribable.

His hand found the hem of my shirt, slipping under it and teasing the sensitive skin of my belly. I moaned, shifting toward him until our bodies were flush, his hardness pressing against my thigh.

We kissed hard and deep, quickly getting one another out of our clothes and down to our underwear.

His cock was stiff, and I couldn't resist pulling it out of his gray boxer briefs and stroking it slowly. It was so warm and thick in my hand, the feeling of his hardness in my grasp making me somehow even more turned on.

Adam sat back, spreading his arms over the back of the couch as I moved my fingers up and down his length. It was bit of work to pump him, a cock that size was no easy feat to please. However, I could tell by the look on his face that he was more than happy with the job I was doing.

After a moment, he took my hand off his cock and pounced on me, kissing me hard and deep, his hand vanishing under the waistband of my panties.

"Oh... oh, *wow*." His fingers found my clit right away, making slow circles around it. The man knew just how to touch me, and all I could do was fall into the pleasure.

Adam kissed my neck, stopping his hand work for just long enough to take my panties down my legs.

"You like when I touch you like that?" he asked, rubbing my clit with the pad of his thumb.

"So damn much."

I needed more, however. Right as I had the thought, he moved a pair of fingers inside of me.

"Oh, *God!*" I clamped my hand over my mouth as soon as the words shot out, totally embarrassed for making such a noise.

"Be as loud as you want, baby," he said, slipping his fingers in and out of me. "No one can hear you but me and the snow." His voice was low and seductive, and as he brought me closer and closer to coming, all I could think about was the stiff cock I'd had my hands on only moments before.

I let out a silent scream as the orgasm broke, my pussy clenching around his fingers as he kissed me hard. Adam guided his fingers out of me as I descended from the peak of delight, the hunger in his eyes letting me know that he was far from done with me.

I turned my attention to his cock, loving the way it pointed straight up into the air.

With a quick pivot maneuver, I positioned myself over his body, reaching down and taking hold of his shaft by the base. I stroked him a bit, teasing him the way he'd done to me. He flashed me a smirk, the smile of a man who was about to get exactly what he wanted.

When he placed his hand on the small of my back, however, I knew he was done waiting. Men like him took what they wanted, and

I was no exception. Adam guided me down, his cock spreading my lips and pushing into my tight passage.

His thickness, his warmth, pushed up into me. He kept his eyes on mine all the while, as if wanting to capture exactly how I looked as he entered me. I opened my mouth and gasped softly, the sensation of him filling me full one I wanted to savor.

"You look so damn pretty when I'm inside of you," he said. "I could watch that all day."

"Tonight's going to have to be good enough," I replied. "After this, you're going to have to bring that sexy behind of yours home safe and sound if you want more."

He clamped his hands on my ass, squeezing my cheeks. "That's as good of motivation as it comes."

He reached around and undid the clasp of my bra, my breasts falling out and into his hands. Adam tossed my bra aside, teasing both of my nipples at once. I focused on how he touched me, how damn good his cock felt buried deep.

My hips grinding on top of him, I leaned forward and kissed him hard. My tits pressed against his chest, Adam's hands eagerly moved over every inch of my body, from my breasts to my hips to my ass to my thighs.

The pleasure built as I rode him, and I could feel another climax on the verge.

"Come for me," he growled into my ear. "I know you're close."

I couldn't even talk, the tight ecstasy between my legs all I could think about.

With one more hard buck, the orgasm released. I moaned, riding hard through it, my breasts bouncing in his face as he sucked my nipples. Adam groaned against me as he came, his cock throbbing inside, his seed filling me.

I stopped at the peak, the pleasure blasting through me.

When it was over, Adam wrapped his arms around my body and pulled me close, my curls dangling over his face. We kissed one more time, long and slow and lingering, before he guided me onto the couch and held me tight.

Silence past as we held one another, our eyes on the stars beyond.

"I'm serious," he said after a time. "About staying here."

"Huh?"

"Being safe. This is the best place, OK? I don't want you to have to worry."

I could sense the concern in his voice.

"Thank you. I mean it. And I *also* mean it when I tell *you* to stay safe."

"Then we'll all be careful over these next couple of weeks."

"Deal."

CHAPTER 21

MARCUS

T en days later...
          I looked out the window from my seat on the cargo plane
we'd caught out of Croatia. The Mediterranean was down below,
blue and sparkling.

"Yo, tough guy." Tyler dropped into the seat next to me. "How
you holding up?"

I snorted. "Didn't take any bullets this time, so good."

Tyler grinned. "Now that's looking on the bright side of things."
He leaned back, shaking his head. "That went pretty damn well, all
things considered, right?"

"If you call getting a fifty-caliber machine gun turned on us at the
damn airport, then yeah. We're lucky this bird didn't have so many
holes in her that she couldn't take off."

He shook his head. "I swear, that Balaban prick wasn't even *kind
of* expecting us."

He was right. We'd planned the mission down to the second,
spending a good week surveying the compound, getting troop move-
ments down. The original plan had been to move in on day thirteen.
When half the stationed troops departed on an emergency mission on

day ten, however, we'd decided to push the timetable up to take advantage of our good fortune.

We'd been expecting a hell of a fight, and that's exactly what we *didn't* get slipping into the compound. A skeleton crew had been left behind, which made getting in and finding the missionaries a far easier task than expected. We'd found the trio beaten and bloody, but alive, and gotten them out of there.

Once clear of the compound, we beelined to our base of operations to pack up and make sure the missionaries were good to travel. They were shaken, but otherwise fine. After that, we hit the road to meet our flight at the local airport.

The mood in the van had been strange. It'd all been too damn easy, but none of us had wanted to say so – that's how you jinx a mission. When we reached the airport, however, things went FUBAR. Balaban and his group intercepted us on the runway, our crew having to lay down some insane cover fire to get the missionaries onboard safely, followed by ourselves.

It'd been a damn miracle that we hadn't been wasted in the process. Not to mention, the missionaries made it in one piece, too. Aside from the small matter of nearly getting shot to pieces on the runway, the mission had been a total success.

As I opened my mouth to say something to Tyler, I spotted Adam coming down the aisle with a shit eating grin on his face.

"What're you so pleased with yourself about?" I asked.

The grin still on his face, he dropped into the seat in the aisle across from Tyler and me.

"Found out how that prick Balaban was able to track us down." With that, he held out his overturned fist. Once our eyes were on it, he opened his hand slowly, revealing a small electronic device that I immediately recognized as a tracker.

"You're kidding me," Tyler said. "Where the hell did you find that?"

"I'd spent the last two hours wondering how the hell Balaban could've found us. He didn't know we were coming, yet he somehow knew just how to track us down at the damn airport. I figured the missionaries had something to do with it. So, I gave them a pat down, found one of these each sewn into their clothes."

"Fuckin' hell," I said. "That Balaban's a bloodthirsty asshole, but he's no dumbass."

"Tell me you turned those off," Tyler said.

"Of course, I snipped the back as soon as I realized what they were."

"Smart," I said. "Balaban could've used those to track down where we're landing. Speaking of which, what's the plan for the drop-off?"

"We're landing in Rome in a couple more hours," Adam said. He tossed the tracker onto the ground and crushed it into electronic dust with the tip of his boot. "Missionaries are going to deplane for medical clearance. From there, we fly into London, then back to the States."

"How long's the trip time total?" Tyler asked.

"Should be touching down in Baltimore in sixteen hours."

Just the mention of home was enough to make me damn near giddy. I kept myself in check, however. A mission wasn't over until you were back on home soil. I was desperate to see the twins and Aubrey again. It was an odd experience for me to feel so damn emotional, but it practically hurt to be apart from them.

"Yo, dudes!" Mac called out to us from his row in the front. "Come up here!"

We climbed out of our seats and headed to Mac. Adam wasted no time sharing the news about the trackers.

"Good work, Adam," Mac said. "But..."

He trailed off, something else on his mind.

"What is it?" I asked.

"We *really* stuck it to Balaban this time," he said.

"Hell yeah, we did!" Tyler exclaimed, his expression eager.

"No, that's not what I mean," Mac said. "We snuck in right under his nose, made him look like a total asshole in front of the entire country. There's not a chance he's going to take this lying down."

"What do you mean?" Adam asked.

"What, you think he's going to come after us?" I asked. "As in, all the way to Maryland?"

As soon as I said the words, a rage that I'd never known before boiled inside of me. I thought about Aubrey, thought about the twins, thought about the possibility of Balaban even coming near them. My heart rate quickened, and my hands instantly formed into tight fists. If Balaban had appeared just then in the plane, I would've ripped the shithead to pieces with my bare hands right then and there.

"Easy, brother," Mac said, seeming to sense my anger. "I'm just thinking out loud. Coming to Maryland to cause trouble would be a hell of a tall order, even for someone like him. I'm talking more about spending some money to have some contacts here in Europe to keep tabs on him."

"Yeah," I said. "Good idea."

I took some deep breaths, working through the anger.

"There's something else, too," Mac said. "Got this as soon as I reconnected our cell phones."

He pulled his phone out of his pocket and showed us the screen. It was a picture of the twins, the message "WE MISS YOU" with a bunch of emoji hearts on it. I hadn't seen a picture of them since we'd left Europe, and I smiled like an idiot at the sight of our little family.

"Another one," Mac said.

He swiped the screen one more time, a picture of Aubrey with the twins. God, it made me feel so damn good to see a picture of her with the twins, looking beautiful as ever. One more swipe revealed a picture of what appeared to be a Christmas ornament up close, the caption, "we have a surprise for you all."

"Surprise?" I asked. "What kind of surprise?"

"That's what makes it a surprise," Tyler said.

"Funny."

"We'll find out in less than a day," Mac said. "Until then, get some rest. I'll keep you all posted if Aubrey sends anything else."

His words reminded me just how damn tired I was. I headed back to my seat, settling in and closing my eyes. Didn't take long at all before sleep began to beckon me, the last thought on my mind was of Aubrey and the twins.

CHAPTER 22

TYLER

The sight of Thousand Acres just ahead was almost too good to be true. I grinned like an idiot as I laid eyes on the place, knowing who awaited all of us inside. The snow had mostly melted, a few patches of white here and there on the ground.

The front was covered in tinsel and lighting, even a little bit of Santa stuff here and there.

"Did she decorate the place?" Marcus asked.

"Looks that way," Adam replied.

"Just texted her," Mac said from the front seat of the truck. "Should be out in a sec."

He pulled to a stop in front of the house, my stomach so tingly with anticipation that I could hardly think straight. I was going to see the kids again, going to see the woman I was crazy about. Coming home safely from a mission was always a joy. There was something about coming home to a family, however, that took it all to another level.

We climbed out of the truck, making our way to the back to unload our gear. We didn't get much of it out before the front doors opened and the three people that I'd been thinking about non-stop for the last nearly two weeks came bounding out.

My damn heart melted at the sight of them. I set down my bag and hurried toward the house. Aubrey and the kids were all dressed in warm winter clothes, big sweaters and jeans and comfy slippers.

"Uncle Tyler!" the twins said in unison, and I couldn't resist scooping them up and bringing the pair into my arms, covering their little faces with kisses.

"There are my dudes!" I said, all smiles as I gave them squeezes then set them both down. I couldn't believe it – it seemed like they'd grown so much in such a short period of time.

"Welcome home," Aubrey said, warmth on her face and in her voice.

"Thanks. I mean it."

I stepped forward and embraced her, Aubrey's body feeling so good against mine that I wanted to scream. She smelled good too, like cinnamon and pine.

The rest of the guys greeted her and the twins, hugs and happiness all around.

"I bet you guys are tired," she said. "Get your handsome butts in here and let me show you the surprise. Well, *surprises*."

"I normally hate surprises," Marcus said. "But I have to admit that I'm a little intrigued."

"He's right about that," I said as we all entered. "You tell him you have a surprise planned for his birthday and he'll practically bust out the interrogation kit to get you to talk."

We stepped into the entry hall, the delicious scents of cinnamon and pine and food cooking in the oven swirling around us.

"Holy crap," Adam said. "This is something else."

The inside of the house was all kinds of Christmassed out. Greenery ran down the stair rail and up across the balcony, bits of tinsel here and big red bows there. Candles were lit, bathing the room in soft lighting. Christmas carols flowed in from another room.

"This is amazing," Mac said. "You did all this?"

"With a little help." We turned to see Aggie at one of the other entrances to the room. "Welcome back, guys. I was in the kitchen finishing up dinner, otherwise I would've come to greet you."

"Hey, Aggs!" I said, stepping over to her and wrapping her up in a big hug. "You helped?"

"We helped too!" Henry exclaimed happily.

"Yeah!" Hattie added.

"They really did," Aubrey said. "You should see the tree... any ornament that's knee-high was their doing."

"There's a tree?" Mac asked.

Aubrey grinned. "Come on and take a look."

Together, we headed into the den. The sight that greeted us there was unbelievable. A huge tree was in the corner of the room, festooned with lights and ornaments, a big star on top. A fire roared in the fireplace, and there were even a few presents.

"This is amazing," Adam said. "How...?"

"Yeah," I said. "We had *maybe* a box of Christmas stuff."

"I kinda cleared out the holiday store downtown," she explained. "Don't worry – got most of it delivered. Same with the tree."

"What're you boys doing standing around?" Aggie asked. "Get some glasses of whiskey in those big hands of yours! Dinner's pot roast with all kinds of sides, some fresh, homemade ice cream and apple pie. My finest feast if I do say so myself. Should be another thirty minutes, so get comfy and I'll call you in when it's done. Oh! And there's eggnog, the boozy kind."

"Thanks, Aggie," I said. "And all of you."

The rest of the boys shared similar sentiments.

"It's our pleasure," Aubrey said. "Figured you guys deserved a little Christmas cheer when you came home. Now, sit. I'll get the whiskey."

The room was so full of warmth and love, I thought my heart might burst. Henry and Hattie climbed up onto the couch, telling us all kinds of stories about what they'd gotten up to while we were gone. Aubrey passed out the drinks, and the next half an hour flew by as we sat wrapped up in love.

By the time Aggie rang the dinner bell, I was starved out of my mind. We piled into the kitchen, gathering round the big farmer's table, the surface loaded with all kinds of good stuff. There was pot roast and veggies and fresh bread – the exact kind of meal a man wanted when he came home.

We piled our plates high, cleared them off quickly, then piled them once again. As much as we ate, there was still plenty of room for pie and ice cream, along with a tall glass of bourbon eggnog. We stuffed ourselves full, the buzz from the food and booze just right.

When the meal was done, Aggie put the kids and then herself to bed. We were more than happy to offer her a room for the night. After that, we headed into the living room for a nightcap.

"Does she know?" I asked after Aggie had said good night to all of us and gone off to bed.

Aubrey smiled. "Oh yeah. Figured it out that first day just like I said she would. She's totally cool with it."

We sat in silence for a time, watching the fire and listening to the music. It wasn't long, however, before we started moving closer to Aubrey, making it clear what other sort of reunion we had on our minds.

"This is nice," Aubrey said finally. "But if you boys aren't too tired, I'd love to give you all a proper welcome back."

I grinned, pleased as hell that she'd finally said the words. "Let's not waste another second."

CHAPTER 23

AUBREY

I was still buzzing from the sight of the guys pulling up in front of the house after nearly two weeks of being away.

The sight in front of me right then, however, each of the guys in nothing but their underwear, was even better.

Once more we were in the third-floor bedroom, that big room with a fireplace and plenty of room to spread out and have some fun. My body yearned for the men, my pussy tight and clenched, every molecule of me seeming to vibrate in anticipation.

"Lay down on the bed, gorgeous," Mac said, his low voice echoing in the room. I loved it when he called me that.

"Oh, are you guys the ones issuing commands here?" I asked with a teasing smile.

"More like a suggestion," he replied with a grin.

I chewed my lip for a moment as I thought it over. Truth was that it was hard to think when you had a small army of four stunning men in front of you, all eager to make you come over and over again.

"Alright," I said. 'Show me what you've got."

I stepped over toward the bed, passing between Adam and Tyler as I did. The men didn't let me get through untouched, Adam stopping me by placing his big hands on my hips and turning me toward him for a kiss.

I was weak in the knees the moment his tongue found mine, and Tyler's touch on my back only added more desire. When Adam had his fill, I turned to Tyler. It was always fun to kiss him, to run my hand through his silky beard as he kissed me long and deep.

I gave Tyler's perfect ass a squeeze as I made my way toward the bed, laying down on top of the soft sheets.

Mac stepped over to the bed and stood above me, his muscular stature and imposing size making me feel so small yet safe. I was in nothing but my panties and bra, and the heat from his stare as he moved his eyes over my nearly bare body set my nerve endings ablaze.

He reached forward, placing his hands on my belly and moving them down, hooking his fingers under the waistband of my panties and pulling them along my thighs, down to my ankles. I helped them off with a little shimmy of my hips, taking a deep pleasure at the idea of being bare before him.

The rest of the guys climbed onto the bed, getting themselves in position as if they'd already had a plan in mind. Tyler took off my bra, Adam covered my belly in licks and caresses, while Marcus captured my attention with deep kisses.

Mac spread my legs open, his mouth moving along my inner thighs and causing me to break out in goosebumps. The guys worked together, and soon I had four pairs of lips on my body – Mac's on my pussy, Adam's on my middle, Tyler's on my nipples, and Marcus's on my lips.

I was in heaven. Truth be told, it was hard to focus on any particular sensation at once. The kisses blurred into one overwhelming rush of feelings, tingles popping like little fireworks all over me.

Mac was an expert with his tongue and lips, his skills bringing me to a warm, rolling orgasm quickly. I moaned, writhing my hips gently as I came. He knew just when to stop, just when to rise in front of me and pull off his underwear, his thick cock jumping out.

"Goes without saying, gorgeous," he said. "But we all missed you like crazy."

I took my lips from Marcus's mouth just long enough to speak. "And I missed you all too. Though, got to say, this reunion is shaping up to be more than worth the wait."

"We're just getting started," Adam chimed in.

As he spoke, Mac took hold of his thickness and brought it close to me. Once more I took my eyes away from Marcus's face to watch as Mac placed his cock between my lips and pushed inside.

I squirmed, moaning as Mac moved deep into me. Marcus kissed me hard as Mac began to drive in and out of me. His lips traveled from my mouth to my cheek to my ear, to my neck, lashing me with kisses as I watched Mac's powerful body work.

The men kissed me all over, but I knew I needed more. I put my hands on Adam's head, turning him gently toward me and guiding him up with a gesture. He grinned, knowing exactly what I had in mind. He and Marcus swapped places, Marcus using his finger to trace my clit as Adam slipped off his underwear and brought his manhood to my lips.

Mac was thrusting into me hard, with Marcus fingering my clit. I focused on the intense pleasure for a moment before wrapping my lips around Adam's shaft, sucking him in earnest.

Having two cocks inside of me was something else. I was filled top-to-bottom, the pleasure immense and intoxicating. My mouth moved quickly up and down Adam's length, my hand cradling his balls as the other brothers made sure I had no shortage of sensations over the rest of my body.

It wasn't long before Mac and Adam's grunts let me know they were both on the verge of climax. Knowing just what I wanted, I took my lips from Adam's cock and spoke.

"Both of you finish at the same time."

Mac pumped into me intently, Adam running his hand through my hair as I sucked him. It didn't take much more of this before Adam let out a hard groan, his cock pulsing in my mouth as he released down my throat. Warm pumps of sweetness shot into my mouth, and I eagerly swallowed them down. Mac released too, his manhood throbbing as he drained himself. I came with them, the feeling of the two men climaxing in unison bringing me over the edge.

When they were done, I let Adam's cock fall from my mouth. He kissed my cheek one more time before rolling away, Mac backing up from the bed and taking a seat near the fire, his big chest expanding and contracting as he collected himself.

The sensation of the two men coming at the same time had been exhilarating, and I wanted to feel it again. Lucky for me, there were two more handsome brothers there, eager to give me exactly what I wanted.

I placed my hands on Tyler's shoulders, guiding him onto the bed. He laid on his back, an eager smile on his face. While I'd been happy to make him come with my mouth the last time we'd all been together, Tyler still hadn't had the chance to be inside of me and I was more than eager to change that.

He shucked off his underwear, his beautiful cock springing out as he did. I climbed over top of him, placing my hands on his solid chest and lowering myself onto him. He felt so good inside of me, his thickness stretching me out in the best way. When he was buried to the root, I raised myself up and lowered slowly, my wetness letting him slide in liquid smooth.

"Just as good as I'd imagined," Tyler said, his hands resting on my hips. "You're damn perfect."

I couldn't help but blush at his words. When I was ready, I gestured for Marcus to come near. He did just that, stepping onto the bed and taking down his underwear. I grabbed his cock with one hand and brought him to my lips, tasting his sweet, saltiness at the tip and beginning to slowly suck, my tongue dragging up and down his length.

Tyler moved underneath me, pumping up, my breasts bouncing from the force of his thrusts.

I gestured for Tyler and Marcus to switch places, Marcus sliding underneath me as Tyler brought his cock to my mouth. One they were both in place, Marcus's solid heat pushing into me and bringing me right to the verge of orgasm, I screamed out in pleasure.

"Please," I moaned. "I need you both right now!"

The men were happy to oblige. Hard grunts sounded from above and below as both men released into me, Tyler's cock erupting into my mouth and Marcus's in my pussy. I came for the third and final time, the intensity so much that I felt on the verge of unraveling.

When I was done, I fell forward onto Marcus. He wrapped his arms around me in response, covering me in kisses. Tyler did the same, the other two men joining us on the bed.

I was spent. A smile on my face, I watched the fire jump and pop, happier than I'd ever been.

CHAPTER 24

ADAM

"This is crazy, huh?"

I sat up from my daze, turning my eyes away from the flames. Mac was coming toward me, dropping into one of the other chairs in front of the fire. I glanced over his shoulder to see that Tyler and Marcus and Aubrey were still asleep in a big pile on the bed.

I, on the other hand, had a lot on my mind.

"Sure as hell is," I agreed.

He reached over to the nearby desk, grabbing the bottle of whiskey and opening it up. He took a quick swig before handing it over to me. I was eager for a drink, bringing it to my mouth and sipping, the warmth spreading in my belly as soon as the booze was down the hatch.

"Can't sleep?"

"Nah."

"The mission?"

"That, sure. I've got a damn good feeling it's not over and done with."

"Same here."

I took another sip, passing the bottle over.

"But... her, too." I nodded backward, in Aubrey's direction.

Mac sipped. "Same."

"What the hell do we do, Mac?"

"What do you mean?"

"This... it's getting really serious, real fast, right? You feel it too, don't you?"

"Sure do."

"I know there's no point in worrying. All the same, this shit is *perfect*. We're crazy about her, the twins are too, and I'm sure she feels the same way about us."

Mac snorted, nodding in a knowing manner. "You know what that is? That's the military man in you talking. You're trying to get everything planned out, every detail down to the last. It's how we get our missions sorted out."

"Yep."

"Love's not like that though. Love... you just have to accept it, let it take you where it will. That's what makes it fun. And you *are* having fun, right?"

I allowed myself a small smile. "How could I not be?"

"Then there you go. Take it from your big bro – don't get so wrapped up in the maybe that you forget about the now. Enjoy this."

He took one more sip, offering me the bottle. I declined.

"I'm heading back to bed," he said. "Try and do the same before too long."

"Will do."

With that, Mac went to join the others on the big bed. I stayed for a time and watched the fire, wondering just what the future might hold for our little fivesome.

I was the last one up, the fire out as I rolled over the surface of the California king. I groaned, my body crying out for more sleep even though I was certain I'd had plenty. Nothing wore a man out like a globetrotting mission, and the fun we'd had last night sure didn't do my weary bones any favors.

I rose from the bed, making my way over to my jeans draped over the back of a nearby chair. I took my phone out and checked the time – a little after eight. I was normally the type to get up at the crack of dawn, so sleeping until that hour was unacceptable for me.

"Wasting the day already." I groaned the words as I dressed myself, heading out of the room and down the stairs when I was done.

A quick check of the house revealed that Tyler was still asleep, Marcus was in the gym, and Mac was up in the office going over some paperwork. I had books to look over, but that could wait until after breakfast and a little time in the gym myself.

When I reached the first floor, however, I realized that we were missing some people, three, in fact - Aubrey and the twins. My heart jumped up a bit when I realized they were gone. I was still wound tight from the last two weeks.

I rushed around the house looking for them, as if the trio might be hidden away behind a bookshelf. On the way down from the second floor, I nearly bumped into Marcus in his workout gear, heading up for a shower.

He gave me a once-over, smirking and shaking his head, as if he knew just what was up.

"Something funny?" I asked.

"Check the kitchen," he said as he headed to his room.

I was a touch annoyed, but all the same I was more eager to get to the bottom of what was going on. I hurried down to the kitchen, spotting a full pot of coffee and a note on the counter, an overturned mug on it holding it in place.

I stepped over and picked up the mug, reading the note with eager eyes.

Took the kids over to Downing to take care of a few things. Be back for lunch.

I sighed, a smile forming on my face as I set the note aside. Of course, that was the explanation. What else could it be? All the same, I wanted Aubrey and the twins back in the house sooner than later – it was safer here, after all.

I wondered if Seth was still lurking around. Just the thought of that prick was enough to make my blood run hot. I poured myself some coffee into the mug that'd been holding the note down, thinking of all the things I'd like to do to him. I tried to push it out of my head, but the more I lingered on the matter, the more I wanted to talk to one of the guys about it.

Mug in hand, I went up to the office. Mac glanced up from his computer, regarding me with an expression of slight curiosity.

"What's up?" he took off his black-framed reading glasses and set them aside.

"I know we talked about stepping back and letting things go last night," I said, sliding into one of the chairs across from the desk. "And I agree with you – when it comes to the Aubrey matter."

"Good to hear. But I'm getting the impression that there's something else you're not as keen to let slide."

I nodded. "Yep. Seth."

Mac said nothing at first, his jaw working as he thought about the man we all wanted to take a crack at. Finally, he sighed and sat back.

"Nothing we can do right now until he pops up and shows his hand."

"You think he might try to get custody of the kids?" I asked. "Play the dad card and try to get them back?"

Just the thought of Henry and Hattie being taken away from us and given to *him* was enough to make me sick.

"He could try. But we've got Kristen's last will and testament. It's in plain writing that she wanted us to be the kids' guardians."

"But he's still their biological father." I shook my head. "God, I wish she would've pushed a little harder to get him to sign those parental relinquishment forms."

"So do I. But we all know what she was going through when that was happening, brother. He was putting his hands on her, getting more and more aggressive. It was only a matter of time before he crossed the line further."

Thinking about that possibility sent a fresh pulse of anger through me.

"I wish she would've listened to us about him from the get-go. We knew he was scum, spotted him for what he was right away. You remember what happened when he found out Kristen was pregnant, right?"

Mac let out a dry, humorless laugh. "When he tried to pressure Kristen into getting an abortion? How the hell could I forget?" He sighed, setting his hands on his desk and leaning forward. "Listen, until he goes into criminal territory, there's not much we can do."

"He could take us to court."

"You're right, he could. But we've got more than enough money to tie the thing up in court for as long as we need to. Hell, with the money we made on this last mission we could hire the best lawyers in the state and let them handle it. The guy's a loser, couldn't even afford an ambulance-chaser to fight us."

"Exactly, and he knows it. Might make him think he's got to be creative if he wants to get to the twins."

"Asshole doesn't even want to be a dad," Mac said, anger in his voice. "He just wants to get his hands on some money. He doesn't give a shit about Henry and Hattie's welfare. We just need to—"

Mac didn't get a chance to finish. A chime sounded in the office, an alert to signify that someone was coming up the road to our place.

"You expecting anyone?" I asked.

"Nope." Mac typed a few keys on his laptop, bringing the security feed from the front gate onto the TV on the wall. We both watched as a rundown SUV pulled up to the gate. A blonde head attached to a pair of scrawny shoulders stuck out.

"Speak of the goddamn devil," I said.

CHAPTER 25

MARCUS

"I'll kill the son of a bitch!"

Rage ran through me.

"You're not killing anyone, bro," Mac said. "We're going to talk to him and keep cool heads about it. Understand?"

"Just tell me your reasoning," I said. "Tell me why you thought it was a good idea to invite him onto our land."

"Well, I really didn't invite him, did I? He just drove up. Not to mention, there's four of us and one of him." He lifted up one side of his shirt, showing off a pistol. "Not anticipating that he's going to be stupid, but we'll be ready if he is."

"But why not stop him at the gate?" Tyler asked.

"Because this needs to get sorted out now," Adam said. "And we didn't have time to throw a committee together to discuss it."

They were right. If Seth was in town, it was only a matter of time until we had a face-to-face. Doing it on our home turf with Aubrey and the twins safe and sound over at her place was about as good of a time to do it as any.

"Alright," I said. "I guess I *do* have a few choice words for him."

"We all do," Adam stated. "But we need to keep cool heads about all of this. If one of us flies off the handle and touches him for no reason, that could be all the advantage he'd need in court to prove us unfit."

It was another good point. "You're right."

"You know that asshole's going to be recording all of this," Tyler said. "He's a sketchy-ass loser, but he's not completely stupid. He's going to be looking for anything he can find that might make us look bad."

"Message received," I said. "Now, can we get this over with?"

The boys and I formed up, heading out onto the front porch just in time to greet Seth. He was driving a beat-up old Bronco that had to be more than twenty years old, the gray and red colors more rust than anything else. The plates were from Maryland, letting me know that he hadn't even bothered to switch them over to California – if he was even still living there.

We stood side-by-side on the porch, our eyes fixed on the Bronco as it came to a stop. The day was mild, a little bit of warmth from the sun in the blue sky above melting the snow by the second, drops falling from the porch's awning here and there.

The driver's side door opened, a blue-jean clad leg sticking out.

Seth stepped out of the vehicle. He was tall and gangly as ever, his face gaunt and his hair messy. He was in such a state that you didn't even need to hear him talk to know that hard drugs and cheap booze were a mainstay in his life.

He stood with his hands on his hips, shaking his head.

"Wow, I get the whole squad, huh?"

"Seth," Mac bellowed, his voice low and deep. "You're a long way from home, and you're on property that sure as hell isn't yours. Say what you came here to say and then turn your ass around."

"Is that a threat?" he asked. "Tell me, are you threatening me?"

On his dashboard I spotted a small camera pointed ahead. I elbowed Tyler, getting his and the rest of the guys' attention, making sure they saw it. They did.

"No threats here," Adam said, raising his palms and bringing a touch of calm to the situation, as he was good at doing. "You came here to talk, right? Well, let's talk. Tell us what's on your mind."

Adam might've been able to be calm, but I sure as shit wasn't. All I could think about was rushing over, ripping him apart limb-from-limb, ending this little problem of ours once and for all.

I kept my anger in check, however.

Seth waited a moment, as if wanting to make sure that Adam's calm demeanor wasn't some trick. When he felt satisfied that it wasn't, he began.

"I came here to tell you that I want the kids back. I'm their daddy, and I have a right to them."

"A *right?*" Tyler spat out the words. "Buddy, you weren't so much a dad as you were a sperm donor. You didn't even wait for those kids to come out before you abandoned our sister."

"Doesn't matter. None of that matters." He spoke with the confidence of someone who felt he had the law on his side. "What *does* matter is whether or not you guys are going to play ball."

I let out a mocking *ooohhh* as if he were trying to be some kind of Billy badass. I couldn't help it.

"You're the one dictating terms now?" I asked. "Try us."

He narrowed his beady little eyes, the circles under them looking worse than ever.

"First of all, I want to see them."

"Not going to happen," Mac said. "We've got custody, and besides, they're not even here."

"But they're *mine!*"

"Seth, we've been over this," Adam said, "We've got custody. It was in the will."

"Not to mention," Tyler added. "They don't even know who you are. That's kind of what happens when you leave when they're barely two months old."

"It's not too late for them to learn. I mean, what, do they think all of you are dad?" He snorted. "Good luck explaining that to them."

"They get it just fine," Mac said. "And when there's so much love and support, you'd be amazed at how much those details don't matter."

I could sense by his body language that he was getting pissed.

"This whole living situation is screwed up! Four men living together... I don't care if you're brothers! And then, on top of it, you've got some slut living here now, taking care of *my*—"

I was already pissed enough at him talking about the kids. Mentioning Aubrey pushed me over the edge. I burst from where I stood, running over to the asshole and getting right in his face. Seth's face flashed with fear as I approached.

"What did you say? Come on, tough guy, please, tell us exactly what's on your mind."

None of the boys said a word. I was getting heated, but I knew better than to go too far.

"You're going to give those kids back to me," Seth said, fear creeping into his words. "They're mine and I have a right to them. Like hell I'm going to give up my flesh and blood!"

"You did that a long time ago, Seth," Mac said. "Now's the time for you to deal with the consequences."

I backed up, letting Mac's words hang in the air, not taking my eyes off Seth.

"Now," Mac said. "You want to get the hell off our land, or do I need to call the sheriff and file trespassing charges?"

Seth stood completely still, and for a moment, I worried he might try something. Instead, he spit, never taking his eyes off of us, then turned to his car.

"This is not over," he said. "Not even close."

With that, he climbed into the car and gunned the engine, squealing his nearly bald tires down the driveway. The four of us watched and waited for him to disappear, making sure that he didn't take a turn heading toward Downing Farm.

I unclenched my fists once he was out of sight. There was no doubt in my mind, however, that it wasn't the last we'd seen of Seth.

CHAPTER 26

MAC

Ten minutes after the "meeting," the four of us were in the kitchen, coffee in hand as we talked over the matter.

In that moment, however, I was furious at my own brothers. I'd learned that Tyler and Adam had kept something from Marcus and me that changed everything.

Seth hadn't just put his hands on Kristen all those years ago, he'd *hurt* her, while she was pregnant. The argument they'd had about the abortion had gotten heated, Seth not just putting his hands on her shoulders, but slamming her hard against the wall, hard enough that she'd been worried she might've lost the babies.

It was a damn good thing that Seth was long gone. If I'd learned what I just had while he was here...

"I want to know why the hell you didn't tell us," Marcus growled. "Why the hell you kept this a fucking secret!"

Adam nodded toward him. "That's why – because of that temper of yours. If we would've told you when we learned about it, you guys would've put him in the damn hospital."

"Or a grave," Tyler added.

Marcus and I shared a look that suggested we knew that he was right.

"Fine. You kept it hidden, but that's in the past. Now we know."

"And there's more," Tyler said. "Kristen took pictures when it happened, emailed them to us for safekeeping."

"You're serious?" I asked.

"Yep," Adam said. "She wanted us to have them in case anything ever happened. She was certain about one thing—that she didn't want Seth anywhere near those kids if anything were to happen to her."

Marcus took a slow sip of his coffee. I could tell that, while he was trying to work through his anger, he was still good and steamed.

"Well, as much as I hate to think of it that way," I said, "Those are good tools to have in our arsenal. If Seth manages to get us into the courtroom, they'll go a long way in making sure he doesn't have a chance of getting Henry and Hattie."

"True," Marcus said. "There's also putting his ass in the dirt – that'd work too."

We laughed at the idea, knowing that, while tempting, it was only an idea.

"Alright," I said. "First step is we get legal shit in order. Adam, you mind getting in touch with our lawyer, giving him the rundown of what's happening?"

"Will do, big brother," he said.

That was one part taken care of. Knowing Seth was still in town, however, didn't sit well with me.

"We need to keep tabs on the prick," I said. "Make sure we know where he is, what he's up to."

"I'd be happy to do it," Marcus said. "I know a few things about recon."

Adam shook his head. "Not a good idea. If Seth finds out that we're tailing him, he could file harassment charges."

"Right," Tyler said. "They got a word for guys who follow people around like that – stalkers. And last I checked it isn't legal."

Marcus nodded. He didn't like it but heard the wisdom in their words.

"Well, then we ought to hire a PI," he said. "I'm with you, Mac – I want to know what he's up to. If he's planning something, we need to hear about it as soon as possible."

"A PI would be great," I agreed. "Marcus, you want to take care of that?"

"Got it."

There was more to think about. At that moment, however, I had major tension inside of me I knew only a workout would untangle.

"I'm going to hit the gym," I said. "Tyler, let's talk after."

"Sounds good."

With that, the meeting was over. I headed up to my room to get changed into some shorts and sneakers and a sleeveless shirt, then went down to the basement gym. The space was huge, filled with all the weights and cardio equipment that four men who wanted to stay on top of their game needed.

Normally, I'd start with a quick mile run, then move into some weight training. That morning however, I was angry. I beelined for the punching bag, turning on the stereo system as I made my way over to it. Pantera's *Cowboys from Hell* blasting, I threw on some gloves and began wailing on the bag, beating it so hard I thought I might break it wide open.

I pretended it was Seth, of course, his smirking, gaunt face shattering into nothing under a barrage of blows. Working over his face in the real world would land my ass in jail, so this was the closest I was going to get.

After about ten minutes, I felt good and worn out, my head a bit clearer.

"Don't need two guesses to know whose face you were imagining on that thing."

I turned, seeing Tyler at the entrance to the gym, a small curl of a smile on his face.

"Yeah. Not exactly a psychological puzzle."

He came over, the smile fading and a tinge of worry replacing it. Something was on his mind.

"What's up?" I asked, opening my water and taking a swig.

"I wanted to say I'm sorry. It wasn't cool to keep that kind of information from you, even if we had our reasons."

I held the bottle of water to my head, letting the cool run through me.

"Thanks. You did what you believed needed to be done. Not to mention, you did what Kristen asked."

He nodded, glancing away for a moment.

"I wanted to kill him too when I found out, rip off his arms and let him bleed out. I wanted him to suffer something sick like that. It's all so screwed up, you know? Our family's nothing but love, yet we've still got this asshole hanging around the edge, wanting to ruin everything."

"You're right. But that's all the more reason for us to stay strong, and to stay together, alright?"

"Yeah. My feelings exactly."

I took another swig of water. "I thought of something for you to do."

"Yeah?"

"Yep. Head over to Downing, check on Aubrey and the twins. And while you're there, let her know what's going on. She has a right to know."

Tyler's expression lightened, and I could tell he was happy to have a task to do, a way to make up for the deception.

"Got it."

I put my hand on his shoulder. "Thanks for everything, brother. We're going to get through this."

"Not doubting that for a second."

He left. I turned my attention back to the punching bag, eager to work out more of my aggression.

CHAPTER 27

TYLER

I pulled the truck in front of Downing just in time to watch as Aubrey led a pair of llamas into the barn. She waved as I stopped, followed by a gesture for me to come in and join her.

God, she looked so damn good. She had on skintight jeans with a light-wash jean jacket, a rancher's hat on her head and boots on her feet. Maybe she'd been a city girl at one point, but as far as I was concerned, she fit right in with this kind of life.

I hopped out of the truck. As soon as my feet were on the ground, I noticed something off in the distance. Dark clouds were gathering in the west. I leaned against the truck, watching them for a time. Whatever was out there would be here soon.

When I was satisfied, I started toward the barn and opened the door. The musky scent of animal and feed greeted me. Aubrey was there, getting the pair of llamas tied up with all the others on the far end.

"You see those clouds?" she asked.

"Sure did. You know anything about them?"

"Surprised you haven't been keeping up with the weather."

"Busy morning; what's the story?"

"Blizzard due to come in sometime in the next twenty-four hours. Supposed to be massive. They're thinking it's going to hit tomorrow morning."

"Damn."

"That's why I'm getting all the animals in now. I don't want to get caught with my pants down if it shows up early."

Just the mention of her pants down was enough to make my cock twitch. My eyes flicked down to her ass, and a small smile formed on her lips when she caught me looking.

"Anyway, what's up?" she started toward the llama feed, grabbing a bushel.

"Wanted to come over and check on you and the kids." That wasn't all, of course. But I'd get to that.

"They're good – sleeping right now. We did some outdoor stuff, so they went down for an early nap."

"Alright. Well, with the storm coming in, you want to stay over at the house? Might be a good idea. We've got a big generator and plenty of supplies."

She glanced aside, giving the matter some thought.

"Sounds nice. But I've got all these guys to worry about and I don't want to put it all on Aggie. Plus, we've got a generator and plenty of food, too."

"Well, there you go. Offer's on the table. If you can get the animals taken care of in the morning early enough to beat the storm, feel free to come over. And bring Aggie, too."

"We'll see how the morning goes." She began breaking up the bushel and tossing out food for the llamas. "But thanks for the offer, really. Might take you up on it if I get lonely." She winked, making it clear what kind of company she had in mind.

"Hey, you got a satellite phone?"

"A what? Like a phone that connects to a satellite dish?"

"Yep."

Aubrey shook her head. "Nope. Why would I need something

like that? Usually get pretty good reception out here, believe it or not."

"In case the storm knocks that reception out and you need to get in touch with someone. Not a bad idea to have one."

She cocked her head to the side. "No, something else is on your mind."

"That obvious?"

"Yep. You're not your usual joking self. Let's hear it."

Aubrey was sharp. It was impossible to get anything by her.

I shut the door and stepped deeper into the barn.

"Wanted to check on you and the kids, no lie there. But I wanted to tell you about what happened this morning after you were gone."

A touch of worry appeared on her face.

"Something happened?"

"Yeah. We had a guest..."

I went into it, telling her about Seth's visit. I told her about what he said, what he wanted, and how we planned to deal with it. She listened with eagerness.

"My God... the kids."

"We're going to make sure nothing happens to them – don't you worry about that."

"OK. Good. And if there's anything I can do, just tell me."

I placed my hand on her arm. "And we want to make sure that nothing happens to you, either."

"You think that I'm in danger?"

"I don't know. He's not the brightest bulb on the tree but you never know what happens when a man reaches the end of his rope."

She turned from me, leaning against the nearest workbench and taking a second to think it all over.

"That explains the satellite phone," she said with a small smile.

"Seriously, it's not a bad idea." I stepped over and leaned back next to her. "Even without all this happening. A bad storm hits and..."

She grinned. "I just run over to your place, spend the blizzard snuggled up in bed with my four favorite guys."

I laughed. "As nice as that sounds, a bad enough storm hits and not even our truck would be able to dig you out until it ended. And don't even think of walking."

She squeezed my arm. "How are you feeling?"

"Huh?"

"Spoken like someone who doesn't deal with that question very often. I mean, how are you handling all of this? You've got some asshole trying to take your niece and nephew from you. I'm sure you're feeling something about it other than concern for me."

I gave the subject a moment of consideration.

"It's... I don't know. I love those kids; don't know how I'd live without them. And I know for a fact we're giving them a far, *far* better home than they'd have with some drug-addled piece of shit like Seth. At the same time, I've been around the block enough times to know that fair doesn't factor into how the world works. We might go to court and some judge might decide that sure, we're nice and all, but Seth is their biological father, and that's all there is to it. If that happened..."

The emotions that ran through me as I considered this possibility were too much to take. I clenched and unclenched my fist.

"God, I'm starting to feel anger like Marcus," I said, forcing a smile.

She grinned. "There's a joke. Now I feel better." She placed her hand on my arm, her touch calming me instantly. "You're right, sometimes these matters are out of your hands. But I just feel that you and the others are the best possible guardians for those two, and that any judge worth a damn would be able to see that."

Her hand stayed on my arm, each second that she touched me making me want more.

"And... you know what else I'm thinking?"

I glanced in her direction.

"What's that?"

She turned to me, gazing up with those big eyes of hers, the corner of her lip curled into a smile.

"I'm thinking that you need a little something to take your mind off things." Her hand moved from my arm to my belly, then down even further.

"That's not a bad idea at all." I placed my hands on her hips, pulling her close to me. I was hard right away, letting her feel it through my pants.

She chewed on her lower lip in that way I couldn't help but find insanely sexy.

"We could go inside," she said. "Kids are sleeping, Aggie's running some errands."

"You kidding?" I asked, moving my hands lower along her legs. "You seriously think I can wait to get you all the way inside the house? No, no, no, Farmer Downing. I'm taking you right here and now."

I leaned in and kissed her hard, ready to take what I'd been thinking about from the moment I stepped out of my truck.

CHAPTER 28

AUBREY

I was more animal than the damn llamas in the barn. We kissed hard and deep, Tyler's hands rushing to my belt buckle and zipper, opening them up and exposing the lilac-colored triangle of the front of my panties.

Arousal gripped me like a fist – there was no denying how I felt, how much I wanted him. As he slipped his hands up the front of my shirt, teasing my belly and moving under the bottom of my bra, it occurred to me how damn strange it was that I wanted all the brothers equally. I was more than happy to be with Tyler in that moment, but my hunger for each of them was the same.

One of them at a time, two or three or all of them, just as long as I was with them, I was happy.

Those thoughts blasted out of my mind as soon as Tyler reached under my bra and touched my breasts, my nipples going stiff at his touch.

I did the same work on his own belt and pants, opening his zipper and reaching down to stroke his cock. He felt perfect in my hand, his length heavy and warm. Tyler groaned as I touched him, closing his eyes and letting his head hang back.

He put his hand on my belly once more, moving it down and under the waistband of my panties, teasing the patch of hair above my pussy before spreading me open. I moaned at his touch, his middle finger rubbing my clit in a way that made me grab hold of the workbench for balance, my legs buckling hard underneath me.

"God, that feels good... so damn good."

He kissed the slope of my neck, waves of pleasure flowing out from between my thighs. He touched me slowly, carefully, as if listening to the intensity of my sighs and moans and adjusting for maximum pleasure. I ground into his hand, yearning for him to keep touching me, not to relent even for a second.

"You gonna come for me?" It seemed more of a demand than a question.

"Yeah, I'm so close."

When he finally moved his fingers into me it was all over. I let my head drop forward, noises of pleasure flowing from my mouth and filling the barn. I came hard on his hand, my nails digging into his thick shoulders.

The orgasm gently faded. The hunger I had for Tyler, however, was even more intense. The look in his eyes made it obvious that he felt the same way. With a growl, he put his hands on my hips and turned me around. I grabbed onto the workbench as he pulled my ass back toward him.

"You want it?" he asked, pressing his erection against me.

"So, so bad."

Without another word, he pulled my pants down, the air cool against my bare ass. The cold only made his warm, rough hands feel even better as he touched me, squeezing my round behind. I grinned, loving the way he handled me, aggressively and tenderly all at the same time.

By the time he finally took out his cock and placed it at my opening, I felt like I might explode. I pushed back against him, guiding his length into me, inch by inch.

"Oh my *God*." The words shot out of my mouth, the sensation of

Tyler moving deeper and deeper inside, stretching me out, almost too much to take. Pleasure rocked my body, my knees buckling as I grabbed onto the workbench yet again for support.

"Man, you feel like heaven." He spoke the words into my ear, his breath so warm that my neck broke out in goosebumps from his nearness.

"You're not so bad yourself," I said over my shoulder with a smile.

He pulled back, his cock sliding out of me for a moment before he pushed back in. I moaned at the thrust, the way he speared me with his manhood, another jolt of pleasure running through my body.

More and more waves of delight ran through me as he bucked hard again and again, the tools on the workbench shifting, the wood groaning as I held onto it. I threw my head back, my hair tossing around me as I looked back at Tyler, savoring the expression of masculine intensity on his face as he took me from behind.

"I'm gonna..." Another orgasm was on the verge of tearing through me.

"Same... same here."

I placed my hand on his hand, wordlessly guiding him to finish. His pace picked up, the tightness inside of me building and building until the release was inevitable.

I yelled out as the second orgasm hit, Tyler pushing into me with the slow, deep thrusts of a man unloading. His cock shot deep into me, warmth flowing as he gave me everything he had.

When the orgasm receded, I let my head hang, my curls falling on both sides. Tyler brushed them away on the right side, leaning in and kissing me on the cheek. I smiled as he placed his lips on me – it was just what I'd wanted after our little tryst.

"Now, as nice as that was, we ought to get going – the llamas are starting to stare."

We kissed one last time as he prepared to leave, the two of us standing in front of the barn.

"Nice stop-and-chat," I said with a sly smile, my hands slipped into his front pockets, his arms wrapped around me.

"I'm definitely in agreement. Just hope we didn't traumatize the llamas."

I laughed. "Don't worry – they're tougher than they look."

One more kiss and he was off, my eyes lingering on his perfect rear packed into those blue jeans as he climbed into his truck. Tyler started the engine, giving me one last wrist-flick of a wave before pulling a U and taking off.

Shortly after he pulled away, I noticed another car coming in on my right. This vehicle was a deep red crossover. I kept my eyes on the car as it approached, slowly pulling to a halt.

The driver's door opened, and Janet stepped out. She was all smiles, as if we were old pals and she was making a planned drop-in. My body tensed at the sight of her, alarm bells going off in my head. She was the one who'd brought Seth into my peripheral at the pizza place. Now I doubted her every move.

"Hey!" she said, marching in my direction with poise and confidence. "Is he gone?" she pointed over her shoulder in the direction that Tyler had gone, disappointment in her voice.

My stomach tightened. Had she seen what had happened between us? Had she seen our kiss?

"He's gone." I didn't elaborate. "Janet, what do you want? What're you doing here?"

She grinned. "I have to ask... are you guys dating?"

I raised my palms. "Seriously, what're you doing here? I get that you're a reporter, but this is private property."

"I know, I know. I wanted to talk to you, but I didn't have your number. So, I figured I'd drive up here and see if you'd be down for a chat. Worst you could do is say no, right?"

I could do a hell of a lot worse than that to nosy trespassers. I kept those words to myself.

"Well, I'm saying no." I started back toward the house, eager to check on the kids.

"Oh, come on," she said, hurrying to my side. "I told you I was doing a piece on second and third generation farmers. Not to mention, there's a lot of interest in those four hunks over at Thousand Acres and you happen to be right next door."

"Good for you. But I'm not about to say anything about it."

"You have to say *something*," she said, keeping pace with me as I made my way to the front door of the house. "It's just..."

"A privacy invasion?" I cut her off, stopping and turning to look at her.

"No, more of a... public interest sort of thing. Think about it – if you were living in town and there was some mansion up in the hills where four possible criminals lived with two kids, wouldn't you want to know more? That's my job as a reporter, after all."

"Wait, what? Possible criminals?"

She cocked her head to the side. "You mean you haven't heard the rumors? Word around town is that those guys are all mercenaries – the 'kill whoever you want for the right price' sort of men."

"That's not true. They do security."

She arched her eyebrows. "Is that right? Or is that what they told you."

I opened my mouth to speak, no words coming out. "That's... no, they're on the level."

Janet kept the grin on her face, as if the conversation were going exactly how she had hoped.

"You sure about that? See, this is why I'm doing this piece. Everybody's got questions. And the fact that they're keeping the kids from their bio dad is—"

"They're not keeping them from anyone," I cut her off, real anger coming into my voice. "The kids' mom wanted them to be with their uncles, and they're great with them."

"Just saying, he *is* their bio dad. And he's got plenty to say about how those four made their fortunes traveling the world and killing for top dollar. Aubrey, this is your chance to tell your side of the story, paint the guys in a good light."

I sighed. Part of me wanted to defend the guys. The smarter part of me knew that I should talk to them before I talked to the press about anything.

Janet shivered, rubbing her hands over her arms. The temperature was dropping, the dark clouds in the distance growing closer and closer.

"You hear about the blizzard?" she asked. "Supposed to be the worst in decades. I wonder how your neighbors will pass the time?"

I'd had enough. "I gotta get inside," I said. "And you should get home before this all comes down." I nodded toward the clouds.

"Sure, sure. Stay safe, Aubrey. And you have my number!"

I made a mental note not to use it, if I did, she'd have mine, too.

With a wave, she was off. I hurried inside, shutting and locking the door then rushing up the stairs to check on the twins. They were still sleeping, but I could sense they wouldn't be down for much longer.

I took out my phone, dialing Adam as his was the first name to pop up.

"Yo, Aubrey. What's up?"

"Hey. Something just happened you guys should know about..."

I filled him in on Janet, telling him that she was poking around in service of some tell-all article about them and the kids posed as a piece on farming. I could almost feel his anger through the phone.

"Thanks. I'll let the guys know. Oh, and just FYI, Tyler's coming back with a satellite phone. Should be there in ten."

"Why is Seth saying you guys are criminals?" the words came out of my mouth in an inelegant blurt.

Silence came from the other line.

"Next time we're together, we'll tell you everything about what we do. In the meantime, don't listen to Seth. Talk soon, alright?"

"Alright."

I hung up, right away feeling guilty about what I'd said.

Then again, what if Seth was right? Sure, he was a scumbag, but his claims only highlighted the fact that I didn't really know that much about the guys' work. They had just returned from a secret mission to Europe they couldn't tell me about. And money had most certainly never been an issue.

I shook my head and told myself I was being ridiculous. With the way all of them made me feel and how much they loved and doted on their niece and nephew there was no way that they could be what Seth said they were.

So why was I still bothered?

CHAPTER 29

ADAM

"If he's here in the states," Tyler said, his arms crossed over his chest and his eyes narrowed, "he sure as shit didn't come for a damn tea party."

I didn't have much time to think about the phone call with Aubrey. The email that chimed in my inbox seconds after talking to her was enough to make my blood run cold, to push aside thoughts of anything else.

It was from Todd Sharpe, a merc I knew based out of the New York region. After the mission with Balaban, I'd spread the word among my contacts to keep an ear to the ground for any signs of movement from him. We'd given him a black eye, after all, and Balaban wasn't the type of guy to take that lying down.

Subject spotted near NYC. Pictures are from a private airfield this morning.

Attached were two security footage shots of a team of men stepping off the back runway of a cargo plane. One of the men was tall and bald, his face covered in scars, his body built like a tank.

It was him.

Without needing to think about it for a second, I'd sent a 911 text to all of the guys. We'd gathered in the office; Tyler having returned from dropping off the phone and picking up the kids. He'd made sure to set the kids up with a movie and snacks in the den, so they were far from the conversation we were about to have.

Mac laid out the pictures that I'd printed out. "He's here for us, no doubt about it."

Marcus, a tight expression of anger on his face, leaned forward. "Then it's simple – we kill him. If he's fine with coming all the way to America to get his revenge, then we're not going to be safe until he's deep underground, buried in his grave."

None of the rest of us said a word. While the idea of doing that particular kind of work on our home turf didn't sound appealing in the slightest, the truth of Marcus's words was clear.

"Aubrey," Tyler said. "He might know about her."

My hands clenched into fists. Just the thought of Balaban coming near her or the kids...

"How would he know?" Marcus asked.

"Balaban's a ruthless son of a bitch," I said. "But he's not stupid. He's not going to enter into America blind. Knowing him, he found some way to track down our location, then did a little recon in the town. Wouldn't take much more than one of his goons asking around to find out where four brothers all lived together in the area – and who they lived near."

Mac nodded. "Then we're going to need to bring Aubrey over here, her and Aggie."

"Already made the offer," Tyler said. "She wants to stay there to make sure the animals are taken care of during the storm."

Something about his words, in spite of everything going on, brought a smile to my face. I shook my head.

"What's so funny?" Marcus asked.

"Just thinking about what Tyler just said. That's one of the things that's great about her, right? She's got a sense of duty, a desire to take care of those animals and everyone else she cares about. And she's as independent as they come. Just some of the things I love about her."

Smiles broke out among the guys, as if they were thinking the same thing.

Tyler, however, furrowed his brow and cocked his head to the side.

"Uh, you hear what you just said, bro?"

"What do you mean?"

He grinned. "You just said the L word."

My first instinct was to tell him that he was wrong, that I hadn't said it.

But I had.

There was no doubt, however, that it was how I felt.

"I feel the same way," Mac said.

Marcus nodded. "Me too."

"I mean, *yeah*," Tyler added.

I chuckled. "Well, this is certainly some new intel."

"But it doesn't change anything," Mac said, his serious expression returning. "We've got danger coming our way, and we need to be ready for it."

"How would Balaban get here?" I asked. "Winds are already picking up outside, and I really doubt he's dumb enough to try a helicopter infil during one of the worst blizzards on record."

I turned my attention to the big, round window over the desk at the back of the office. The dark clouds were growing nearer, snow beginning to fall in the distance. The branches of the nearby trees whipped back and forth, the wind already picking up.

"He'll drive," Mac said. "Easier to do, safer. Assuming he's coming in from the NYC region, that's about a six hour drive. He'll want to supply up and take his time, so let's say twelve hours before any kind of attack."

I peeked out into the den to check on the twins, watching them play and watch their movie, both blissfully unaware that possible danger was near. The idea of anything happening to them was too much to bear.

"What about Aubrey?" Marcus asked. "Animals or not, we need to get her and Aggie over here."

"We've got space in the barns for her animals. It'll take some doing to get them all over here, but we could do it." I sat forward after I spoke. "Not to mention I told her that we'd fill her in on everything about our work."

"That's as good a time as any to tell her about Balaban," Tyler said. "I'll try to smooth talk her into coming."

Mac leaned forward. "Once she's over here, we can start talking about how we're going to plan for the attack. Adam, check the weapon stash and make sure we're ready to rock if it comes to that. Marcus, check the security system, then get the animal transport truck geared up. Tyler, you make the call to Aubrey. We need to get moving now before this weather gets any worse."

We had our duties. It was time to act.

CHAPTER 30

AUBREY

"What's the reason they wanted to come here?"

Aggie and I were seated at the kitchen table, mugs of tea in front of us.

How the hell could I even begin to answer her question?

"Don't tell me they all want one-on-one time. Or four-on-one." She leaned in with a mischievous look on her face.

"Aggie!" I playfully slapped her hand.

"Seriously! I mean, I know that you guys are all a thing, but you've never told me how it all works."

"You're awfully curious about the logistics of our bedroom activities for a lesbian."

"Hey, sexual orientation has nothing to do with it. I'm just curious how one woman can be with four guys at the same time."

I laughed. "You want me to draw you a chart or something? Label everything?"

"You laugh, but that might help."

I sat back, thinking the matter over. "You would think it's complicated. But... it's not. In fact, it's easy – the most natural thing in the world. We just get together and start kissing and..."

I trailed off, just the mention of being with all of the guys enough to make me tingle down below.

"We can talk about it later," she said, getting up. "And we *will* – make no mistake. But the guys are here."

I rose from my seat, making my way over to the kitchen window. Three cars pulled up – the Tahoe, the F-350, and a huge cargo truck with a compartment in back big enough for animals.

What the hell was going on?

The guys climbed out of the vehicles, the twins with them.

"Looks like the whole crew's here," Aggie said.

It seemed a little much for just a chat. Either way, I opened the door and greeted them. Off in the distance, the clouds grew closer and closer.

"Hey!" I said to the twins, both of them running up to hug me.

"George is coming over!" Henry said. "And Larry too!"

I was confused. "George is coming where?"

I let the kids go and turned my attention to the guys.

"You all want to tell me what's going on?" I asked, stepping aside to let all of them in.

"Gladly," Mac said.

Moments later, we were all seated with mugs of our beverages of choice. Aggie was with the kids in the corner of the kitchen, playing little games with them.

The guys regarded one another, not sure where to begin.

"Your jobs," I said. "Start with that."

Mac nodded. "Yeah. Well, not sure what else to say on that score, Aubrey. We're mercs, yeah. And we were telling the truth about the kind of mercenary work we do."

"Exfils?" I asked. "That was the word?"

"That's it," Adam said. "When the four of us finished our last tours with our branches of service, we were all certain of one thing— we didn't want to use our skills to hurt people any longer."

"Unless they deserved it," Marcus interjected. "Unless *they* were going to hurt innocent people."

Mac went on. "We figured the best way to do that would be to stick to rescue missions. If there's a war going on, we offer our services to get any innocent people out of harm's way. We charge for our skills, but nothing exorbitant."

"And we offer exceptions for anyone who needs our services but can't afford it," Tyler said. "There's no shortage of people in the world to help."

Their words were putting me at ease. I'd never gotten an evil vibe from any of them; just the opposite, in fact.

"Trust me," Adam said. "If we wanted to make a living as hired guns, the type of lowlife mercs who will turn their weapons on anyone for the right stack of cash, , we could do it. Lots of greedy men and women out there who are looking for exactly that."

"By the way we're constantly turning down those kinds of offers," Tyler said. "We always tell them the same thing; we don't do that kind of work. We're not in the business of hurting people."

Each word they spoke calmed me a bit more. All the same, I could sense there was something they weren't telling me.

"I believe you," I said. "Thank you for explaining it to me. Now, why are all of you here with the trucks and trailer?"

The guys looked at one another with an expression that tightened my stomach.

Something bad was about to happen.

"Our last mission," Mac began, "It was in Croatia. We were sent to rescue some missionaries from a man named Balaban. Real scum-of-the-earth type, the sort of man who'd toss his own mother off a boat if it meant he'd have a chance at a little more power."

"We've come up against him before," Marcus said, placing his hand against his shoulder. "Got a bullet wound as a little souvenir."

I said nothing, letting them go on.

Mac continued. "The mission was a success. We'd gotten in, rescued the missionaries, and gotten the hell out. Each of them was safe, and we got paid a nice sum for our trouble. Along with a chance to stick it to Balaban."

"But apparently, he's not done with us. We just got news this morning that he's in the states, and—"

"Wait," I sat forward. "Please don't tell me some Croatian warlord is in the country and coming here to hurt you."

The boys shared another look.

Shit.

"That's what we're fearing," Mac said. "Can't think of any reason why he'd risk coming to the States unless it was for revenge."

Little by little, the situation began to take shape.

"And he's not coming here just for you guys. He's got the kids in his sights, too."

"And possibly you," Adam said. "All he'd have to do is ask around a little to find out that there's some woman up here that we've been really friendly with."

I realized I hadn't even considered that I could be in danger too, by association. I'd been too focused on the kids.

Now that Adam had said the words, however, I began to feel sick to my stomach.

"I get it now. That's why you're all here. You're here to what, throw me in a vault in the basement of your fortress until this is all over?" I stood up and began pacing. I was angry; not just about me, but about how the twins were in danger from all of this, too.

"We didn't want you to get dragged into this," Adam said, rising from his seat and coming over to me. "But we're going to make sure you're safe." He put his hands on my arms and held me still. The instant he touched me I realized how panicked I'd become. I turned to see that Aggie and the twins were watching me, worried expressions on all of their faces.

"Is Miss Aubrey OK?" Hattie asked.

Shit. Last thing I wanted was to scare the kids. I closed my eyes and took a slow deep breath, trying to calm myself.

The anger was still there, however. I felt betrayed, I felt like the men had been careless with my life, not to mention the lives of the twins.

Without another word, I stormed from the kitchen, furious.

CHAPTER 31

MAC

The boys and I shared a look that suggested we'd just blown it – *hard.*

"I think you guys have some explaining to do," Aggie said, turning away from the twins. "Or, if you want my advice, apologizing."

She was right.

"Let's go," I said to the guys. "Can you handle them?"

Aggie nodded. "Of course. And tell me what's up when you guys decide on a plan."

"Will do," Adam said. "Thanks, Aggie."

We rose from our seats and headed out of the kitchen and down the hall toward the living room. Aubrey was there, standing in front of one of the big windows, her hands clasped behind her back watching the snow come down.

"Last thing I said to my mom was how I'd never abandon this place," she said. "And now that's just what you guys are asking me to do."

"Only for a short time," Tyler assured. "A few days, at the most."

She turned, her dark eyes flashing with anger. "And what about the animals? I've got lives that I'm responsible for, you know. And now I have to uproot everything that I've built because you four dragged me into some mess with a psycho warlord?"

The guys and I glanced at one another again. I nodded to them, letting them know I'd be taking point on this one.

"Aubrey," I said.

She said nothing, keeping that fiery stare on me.

"We're sorry."

Just like that, the anger seemed to have been taken out of her sails. Her expression softened, her shoulders slumping. Aubrey was a woman who wasn't afraid to stick up for herself, to get angry when she needed to. At the same time, she wasn't the sort to hold onto a grudge, either.

"You're sorry," she said, softly repeating the words.

"We're sorry as all hell," I said again, stepping over to her and taking her hands.

"And he speaks for all of us," Adam chimed in. "You don't deserve to have to deal with this."

I held her hands in mine, feeling them shake slightly. The shaking let me know that she wasn't just angry, she was scared.

"I know we're asking a lot. You've got a life here, one that you've busted your butt building. And here we are, expecting you to pick it all up and take it to our place. Even if it's for a short time, that's no small thing."

I closed my eyes for a moment, knowing what needed to be said next.

"But Aubrey, we love you."

She opened her mouth slightly, knitting her brow.

"You what?"

"We love you. I love you."

"So do I," Adam said. "I love you, Aubrey."

"Same here," Tyler added. "I love you like crazy."

Marcus grunted. "I never thought I'd say this to a woman, but yeah. I love you, too."

"I don't know if you feel the same way," I went on. "For all I know, we just ruined everything with our admissions but none of us are the type of man to live dishonestly. With that said, there's no way we could ask this of you without you knowing how we feel about you. Hopefully, that helps to explain why we are so adamant about keeping you safe."

Aubrey shifted her weight from one foot to the other, her eyes jumping from man to man. She blinked hard, a tear trickling down her cheek. Without thinking about it, I took her face into my hands, wiping the tear away with the side of my thumb. She smiled, closing her eyes once more.

"I love you all, too," Aubrey said, opening her eyes, her gaze on me. "I don't know what kind of thing we're building together here, but I can say for damn sure that there's a lot of love involved."

I wrapped her in my arms and held her close, Aubrey pressing her face against my shoulder.

"And I have to admit, I'm scared."

"You don't have to be," I reassured her. "We've got each other. And we're going to get through this."

"Come on, Larry!" Aubrey stood at the back of the animal transport truck, clapping her hands on her knees. It was a few hours later over at our place, the last of the animals having been unloaded into our barn. It was a tight fit, and I could sense that our animals weren't too happy about the arrangement, but it'd have to work for the next few days.

Larry, her llama, was still in the truck, not wanting to budge. By then, the snow had begun to come down hard. While I knew enough about llamas to understand that they didn't mind the snow, all the same, I wanted to make sure that all of us were tucked safely inside before the weather got any worse. Besides, I didn't like being exposed out there knowing Balaban could be around.

"Come on, bud! Get your butt down here!"

Larry didn't move, his tongue hanging out of his mouth.

"I know you love him," I said. "But this has got to be about the dumbest animal in God's creation."

Aubrey smiled in my direction. "I know. But it's part of his charm. Larry! Get down here now!"

He didn't budge.

"Come on, Larry!" Henry, who'd been on the porch with Tyler and Adam, came trundling over. "You have to go inside!"

"Yeah, Larry!" Hattie said, joining in. "It's not safe out here! It's going to get cold!"

It was already cold, but I understood what she meant.

The kids began gesturing to Larry, shouting and guiding him into the barn. To my surprise, Larry finally got his butt in gear, coming down the ramp.

"There!" Henry said. "Now go into the barn!"

Larry obeyed, making his way into the open doors of the barn. Aubrey was close behind, guiding him into his stall, then shutting the building up with a sigh.

"Should've known I'd need the llama whisperers!" she said, coming over and mussing the twins' hair.

A smile on my face, I turned my attention to the house.

"Just a matter of getting the rest of the place locked up tight. Come on, everyone, we've got a lot of work to do."

CHAPTER 32

MARCUS

The next morning...

The snow came down hard, the sky nearly black. As I stood in the kitchen behind the bulletproof windows, part of me couldn't help but think how nice it would be to just get snowed in without a care in the world, not having to worry about international psycho criminals coming for revenge.

Out of the corner of my eye, I watched as Mac came into the kitchen and headed over to the fridge.

"Any word?" I asked.

"Well, on the weather front, I'm sure you don't need me to tell you that we're in the thick of it. Supposed to come down for another eighteen hours like this."

"Damn. So much for running into town to grab some Ben and Jerry's."

Mac cocked his head to the side as he approached, a cocky grin on his face, a bottle of water in hand. "Was that a joke? Out of you?"

"Hey, Tyler's not the only one allowed to issue the wisecracks."

He chuckled. "Anyway, we're set up. Aggie and the twins are in the basement theater having a Pixar marathon, windows and doors are sealed shut, alarms are activated, shades all pulled tight... there's no way for anyone to get in here without one hell of a fight. And if we need to get to town for some emergency reason, we've got the truck hooked up with the plow."

"Good. So, we're in fortress mode, right?"

"Almost. Aubrey's out in the barn right now."

"You serious? In this weather?"

"Mmm-hmm. Wanted to take one more check on the animals before we lock down for the next twenty-four hours."

"She's a committed rancher, I'll give her that much. Any news on Balaban?"

"Not a peep."

"What do you think the odds are that he came here to take a nice, relaxing vacation in the Big Apple? Who knows? Maybe he's on the top floor of the Empire State Building right now taking some selfies."

"Another joke," Mac said. "I'm beginning to get impressed. And to answer your question, slim to none."

"Yeah, I know. He's going to show up sooner or later."

"Don't forget we've got home field advantage, not to mention as shitty as the weather is, it could help us out. If he mounts an attack in the blizzard, it means he's counting entirely on the element of surprise. There's no way he'd be able to take us otherwise."

"Even so, it would be a bad idea on his part. We could easily wreck him when he attacks. We're armed, we've got a fortress here, and there's the little matter of how I'll rip his fucking arms off if he threatens the people I care about."

"He's being reckless," Mac agreed. "But that doesn't mean he can't do some damage."

I sighed, running my hand through my hair. "I'm going to go check on Aubrey, see if I can't get her to come inside so we can lock up."

"Good call. I'll do one more patrol with the rest of the guys, then we can finish hunkering down."

With that, we split up. I threw on my heaviest coat and headed outside, keeping my head low against the whipping wind. Didn't take long before I was at the barn doors, pulling them open and stepping inside.

"Damnit, Mike, you can't eat that!"

I turned my attention in the direction of Aubrey's voice. She stood in front of one of her half-dozen goats, the animals packed into one corner of the barn. Between them and the llamas and the chickens, the place was crowded. Good thing we had two barns on our land, so there was plenty of shelter for all of the animals. It was comforting to know that they were in the barns instead of in the cold.

"What's he doing?"

"Trying to eat the barrier," she said as I came over. "Doesn't understand that the world's not his tin can chomp on."

"He's just nervous," I said. "Knows something's off."

"Yeah, an anxious eater, it looks like."

"They're holding up alright, though?" I asked. "No issues?"

She put her hands on her hips, giving Mike one last annoyed look before turning her attention to me.

"They're fine. I mean, a little shaken up from the move, but they'll be OK."

Silence fell, the real question on my mind surfacing.

"And how are *you* feeling? I mean, about everything?"

She pursed her lips. "Good. I think. Scared, but good. I've got a hell of a lot to process, but we've got other matters to worry about, you know?"

"Oh, I know."

"What about the twins? They're OK?"

"They're with Aggie, they're good. If anything happens, they won't even know about it. The basement's soundproof and bullet-proof. Basically a giant panic room we can seal off with a button if needed."

"Thank God."

I glanced aside for a moment. "And we've been talking."

"Yeah? About what?"

"About this arrangement we have going on, with you living here. We were thinking that, if you wanted, we could make it a little more permanent."

"More permanent? What do you mean?"

"I mean you'd live here with us, full time. You could have that big room on the top floor all to yourself if you want. Maybe put Aggie in charge of Downing, check in on her and the animals every day if you need to. How it'll all look, I don't know. The point is that we all want you to be here with us. That is, if you want it, too."

I placed my hands on her arms.

"I'm not good with words, Aubrey. But I love you. We all do. If you want, we can start something real, the five of us, together."

She smiled, tears forming in her eyes. Silence took hold, and I waited eagerly for whatever she might have to say next.

"Marcus, I—"

It was all she got out before a *bang* cut through the air.

"What the hell was that?" she asked.

I knew right away what it was, a sound that I'd heard hundreds of times before.

I jumped forward, diving onto Aubrey and pinning her to the ground.

"Stay down!" I shouted. "We're under attack!"

CHAPTER 33

TYLER

A barrage of bullets sounded out, sending me diving into the snow face-first. I did it just in time as another round of gunfire slammed into the side of the house.

"Shit!" I reached into my coat, taking my pistol out of the holster and flipping around to face the falling snow and the nearly black sky overhead. I flicked off the safety and took aim into the flurries, spotting a pair of vans pulling toward the house and firing off a quick triplet of shots.

More gunfire came from the vans. I stayed down, the shots hitting far above me.

This was it; the fight was here.

I rolled over onto my belly, army crawling forward and getting away from the gunfire.

"Mac!" I shouted. "Get your ass out here!"

Before I even finished the sentence, one of the side doors to the house opened. Mac stepped out with a semi-automatic rifle in his hands, raising it to shoulder-level and firing round after round at the vans. One of the men piling out dropped, Mac's shot hitting home and relief washing over me at the sight of one of the bad guys getting taken out.

I took advantage of the chaos, crawling toward Mac and hurrying into the house. Once inside, I fired off a few more rounds at the vans, Mac shutting the door behind us.

"What's the status?" I asked.

"Good question. Adam!"

I sat up and Mac gave me a look over. "You're hit."

"Huh?" I glanced up and down my body. Sure enough, a shot had gone through my upper arm. I quickly peeled off my coat to see that, to my relief, it was a through and through shot through the fatty part of my skin. "Damn it!"

"Can you still shoot?" he asked.

"You just saw me do it, big brother."

"Good, because we're going to need all the hands we can get."

Adam hurried into the room, a shotgun in his hands.

"What's the status?" Mac asked.

"Was watching on the monitors, we've got seven men in total. Well, six now. The house is mostly locked up, Aggie's in the basement taking cover with the kids. I've sealed the room up tight, so no one is getting near them. And I used the satellite connection to put in a call to the local PD. They'll be a while in the storm, but they're on their way and bringing the State Police with them."

More relief took hold.

"Is he hit?" Adam asked, referring to me.

"I'm fine." I pushed myself off the floor, the pain in my arm stinging as I stood up. "Fine. What about Marcus and Aubrey?"

"They're in the barn. If we can get them into the house, we can hole up and keep safe inside. But—"

"But that's going to involve going out there and putting all of us in danger," Mac said.

I grinned. "We're warriors – danger's what we do."

The guys grinned right back at me.

"Alright," Mac said. "Here's the plan..."

Moments later, I was positioned at the front doors on the other side of the house. Balaban and his men were on the opposite side, evidently putting all of their manpower into a flank attack. He was desperate, coming after us when he was weak, hoping to catch us off guard.

We were ready for him.

More gunfire sounded out, most likely Marcus shooting back at the attackers. I snuck around the house, the wind bitter and cold. I inched my way along the wall, pistol in hand. Before too long, I was at the corner looking out over the barn.

I saw him. Standing among his troops was the familiar sight of Balaban. He was easily a head taller than the rest of his troops, dressed in winter camo, his bald head bare. He shouted something in Croatian to his men, all forming up around him and preparing to attack the barn.

The sight of the half-dozen armed men made my gut tense. I wasn't worried about myself—I was worried about Aubrey.

All the same, I had my orders. When I gave the signal, the counterattack would begin.

Taking one more slow, deep breath, I raised my pistol and took aim.

CHAPTER 34

ADAM

Tyler was a damn good shot.

Gunfire rang out as he opened up with his pistol from his position on the far side of the house, two of Balaban's men dropping like the plug had been pulled from them.

That was the signal for the rest of us to move. I pulled open the door to the garage, running in and jumping into the truck with the plow attached. After clicking the garage door opener, I gunned the engine and drove forward into the snow.

"Come on, assholes!" I shouted, steering the truck around in a half-circle toward the vans. "You wanted a fight! Here it is!"

I slammed onto the gas, driving forward and crashing into one of the vans. Just as we'd hoped, the display totally took them by surprise. From my cover, I took aim with my shotgun and fired a pair of blasts, taking down another of Balaban's men.

Balaban's ugly mug turned surprised, and he barked more orders to his men in his native language that I didn't understand. They didn't get the chance to execute them, however. Mac threw open the front door, marching out with his rifle in his hands and opening fire.

Two more men dropped, leaving only Balaban and one other

remaining. I watched as they made a mad dash for the barn, slamming open the door and running inside before we had a chance to drop them.

Fuck.

I hopped out of the truck and ran over toward the house, Mac and Tyler coming to join me.

"Tyler! Barn window!" Mac barked. "Adam, come with me!"

We split up, running toward the barn's side door. Anger and fear took hold of me in equal measures. The plan had gone off without a hitch so far, but nothing mattered until Aubrey and Marcus were safe and Balaban was neutralized.

Screaming sounded inside, followed by gunfire. Mac and I shared the same horrified expression as we stood on both sides of the door.

"Alright, what's the plan now?"

"I take Balaban, you take the other asshole."

"What if I want to take Balaban?"

"Older brother privilege. On three – one, two..."

He stepped forward, smashing his huge shoulder through the door. It flew open, the two of us rushing inside and sizing up the situation.

Aubrey and Marcus were there, Marcus on the ground holding his shoulder – he'd been hit.

Balaban was behind Aubrey, using her as a human shield, a gun to her head. The other man was down, likely having been killed by Marcus.

"Here's the deal," Balaban said, his thickly accented, booming voice filling the barn. "Not one of you is going to take another step. If you do, I won't hesitate to put a bullet in her head."

"Cops are on their way," I said. "You let her go and we can end this peacefully."

He laughed. "You think I came here for *peace*? No, I came here to hurt you just as badly as you hurt me. And going by the looks on your faces as I hold my gun to this pretty little thing's head, I know just the way to do it."

As he spoke, I caught sight of something on the ground. The fallen merc had dropped a pistol, small and black. Most importantly, it was near Aubrey's foot. I caught her attention with my gaze, glancing down at it. She blinked in response.

Behind her, I spotted Tyler on the loft. He moved slowly and silently.

"First," Balaban said. "You're going to let me out of here with her. Once we're clear, I'm going to be in touch, send you the number for a bank account into which you'll deposit every last cent of the money you made on your last mission. Then—"

I was done listening to this prick talk.

"Tyler, now!"

With a grin, he jumped down right in front of the llama pen. With a quick motion, he opened it up and began calling out, George and Larry and the rest of the llamas running wild and free.

"Huh?" Balaban was totally taken by surprise, not having expected a stampede of runaway llamas to deal with.

The distraction was enough for Aubrey to pull her arm forward and slam it into his belly. He let out a rush of air as she dropped, grabbing the gun off the ground and turning it toward him. She pulled the trigger, only a *click* sounding out.

The safety.

"You bitch!" he screamed as he raised his weapon.

I opened fire, filling the asshole with lead. He twitched back and forth where he stood, his eyes going wide with surprise as he dropped to his knees, then into a heap on the ground.

That was it, Balaban was dead. One look at Tyler and Marcus, however, let us know right away that our problems were far from over.

CHAPTER 35

AUBREY

I felt like I was being totally babied, and not in a good way.

"I'm *fine!*" I said, the nurse fluffing my pillow underneath me. "The guys are more important than my stupid pillow."

The nurse, a no-nonsense middle-aged woman, smirked as she backed away from the bed. We were in one of the rooms at the ER of the local hospital, the walls covered in Christmas décor.

"You twisted your ankle hard," she said. "The adrenaline going through you right now means you're not going to feel it for a little while. But when you do, you're going to be glad we took care of you."

I sighed. "OK, maybe you have a point."

"I definitely have a point."

"But what about the guys?"

"They're fine. Both wounds were surface level. We're going to do a little stitching up and, with a little luck, you'll all be out of here at the same time."

"What about the blood work?" I asked. "Was that really necessary?"

"Standard protocol. Might as well check everything while you're here, right?"

As she spoke, I began to come to my senses.

"Listen," I said. "Sorry to be a brat. It's just that less than two hours ago I was in a gun battle. Those kinds of things have a way of jangling up your nerves."

"I'll have to take your word for it. Anyway, the results from the bloodwork should be coming in any moment. I'll let you know when they do."

"Thanks again."

She smiled at me one more time before turning toward the door and heading out. Adam and Aggie stepped into the room as she left, each of them holding one of the twins.

"There are my dudes!" I said, sitting up.

"Miss Aubrey!" Henry held out his little arms toward me, a big smile on his face. I took him, Hattie hugging my head from Adam's arm.

"OK!" I said. "Kinda need to breathe!"

They set the kids down, the pair wasting no time exploring the small hospital room.

"How you feeling?" Aggie asked, looking me over with eager eyes.

"Fine, I think. Still feeling like I'm on the set of an 80's action movie, but other than that, not bad. How're the boys?"

"Doing great," Adam said, sitting down in the chair next to the bed. "Getting stitched up right now. Cops are all over the property. God, the paper's going to have a field day with this one."

I thought about Janet, hoping that this little story might give her something more interesting to write about than my love life.

"Listen," I said. "I wanted to thank you guys."

"Even me?" Aggie asked. "Hell, I was downstairs watching *Encanto* while it was all going on. We didn't even know anything was happening."

"You were with the kids, making sure they were safe. And because of you, they're not going to have to deal with the trauma of having lived through a damn warzone." I turned to Adam. "And you guys... you kept me safe. I don't know what to even say to that."

"Just doing what needed to be done," Adam said. "We're family. Or something like it, at least."

Before the conversation could go on any further, a knock sounded at the door.

"Come in!" I called out.

The door opened, the doctor who'd taken my bloodwork stepping through. He was a younger man, tall and blonde with a prematurely wise look to his face, his eyes behind wire frame glasses.

"Miss Downing," he said. "How are you feeling?"

"Good, all things considered."

"Excellent." He let out his breath, clasping his hands behind his back. "Would it be alright if we spoke in private?"

"Uh, why?"

"I just wanted to go over your test results with you."

Adam and Aggie both glanced at me, their expressions seeming to say, "we'll stay if you want."

"It's... sure. Yeah." I nodded to Aggie and Adam. "It's fine."

The pair gathered the kids, the twins leaving with me making the promise that we'd get pizza on the way back.

Once we were alone, the doctor took another deep breath.

"What is it?" I asked.

"You're pregnant, Miss Downing."

"I'm what?"

I couldn't believe what I was hearing. The surreal mood in the room became even more so.

"I can't be pregnant. I'm on the pill."

"Remember, it's not one-hundred-percent effective."

I opened my mouth to dispute him, but no words came out.

"Th...thank you, doctor. Can I have a minute alone?"

"Sure. I'll be here if you need anything."

Seconds later, he was gone.

I knew I should've been worried, maybe even a little scared. After all, who the hell was the father? Did it even matter?

Instead of that, however, I let out a shriek of happiness.

I was going to be a mother. And more than that, I now had the best present for the guys, one that would make this Christmas one to remember forever.

EPILOGUE I

TYLER

I t was about as perfect a Christmas morning as I could imagine. The whole gang was gathered at the house, even Mom and Dad were there visiting from West Palm Beach. All of us were sipping our coffee in front of the fire, the snow from the most recent fall still fresh outside.

Dad, tall and broad-shouldered like his sons, with the notable difference of far less hair on top, called over to us from his conversation with Aubrey.

"Boys, you didn't tell me she had llamas at her place! Why didn't you say something?"

I laughed. "What were we supposed to say? 'Can't wait for you guys to meet Aubrey. Oh, she's got llamas.'?"

Dad shrugged.

"More coffee?" Mom, who looked so much like Kristen that it was startling, came into the den then with a pot of coffee. She topped up whoever wanted more, leaning in and saying something to Aubrey that I couldn't quite hear, both of them breaking out into laughter.

"Alright," Mac said. "I'm about ready to tear into those presents." He nodded toward the massive pile underneath the big tree.

"I swear," Marcus said. "The twins are the only kids on earth that don't wake up at the crack of dawn on Christmas morning to open their gifts."

"They slept in the living room hoping to catch Santa," Adam said. "You'd think we would've woken them up."

"Oh, speaking of the little munchkins," Mom said.

We turned to see Hattie and Henry, both of them coming into the room with sleepy eyes.

"Morning," they both said at the same time. Of course, their eyes lit up as they saw the tree, both running over to the presents.

"Can we start?" Henry asked. "Please-oh-please-oh-please?"

"Easy, buds," I said, getting up and scooping Hen off the ground and planting a kiss on the top of his head. "You know how we do this – pass out the presents one at a time."

My stomach tingled as I mentioned the gifts. There were tons of presents under the tree for everyone but the one gift I was interested in most was the small one right near the edge for Aubrey.

We went to work passing out the gifts, making our little piles. I sipped my coffee, putting my slippered feet up on the coffee table, Mom smacking them off with a scold, of course. As we unwrapped, I thought about the last few weeks, how much had happened.

The gunfight had been the talk of the town. It had also blown the lid off any privacy that we'd hoped to have here at Thousand Acres. Janet, the reporter in town, pounced on the whole thing, using it as fodder for her article. She even got Seth to throw in an unkind word or two before he turned tail and headed back to whatever rock he'd crawled out from under. We hadn't heard from him since.

Wasn't long before everyone knew about our situation. At first, I was worried—more for Aubrey than anything else. To our pleasant surprise, however, she didn't care. She didn't run like Tiffany had. In fact, she'd found the attention more amusing than anything else.

On top of it all, the news getting out pushed her to make a decision on moving in with us. We'd drawn up plans for expansions to the farms, a few buildings between here and Downing where Aggie would be in charge of her own crew with long-term intentions of connecting the lands into one big farming kingdom.

That was all down the road, however. For now, I had bigger things on my mind.

The kids went wild opening their gifts, not wasting any time playing with their new toys as the rest of us opened our presents. In the middle of it all, Aubrey rose and hurried over to the tree, snatching up four, identical, fist-sized boxes.

"Here you guys," she said. "A little something for all of you."

The guys and I shared the same look of confusion.

"But you have to open them in order."

"In order?" Mac asked, looking at the underside of the box as if it might hold some clue to what it contained.

"Yeah. So, Mac goes first, then Adam, then the twins. Marcus first, since he's a little older."

Adam smirked. "So, it's a seniority thing?"

"You'll see. Open them!"

The guys and I shared a look before Mac opened his box, all of us craning our necks to get a look inside. There was nothing but a small, folded up piece of paper. Mac picked it up and opened it.

"I'm."

"'I'm'?" I asked. "That's it?"

"That's it."

Adam, his eyes narrowed in suspicion, opened his next.

"Having."

My stomach jumped. I had a sense of what was coming.

Marcus opened his. "A."

Ho-ly shit. I looked over at Mom and Dad, who seemed about ready to explode from excitement.

"Open yours, baby brother!" Marcus said, giving me a shove.

"Alright, hold on!"

My hands practically shaking with eagerness, I opened the package.

"Baby."

The celebration started right away, all of us yelling out with happiness. Hugs went all around.

I couldn't believe it. We were about to welcome another child into our family.

"I guess this is a pretty good time for *our* gift," Mac said, stepping over to pick up the small box for Aubrey.

She took it from Mac, opening the wrapping and revealing a small box of black satin. She popped it open, a gorgeous diamond ring inside.

Mac cleared his throat, ready to begin the big speech we all had planned.

"Aubrey, we—"

"Yes!"

I laughed. So much for speeches.

She threw her arms around Mac, then kissed each and every last one of us. Mom was in tears, and Dad looked to be on the verge.

"Are we going to have a little brother?" Henry asked, seeming to grasp what was going on.

"Or sister!" Hattie added.

Brother, sister, it didn't matter. We had each other. We were a family.

Everything was wonderful.

EPILOGUE II

AUBREY

Two years later...

There were a few sights I never got tired of. The first was the kids sleeping, looking innocent and precious as they slumbered. The second was my husbands all piled into bed at night, waiting for me to come join them. The third? My kingdom, of course.

I stood at the window on the third floor of Thousand Acres ranch, the land spreading out into the distance, the early spring air inviting and fresh. A handful of pens were down below, each containing pigs or goats or horses and, of course, llamas. We'd built them all, along with a pair of new barns, over the course of the last couple of years.

Beyond them were the crops, the fields low before the harvest. Off toward the east, toward Downing, was a little cluster of guest homes where the dozens of hands we hired stayed. We had just gotten through winter, which meant we'd been running a skeleton crew to handle the animals. When planting season came, however, this place would be like a small village.

I couldn't wait for the upcoming year. Mac and the boys had put the finishing touches on selling their mercenary business to the B-team they'd been using for most of their rescue ops, which meant that they were ready to devote themselves fully to the farm and their family.

"Mama?"

I turned, greeted by the sight of Mac holding Austin, our fourteen-month-old baby boy. The little man beamed as he laid those big brown eyes on me, his hair a tussle of my dark curls. Mac set him down, Austin taking careful, cutely awkward steps over to me.

Once he was near, I bent down and opened my arms to him, Austin coming over and letting me wrap him up in my hug.

"My little man!" I said, hoisting him off the ground. "Or my *big* man!"

I grunted as I picked Austin up. "I swear, he gained five pounds since last night."

"Sometimes feels like it, doesn't it?" Mac asked. "Anyway, just wanted to let you know we were about to send the other two off."

"Henry and Hattie are about to go to school?"

"Yep. Tyler's taking them."

"Then let's get a move on. Got some stuff going on over at Downing I wanted to tell you about."

We walked and talked, Mac filling me in on what was happening over at the other property. Aggie was in charge of the place now; her girlfriend Chrissie having been serving as her second-in-command for the last year. A few new constructions were going on, including space for more llamas, along with some alpacas. Last year had been wildly profitable, and I had high hopes for the upcoming one.

The conversation ended when we reached the bottom floor, Hats and Hen all dressed and ready to go, looking as cute as ever in their spring clothes and little backpacks. Tyler and Adam and Marcus were with them.

"Mom?" Henry asked, looking such like a little man I could hardly believe it. I had no doubt he was going to grow up to be as tall and handsome as his uncles. "Can you pick us up from school today?"

"Yeah!" Hattie said. "I want to go to Downing and play with the new llamas!"

"But pizza first!"

I laughed, coming over to hug them both.

"I think we can work something out. Aggie would love to see you guys."

"I want to see Aunt Aggie!" Hattie said, her eyes lighting up.

"Well, be good at school and we can make it happen." I leaned in to kiss them both. "Love you guys."

"Bye, Austin," Hattie said, coming over to hug her little brother.

"Bye-bye!" Austin said as Hattie let him go, Henry giving the little man a hug of his own.

"Be back in a bit," Tyler said. "Oh, and did you tell her about the meeting?"

"The what?" I asked.

Tyler smirked. "The meeting. You know."

"Oh yeah," Marcus said. "The meeting."

"Right," Adam added. "The meeting. It's happening when Tyler gets back. Important stuff. But let's finish breakfast first."

"What! You guys seriously can't act like that and then not tell me more."

"Watch us," Tyler said. "Anyway, bye!"

With that he was gone, leaving me with the rest of them. I pried a little more, but none of my husbands would say a word. We finished breakfast, talking about the tentative plans for the day ahead. It wasn't long until Tyler came back just as I was putting Austin down for his morning nap.

"Meeting time!" he said, sticking his head into the den. "Let's go! Upstairs!"

The guys all gave me a look as we rose, the whole group heading up to my bedroom.

"Alright," I said. "What's this all about?"

The boys shared another look.

"Just been thinking about how busy we've been over the last few weeks," Mac said.

"Yeah," Adam added. "With the kids and the farm and the business sale and all that."

Tyler smiled. "Got us talking about how we hadn't had much time to spend together, you know? Like, quality time."

To make his point, Marcus pulled off his shirt, revealing his gorgeous body. "Yeah, a certain kind of quality time."

I got wet at the sight of them, the rest of the guys taking off their shirts too.

"So we figured we were due for a meeting," I said with air quotes.

I laughed, Tyler wrapping me in his arms and kissing me hard.

From there, we fell into it. We stripped, the group moving over to the bed. My men did what they did best, pleasuring me every which way, the five of us taking our sweet time. I came again and again, each of the guys making sure they had a chance to make me come. I returned the favor with my mouth and hands and body.

When we were all done, we laid together in a big pile on the bed, the late morning sun streaming in.

"Love you, Aubrey," Mac said.

"Yeah, love you like crazy," Tyler added.

"Like nothing else," Adam agreed. "Well, except for our amazing family."

"Right," Marcus said in his gruff voice. "Nothing but love."

"And I love you guys too. I can't wait to see what the year ahead has in store."

I meant it. Life was nothing but hope and promise. And I had the four best companions that a girl could ask for to share it with.

THE END

Printed in Great Britain
by Amazon

40553459R00136